Dangerous Alliances

Diana Cole

Published by Diana Cole, 2024.

This is a work of fiction. Similarities to real people, places, or events are entirely coincidental.

DANGEROUS ALLIANCES

First edition. November 6, 2024.

Copyright © 2024 Diana Cole.

ISBN: 979-8227702654

Written by Diana Cole.

Chapter 1: The Storm Within

The clouds overhead mirrored my turbulent thoughts, dark and brooding, threatening rain as the sun began its slow descent behind the skyline. I leaned against the cool iron railing, the rusted paint flaking beneath my fingers as I gazed out at the chaotic beauty of Brooklyn. The streets below buzzed with life, but here on the balcony, the world felt oddly distant, as if the vibrant city thrumming with energy had become a mere backdrop to the tempest raging within me. My thoughts drifted back to Nathan, the way he had looked at me during the meeting, a mixture of challenge and intrigue sparking in his deep-set hazel eyes.

His laughter had been a rich, dark sound that cut through my carefully crafted points, leaving me flustered and eager to reclaim my ground. "You really think that's the best solution?" he had asked, his voice smooth like silk yet laced with a sharp edge. I had felt the heat rise to my cheeks as the other board members shifted in their seats, watching the exchange unfold like a carefully scripted play. I had fought back with all the poise I could muster, but his smirk had been my undoing, igniting a fire that I couldn't ignore. It was infuriating. I hated him, and yet, there was an undeniable thrill in our sparring, a crackling tension that I couldn't quite place.

Turning away from the bustling streets, I stepped back inside, the warmth of my apartment embracing me like a long-lost friend. The walls were adorned with artwork I had collected over the years, vibrant splashes of color that mirrored the chaos of my emotions. Each piece told a story, much like my life—a mosaic of triumphs and disappointments, love and loss. I poured myself a glass of red wine, the rich aroma swirling up to greet me, a small comfort amidst the storm brewing in my mind.

I sank into my favorite chair, its fabric soft against my skin, and closed my eyes, letting the evening's chaos settle. The sound of traffic below became a soothing melody, punctuated by the occasional laughter or shout from the street. I thought of Nathan again, of the way he had challenged me—not just in our professional rivalry, but in a way that felt personal. Each interaction was a carefully balanced dance of power and vulnerability. I could see the legacy of our families' animosity reflected in the way he moved, confident and poised, a man accustomed to getting what he wanted. Yet beneath that facade lay something else, something deeper that intrigued me.

"Are you going to brood all night or actually do something productive?" I muttered to myself, shaking my head at my own melodrama. I could be passionate, fiery even, yet Nathan had a way of making me question everything I stood for. A knock on the door interrupted my thoughts, pulling me back to the present.

"Who is it?" I called, feeling a mix of irritation and curiosity.

"It's Matt. I brought the project files you wanted."

I swung the door open, revealing my friend and coworker, Matt, standing there with a stack of papers in one hand and a bright smile on his face. His sandy blonde hair was tousled as if he had run a hand through it in frustration, and his blue eyes sparkled with mischief.

"Ah, the savior of the day! Come in," I said, stepping aside to let him enter.

"Nice balcony view," he remarked, glancing out as he set the files on my coffee table. "But I'd rather not end up a human kite if the wind picks up. You know how this place is in storms."

I chuckled, taking a sip of my wine. "Maybe I should just attach a harness next time I feel like contemplating life. Or more accurately, contemplating Nathan Grayson."

Matt raised an eyebrow, the smile slipping into a knowing grin. "Ah, the infamous Grayson heir. What's he done this time? Bring you a gift wrapped in disdain?"

I rolled my eyes, recalling the earlier confrontation. "It's like he thrives on pushing my buttons. Every time I think I'm making progress, he swoops in with his sarcastic quips and derails me."

"Is it bad I find that amusing? He seems like the kind of guy who could goad a saint into swearing."

"True, but it's not amusing when I'm trying to impress the board and he's trying to play the devil's advocate. I'm here to make a name for myself, not to engage in some twisted battle of wits."

Matt leaned back against the couch, his arms crossed. "Or is it a challenge you secretly enjoy? Maybe a little tension keeps you on your toes?"

"Stop it," I said, half-laughing and half-serious. "I refuse to admit that Nathan's presence makes my heart race for any reason other than pure frustration."

"Right," Matt replied, his smirk growing. "Just remember, in the game of office politics, every rivalry can lead to unexpected alliances—or sparks that fly."

With a heavy sigh, I sank deeper into the chair, allowing my mind to drift back to Nathan. He was undeniably captivating, his dark charisma wrapped in layers of complexity that I had only begun to scratch the surface of. But then again, the closer I got to unraveling him, the more danger it posed to my carefully constructed walls. And if there was one thing I knew, it was that opening those walls could lead to devastation. But there was something thrilling about the unpredictability of it all, something that sent a shiver down my spine.

"Keep your enemies closer, right?" I said, my voice barely above a whisper, as I gazed out into the encroaching night.

As the night deepened, the city transformed beneath a veil of shimmering lights, casting a warm glow over the streets like scattered stars fallen to Earth. The whir of cars and distant laughter floated through my window, mingling with the cool breeze. I took another sip of my wine, savoring its boldness as if it could somehow bolster my courage. Just as I settled into a moment of calm, the doorbell rang, pulling me back from my contemplations.

"Must be the universe sending me a distraction," I murmured, setting down the glass and padding over to the door. Swinging it open, I was met not just by the familiar face of Matt, but by an unexpected guest standing right behind him. Nathan Grayson. His presence was as commanding as it was jarring, like a thunderclap in an otherwise peaceful night.

"Surprise!" Matt declared, grinning widely as if this was the most normal occurrence in the world. "I thought we could use a little more... intensity in our evening. Nathan was just passing by, and I thought he might want to join us."

I blinked, momentarily speechless. Nathan, clad in a tailored black jacket that hugged his frame just right, looked at me with that infuriating smirk, a hint of amusement dancing in his eyes. "I didn't know this was a private party. Do I need an invitation or can I just barge in unannounced?"

"You've clearly mastered the art of barging," I replied, crossing my arms, determined to play it cool despite the flutter in my stomach. "But you might want to reconsider if you're planning to take over my space like it's your own. I promise the views are just as lovely from the street."

Matt stepped inside, a look of pure glee on his face. "Now this is the kind of banter I live for! Let's keep the fire going. Wine?"

I gestured toward the bottle, still half-full, feeling a swell of uncertainty. Could I keep the competitive energy alive while balancing the tension that Nathan brought with him? As he stepped past me into the living room, his presence seemed to fill the space in a way that was both irritating and intoxicating.

"Just one glass for me, thanks," Nathan said, flashing that crooked smile that made my insides twist. He settled into an armchair, casually crossing one leg over the other as if he owned the place.

"What do you mean, 'just one'? We're here to have fun!" Matt chirped, pouring Nathan a generous glass. I couldn't help but watch as Nathan accepted the glass, his fingers brushing against Matt's, a small interaction that sent my thoughts spiraling.

"What's your idea of fun?" Nathan asked, turning his gaze to me, his expression unreadable. "Chess? Or perhaps a spirited debate on corporate ethics? I have some pretty strong opinions about the latter."

"Oh, I bet you do," I shot back, trying to ignore the heat rising in my cheeks. "But I'd prefer something less... predictable. How about a round of 'who can outwit the other' instead?"

"Sounds intriguing," he replied, leaning forward slightly, the playful challenge lighting his eyes. "But let's not kid ourselves. We both know I'd win."

"Is that so?" I quipped, raising an eyebrow, aware that my heart was racing again. "Maybe I've just been holding back all this time. After all, I wouldn't want to ruin your confidence."

Matt laughed, caught between us as if he were watching a thrilling tennis match. "I can already see the sparks flying! Can I take bets on how long before you two start throwing insults that are actually compliments?"

I shot him a mock glare. "Don't encourage him."

As we settled into easy conversation, the wine began to take effect, loosening the tight coil of tension that had knotted my stomach. I leaned back in my chair, watching as Nathan and Matt shared jibes, their camaraderie surprisingly effortless. But no matter how easy the atmosphere became, I couldn't shake the nagging feeling that the air was charged with more than just playful competition.

At one point, Nathan turned to me, a more serious expression taking hold. "So, tell me, what's it like being the underdog in this never-ending feud?"

"Underestimated, you mean?" I replied, a smirk playing at the corners of my mouth. "It's a position that comes with its perks. People often overlook the underdog until it's too late."

"Interesting perspective," he said, his tone thoughtful. "Maybe that's where you're wrong. Sometimes, the underdog can become the fiercest competitor."

Our eyes locked for a brief moment, and something electric crackled in the space between us. It was as if he were peeling back layers, searching for the person beneath the exterior.

Just then, my phone buzzed, breaking the spell. I glanced down to see a message from my boss, reminding me about an upcoming deadline that loomed like a storm cloud. With a sigh, I shoved the phone back into my pocket. "As much as I'd love to stay in this cozy bubble, reality calls."

"Come on," Matt said, nudging me. "One more round of witty banter before we return to the grind? Or are you afraid Nathan will outsmart you?"

"Afraid?" I scoffed, crossing my arms defiantly. "I'm merely cautious. One could argue that Nathan's wits are a double-edged sword."

Nathan chuckled, the sound rich and warm. "I'll take that as a compliment. But I assure you, I'm only dangerous if provoked."

"Is that a threat?" I asked, feigning innocence.

"Not a threat, merely a promise."

Matt raised his glass, clearly enjoying the show. "I love it! Who knew rivalry could be so entertaining?"

Before I could respond, Nathan leaned closer, his voice dropping to a conspiratorial whisper. "Just remember, the line between rivalry and attraction can often blur. Especially in a high-stakes game."

The air shifted, thickening with an unspoken tension, leaving me momentarily breathless. My mind raced, wrestling with the implications of his words. Attraction? Was I really going to acknowledge that dangerous possibility, or would I keep deflecting like a seasoned pro?

"Let's see where this game takes us then," I finally said, my voice steady despite the thrill coursing through me. "I'll bring my A-game."

"Then it's settled," Nathan replied, leaning back with a satisfied smile. "Prepare yourself. You'll need it."

And just like that, we dove back into the banter, but the stakes had subtly shifted, the atmosphere charged with a mixture of challenge and something else entirely.

As the evening wore on, the banter between Nathan and me wove an intricate tapestry of teasing jabs and undercurrents of something deeper. Matt had settled in for the long haul, cracking jokes and filling the room with warmth, yet I couldn't shake the feeling that Nathan's smirk held secrets I was dangerously curious about.

"Alright, since we're so full of enthusiasm," Matt declared, plopping down on the couch and gesturing grandly, "how about a little game to keep things interesting? Something that lets us explore this friendly rivalry of yours?"

I raised an eyebrow, intrigued despite myself. "And what exactly did you have in mind? A trivia contest? I'm pretty sure I can take both of you down."

Nathan leaned back, folding his arms across his chest, his eyes glinting with mischief. "I'd love to see you try. But let's not waste our talents on trivial knowledge. How about a round of Truth or Dare?"

"Ah, a classic! And so very high school," I scoffed, but inside, I felt the familiar thrill of competition spark to life.

"Admit it, you love a good dare," Matt chimed in, egging me on with a grin. "Plus, this way we can get to know each other a little better—especially the mysterious Nathan Grayson."

"Fine, I'm game," I said, pretending to roll my eyes but unable to hide my smirk. "But don't expect me to hold back just because we're in a living room instead of a playground."

Nathan leaned forward, a predatory glint in his eyes. "Then let's make it interesting. No backing out. Once you choose, you have to stick with it."

Matt clapped his hands, clearly excited by the prospect. "Alright, Nathan, you start! Truth or dare?"

"Dare," Nathan replied without hesitation, his confidence unwavering.

"I dare you to call your mother and tell her you're spending the evening with two of your greatest rivals. And that you're having a blast," Matt announced, barely able to contain his laughter.

Nathan rolled his eyes but pulled out his phone, an amused smile breaking through. "You're not serious."

"Totally serious. The stakes have been set!"

With a dramatic sigh, Nathan dialed, his expression transforming into one of exaggerated earnestness. "Hey, Mom. You wouldn't believe it, but I'm spending the evening with the enemy. Yes, we're having a blast." He paused, clearly listening, then added, "Of course, they're trying to distract me from world domination."

Matt and I burst into laughter as Nathan expertly navigated the call, leaving his mother in stitches. "Alright, your turn," he said, clearly pleased with himself as he hung up.

"Very well played," I said, nodding in admiration. "But now it's my turn. Truth or dare, Nathan?"

"Dare, obviously."

"Alright, I dare you to..." I paused for effect, the possibilities swirling in my mind. "I dare you to tell us something you've never told anyone else. Something juicy."

His expression shifted, and for the first time, I saw a flicker of hesitation. "You sure about that?"

"Absolutely. You challenged me to bring my A-game."

He leaned back, a contemplative look crossing his features. "Fine. You want juicy? Here it is. I once got expelled from a prep school for a prank gone wrong."

"Really? What happened?" Matt leaned in, clearly enthralled.

"I filled the headmaster's office with balloons—like, thousands of them. But I underestimated the weight of all that helium. The entire office ceiling collapsed," Nathan said, his voice dripping with mischief.

"Wow, I can't believe that actually worked out for you," I said, laughing. "And I thought you were just the brooding heir type."

He smirked, a glimmer of something genuine shining through the facade. "I'm full of surprises."

As the game continued, the air thickened with laughter and camaraderie, but beneath it all, an undercurrent of tension lingered. I found myself oddly invested in Nathan's stories, the flicker of vulnerability in his gaze catching me off guard. Matt's lightheartedness made the evening enjoyable, yet I felt a tug toward the darker, more complex layers that Nathan exuded.

"Okay, my turn again!" I said, feeling emboldened. "Nathan, truth or dare?"

"Dare," he replied, his eyes sparkling with challenge.

"I dare you to... call your mother back and tell her you love her," I said, feeling a sense of satisfaction at how simple yet profound my dare was.

He opened his mouth to protest, then paused, clearly considering the weight of the request. After a beat, he sighed and dialed again. "Hey, Mom... Yes, I'm having a great time. I just wanted to tell you I love you. Okay, bye."

I blinked in surprise as he ended the call, the warmth of the moment lingering in the air. "That was... sweet," I said, surprised by the genuine tone in his voice.

Nathan shrugged, his nonchalance only partially hiding the softness in his expression. "She worries too much. Thought I'd ease her mind."

Matt grinned, leaning back triumphantly. "Look at you both! Rivals turning into... friends? Enemies? I can't even tell anymore."

I felt my heart skip a beat, the idea of us being anything more than adversaries swirling tantalizingly in my mind. "Your turn, Matt. Truth or dare?"

"I'll take dare, of course."

"Okay, I dare you to... serenade us with a love song."

"Absolutely not!" Matt exclaimed, feigning horror.

"Oh, come on! It's only fair," I teased, laughing.

With exaggerated reluctance, he stood and began to belt out a pop ballad, the kind you'd hear on the radio during a late-night drive. His voice, though not the best, was earnest, and we couldn't help but join in, laughter mingling with the melodies as we teased him mercilessly.

Just as he hit a particularly high note, the doorbell rang again, interrupting our moment. I shot a glance at Nathan and Matt, a frown crossing my face. "Who could that be?"

"Maybe it's your future rival?" Nathan quipped, but I felt a sense of foreboding creeping in.

"Could be anyone," I said, rising from my seat. "Stay here."

As I opened the door, my heart raced. A figure stood silhouetted against the hallway light, someone I didn't expect—a shadow from my past that had long been buried.

"Hello," he said, his voice smooth but laced with something darker. "We need to talk."

The world around me faded as I stared into those familiar, unsettling eyes.

Chapter 2: The Mask of Rivalry

The evening air shimmered with excitement as I stepped into the grand ballroom of the Astoria Hotel, a swirl of silk, laughter, and the clinking of champagne glasses enveloping me like a plush cocoon. The walls were draped in deep emerald fabric, contrasting dramatically with the opulence of golden chandeliers that hung from the ceiling like the sun captured in glass. Each beam of light refracted into a thousand dancing sparks, illuminating the room in a warm glow that invited indulgence and celebration. I took a deep breath, the scent of expensive perfumes and fresh flowers mingling in the air, trying to anchor myself amidst the whirlwind of emotions swirling within.

My family's charity gala was a tradition, an attempt to bridge the longstanding rivalry with Nathan's family, which had become a legacy of feuds and whispered grudges. I had sworn to uphold the family honor tonight, and despite my heart racing at the thought of seeing him, I was determined to maintain my composure. As I navigated the sea of elegantly dressed guests, my mind was a storm of strategy. This was not just a social gathering; it was a battleground. I needed to engage, to smile, to charm, and most importantly, to remind myself of the stakes at hand.

But then there he was, like a lightning bolt across the room, standing near the bar with an air of effortless charm that made the surrounding guests gravitate toward him. Nathan wore a perfectly tailored tuxedo that accentuated his broad shoulders, his dark hair expertly tousled, and his piercing blue eyes—those damned eyes—sparkled with mischief. I felt my breath catch for a moment, a visceral reminder of how easily he unraveled my carefully constructed defenses. A sly grin played on his lips, as if he sensed the effect he had on me, and I could almost hear the taunt in the silence that lingered between us.

Determined not to give him the satisfaction of my disquiet, I turned my attention to the room, feigning interest in the various art pieces lining the walls. Each painting told a story, vivid and bold, yet my thoughts kept drifting back to him. My best friend, Clara, materialized at my side, her golden dress shimmering like a beacon amidst the crowd. "You're going to have to confront him at some point," she said, her voice low but teasing. I shot her a glare that was meant to silence her, but it only made her grin wider.

"Confront?" I echoed, forcing a laugh. "I'd prefer to think of it as a casual encounter, an innocent exchange of pleasantries."

"Pleasantries with a side of daggers?" she quipped, nudging me playfully. "Come on, you can't deny there's something electric between you two. It's practically crackling in the air."

Before I could respond, the orchestra struck up a lively waltz, and Clara grabbed my hand, pulling me toward the dance floor. "Let's shake off this tension," she declared, her enthusiasm contagious. As we twirled and spun, I forced my thoughts onto the music, but every note reminded me of Nathan.

In the midst of the dance, I caught him watching me, his gaze unwavering, a mixture of challenge and intrigue. My heart raced as I met his eyes; there was a spark there, an undeniable connection that felt like both a trap and a promise. I could see it clearly now—this gala was not just about charity or rivalry; it was a stage set for a performance that neither of us had rehearsed.

The waltz concluded, and I stumbled back to Clara, breathless and flustered. "I need a drink," I announced, more to steady my nerves than anything else. As I made my way to the bar, I could feel Nathan's eyes on me, a heavy weight that both thrilled and terrified.

"Chardonnay, please," I ordered, and the bartender nodded, expertly pouring the pale liquid into a crystal glass. I took a sip, savoring the crisp flavor that washed over my tongue, but the comfort was fleeting. Nathan sidled up beside me, a casual confidence radiating from him as he leaned against the bar, mirroring my posture with a relaxed elegance.

"Enjoying the gala?" he asked, his voice smooth as silk, effortlessly disarming.

"Enjoying the theatrics, you mean," I shot back, raising an eyebrow. "This is a glorified family reunion with a side of PR, Nathan. You know that as well as I do."

"Touché," he replied, his grin widening. "But I must admit, it's nice to see you in your element. You look... remarkable."

"Flattery will get you nowhere," I replied, trying to keep my tone light, even as my cheeks betrayed me, warming under the intensity of his gaze.

"Is that so?" He leaned in slightly, the intoxicating scent of his cologne enveloping me. "What if I say I admire your tenacity? You're brave to step into this arena, especially with our families' history."

I paused, taken aback by the sincerity in his tone. "Brave or foolish, I suppose it depends on who you ask," I replied, the wry edge to my words softening as I met his gaze.

"Maybe a bit of both," he countered, a hint of admiration threading through his voice. "But I have to say, I respect it. You've never backed down from a challenge."

My pulse quickened, an unfamiliar warmth blooming in my chest. This wasn't just a rivalry anymore; it felt like a dance on a knife's edge, a precarious balance between animosity and something undeniably deeper. The room buzzed around us, but in that moment, it felt as if we were cocooned in our own world, two opposing forces circling each other, drawn together despite the barriers built by our families.

"I can handle myself, Nathan," I replied, injecting a challenge into my tone. "Let's see how well you can handle me tonight."

And just like that, the mask of rivalry slipped, revealing something raw and electric that neither of us had anticipated. The tension crackled in the air, a promise of what was to come, but for now, I stood firm, refusing to let him take control.

The laughter and chatter of the gala swirled around me like a heady perfume, sweet yet slightly cloying. I could feel the weight of the evening's expectations pressing down on my shoulders. Each smile I offered felt like a carefully calculated move in a game of chess, where every glance and gesture was scrutinized, especially by the members of both families, who hovered like hungry wolves, ready to pounce on any sign of weakness. I'd worked tirelessly to prepare for this night, to ensure I could charm and dazzle while maintaining the upper hand.

"Don't forget to smile, darling," Clara whispered as she flitted past me, her shimmering gown trailing behind her like a comet's tail. "You look like you're plotting a coup."

"Maybe I am," I replied, tossing her a grin that felt a little forced. The truth was, I was grappling with a turmoil that bubbled just beneath the surface. Nathan had a way of rattling my composure, and with every moment spent in his orbit, I felt the barriers I'd constructed around my heart begin to tremble.

As the evening progressed, I was swept into a whirlwind of pleasantries and small talk, engaging with various guests who seemed eager to weigh in on the family feud. Their chatter droned in the background, punctuated by the occasional clinking of glasses and the sound of laughter that echoed through the lavish space. I found myself at the buffet table, meticulously choosing delicate hors d'oeuvres while keeping one eye on Nathan, who was entertaining a group of well-heeled patrons nearby.

"Isn't he just the most infuriatingly charming man?" Clara nudged me from behind, and I could hear the mischievous grin in her voice. "I can practically feel your heart rate quickening from here."

"Please," I scoffed, trying to project an air of indifference. "He's just a thorn in my side—an annoying distraction in a tuxedo."

Yet, even as I uttered the words, I could feel the tug of attraction pulling at my resolve. There was a certain magnetic quality to Nathan that was impossible to ignore. As he spun tales with a charismatic flourish, laughter erupted around him, his humor weaving through the crowd like a ribbon of silk. I hated that I was enchanted, that his mere presence sent ripples of excitement through the room—and through me.

As if sensing my scrutiny, Nathan turned, his gaze locking onto mine. It was a moment suspended in time, where the cacophony of the gala faded away, leaving just the two of us in a bubble of charged tension. He raised his glass in a mock toast, his eyes sparkling with mischief, and I couldn't help but roll my own. I had to remember who I was—a determined advocate for my family's legacy and a woman who wouldn't be outmaneuvered.

"Feeling brave tonight?" he called out, his voice smooth, cutting through the crowd. "Or are you just pretending for show?"

"Show's all I've got, Nathan," I shot back, summoning my bravado. "I'd hate to think you actually believe I'd let you get the better of me."

With a dramatic flourish, he leaned against the bar, a playful smirk on his lips. "You really think I'm trying to get the better of you? I'm just trying to enjoy the view."

"Good luck with that," I retorted, attempting to stifle the heat rising to my cheeks. "There's not much to see here but overpriced cocktails and family drama."

"Ah, but the drama is the best part," he said, tilting his head. "I mean, who doesn't love a little tension? It makes for the best stories."

Before I could respond, an older gentleman approached, extending a hand to Nathan. "Young man, do you remember me? We met at the gala last year. You were charming even then."

"Mr. Hayworth!" Nathan greeted him with an infectious enthusiasm that took me by surprise. "Of course, how could I forget? Your stories about the war were more riveting than anything else at the event. Care to enlighten me again?"

As Nathan engaged the man, I stood there, momentarily forgotten, feeling like an unwanted spectator in a play where I was supposed to be the star. The familiarity with which he navigated the social dynamics around him only served to amplify my frustration. How could he be so effortless, so likable? I fought against the rising wave of envy as I realized that perhaps it wasn't just his charm that had me so rattled—it was the depth of his charisma and the ease with which he connected with others.

As if sensing my turmoil, Clara appeared at my side, holding two glasses of sparkling water. "Here," she said, handing one to me. "You look like you could use this. A little refreshment to wash away the bitterness."

"Thanks," I muttered, sipping from the glass. The coolness was a brief reprieve from the heat in my cheeks. "What's the plan now?"

"Let's mingle," she suggested, her eyes gleaming with mischief. "How about we dance? Show Nathan just how radiant you can be when you're not fixated on his blue eyes."

With a reluctant nod, I allowed Clara to drag me onto the dance floor. The music swelled around us, the rhythm infectious, pulling me into the swirling mass of couples. I lost myself in the beat, twirling and laughing, forgetting for a moment the rivalry that loomed over me like a dark cloud.

But then, out of the corner of my eye, I caught Nathan watching me again, his expression inscrutable. I could see the way his gaze flicked from me to Clara, and suddenly, the carefree atmosphere around me felt charged with something deeper, something that threatened to unravel all my efforts to maintain control.

"Are you going to let him get to you like this?" Clara whispered as we moved to the side, catching our breath. "You know he thrives on it. Don't give him that power."

"I'm not letting him do anything," I replied, a note of defiance in my tone. "I just... I need to play this smart."

"That's the spirit!" she cheered, giving me a playful shove. "Now let's make him work for it. We're not just here to look pretty—we're here to take charge!"

With a newfound determination, I strode back toward Nathan, who was still conversing with Mr. Hayworth, his laughter ringing out like music in the crowded space. I approached, each step a calculated decision, every glance a challenge, feeling the electric tension rise once more. "Mind if I join the conversation?" I asked, injecting a hint of playfulness into my voice.

"Only if you promise to be just as charming as Mr. Hayworth here," Nathan quipped, a glimmer of approval lighting his eyes. "What do you say, Miss Charisma?"

"I think I can manage that," I replied, refusing to let him take the lead. I focused on Mr. Hayworth, engaging him in conversation, savoring the way the older gentleman's eyes lit up as I asked about his experiences. But even as I spoke, I could feel Nathan's gaze on me, a weight that both anchored and distracted.

With every word exchanged, the stakes felt higher. This evening had become a high-stakes game of strategy, where every move was scrutinized and every glance could tilt the balance of power. I could see it in Nathan's eyes—a challenge, a dance we were both reluctant to admit we were enjoying. The gala was no longer just an event; it was a proving ground, and I was determined to emerge victorious.

I felt the energy of the room shift as I approached Nathan, the air thick with anticipation and an undercurrent of tension. Conversations around us flowed like a river, but I was keenly aware of the island we had created in the midst of the swirling crowd.

His charm was disarming, yet every smile he flashed held a hint of challenge, a subtle dare that had me on edge. "You really know how to make an entrance," I said, raising an eyebrow as I took a sip of my drink, trying to maintain my composure.

"Only when it's worth the effort," he replied smoothly, leaning closer so that his voice dropped to a conspiratorial whisper. "And I must say, the competition tonight is quite fierce. You're holding your own, though."

"Flattery, Nathan? I expected more from you," I shot back, crossing my arms in mock defiance. "Or do you just find it hard to resist the allure of my family name?"

He laughed, a low, melodic sound that cut through the cacophony of the gala. "No, I genuinely appreciate the challenge. Your family may have a reputation for being formidable, but it seems you're the real prize."

I fought to suppress a shiver at his words, the thrill of the compliment both welcome and disconcerting. It was infuriating how easily he could twist my resolve, like a master puppeteer tugging at invisible strings. I needed to shift the power dynamic back into my hands, so I decided to play his game.

"Since we're trading compliments, let's talk about your ability to charm every person in this room," I remarked, gesturing toward a group of well-to-do socialites who were hanging on his every word. "Do you practice in front of a mirror, or is it all natural talent?"

"Oh, a bit of both," he replied with a wink. "But I have to admit, standing next to you makes my efforts seem minuscule. You shine like a beacon."

His gaze bore into mine, a fire igniting between us that felt both exhilarating and dangerous. I couldn't deny that the flutter in my chest was alarming, yet I couldn't quite bring myself to extinguish the spark.

"Enough with the sweet talk, Nathan," I said, trying to mask my sudden vulnerability with bravado. "What are you really after tonight? I know you're not just here to compliment your rival."

"Fair point," he admitted, his demeanor shifting ever so slightly as he straightened up. "I'm here to understand the lay of the land. This charity gala isn't just a social affair; it's a strategic battleground. Your family and mine? We're not so different, are we? Both fighting for our legacy."

"Your legacy is built on undermining mine," I countered, feeling the competitive fire reignite. "It's hard to forget that."

He chuckled softly, the sound rich and smooth. "Touché. But perhaps we can find a way to turn that rivalry into something productive? A truce of sorts?"

"A truce? You're a bold one," I replied, feeling the weight of his suggestion settle in the air between us. "What would that even look like? Sharing the spoils of our families' conflicts?"

"Maybe it means joining forces to take on a common enemy," he said, leaning forward, his voice low and serious. "Or at least working together to ensure neither of us ends up in the crossfire."

I considered his words, the idea of collaboration sparking a flicker of intrigue amidst my caution. There was merit in his proposition, yet a part of me resisted the notion of teaming up with him. Could I really trust Nathan, even if we were aligned in our interests?

"Who's the common enemy?" I pressed, unwilling to let my curiosity override my skepticism.

"Let's just say our families aren't the only players in this game," he said, glancing around the room as if searching for unseen threats. "There are others who would love to see us fall. If we don't start watching each other's backs, we might just find ourselves fighting the wrong battles."

The weight of his words hung heavily in the air, and I couldn't shake the sense of urgency in his tone. Perhaps there was more at stake tonight than I had initially realized. "I'll consider your offer," I finally replied, trying to sound nonchalant. "But don't expect me to trust you completely."

"Fair enough," he agreed, a smirk playing on his lips. "Trust is earned, after all. And what better way to earn it than a little cooperation?"

Just then, the lights flickered ominously, momentarily casting the room in shadows. Conversations halted, and a hush fell over the crowd. An uneasy ripple of concern passed through the guests, and I could see a few of the older attendees exchanging worried glances.

"What was that?" I asked, my instincts sharpening as I scanned the room. Nathan's expression shifted, his earlier playfulness replaced with something more serious.

"I don't know," he replied, tension threading his voice. "But we should stay alert. Something feels off."

Before I could respond, a loud crash erupted from the back of the ballroom, drawing our attention. Guests turned toward the sound, confusion etched on their faces. I felt Nathan's hand on my arm, an instinctual gesture that sent jolts of electricity coursing through me.

"Let's check it out," he suggested, his tone decisive. We pushed through the throng of guests, making our way toward the commotion. As we approached, the scene unfolded before us like a cinematic moment gone awry. A large table had toppled over, glasses shattering on the floor, sending shards flying like tiny, dangerous stars.

The cause of the chaos soon became apparent—a group of men, dressed in dark suits, stood amidst the wreckage, their expressions menacing. They were strangers, yet something about their presence felt all too familiar, as if they were the embodiment of every unspoken threat our families had faced. My heart raced, instinctively recognizing that the gala had transformed from a mere social affair into something much darker.

"What do they want?" I breathed, my voice barely audible over the rising murmur of confusion.

"Stay behind me," Nathan instructed, stepping in front of me, a protective stance that sent a rush of conflicting emotions through me.

Before I could respond, the leader of the men stepped forward, his eyes scanning the crowd before landing on Nathan and me. A smirk curled on his lips, one that sent a chill down my spine. "So, the infamous heirs have decided to play nice at last?" he taunted, the mockery in his voice cutting through the tension like a knife.

The air was thick with uncertainty, and in that moment, it felt as though the very foundation of everything I had known was crumbling. With Nathan by my side, the stakes had risen, and as the unfamiliar man's gaze locked onto mine, I realized I was standing at the precipice of a conflict that threatened to engulf us both, a battle that would test not just our families but our very identities. The evening was no longer just a gala; it was a declaration of war, and I was caught in the crossfire.

Chapter 3: Unraveling Threads

The ballroom was a spectacle of opulence, draped in silks and glittering with crystal chandeliers that spilled light over the polished marble floors. But beneath the sheen of luxury, an undercurrent of anxiety crackled like static in the air. The guests, adorned in their finest attire, shifted restlessly as whispers echoed through the gilded space. It was a night meant for celebration—a fundraiser for the local arts program, an evening of laughter and dancing. Yet here I stood, heart hammering, as the truth clawed its way to the surface.

Nathan stood before me, a storm brewing in his hazel eyes, his usually charming demeanor eclipsed by fury. "You think this is a game, don't you?" he spat, his voice low and edged with a sharpness that made my stomach drop. The weight of his words clung to me like an unwelcome shroud. I could feel the watchful gazes of the guests brushing against us, a thousand ears poised to catch our exchange.

"Is that really what you think?" I shot back, my voice steadier than I felt. It was absurd to think I would engage in whatever tangled web of deceit he was insinuating. The last person I would conspire with was him. But there was a twist in my gut, a magnetism that tethered me to Nathan, despite the accusations hanging between us like a suffocating fog.

He stepped closer, his anger palpable, and I couldn't help but notice the way the soft light caught the contours of his jaw. "You have no idea what's at stake here." His words dripped with intensity, and for a moment, the ballroom faded, leaving just the two of us suspended in this confrontation. A part of me wanted to fold under the weight of his gaze, to let his frustration sweep me away into the depths of whatever twisted scenario he envisioned. But I couldn't—there were too many questions swirling around us, a chaos that begged for resolution.

"Neither do you!" I countered, feeling a flicker of defiance spark within me. "If you think I'm in on this, then you don't know me at all." The night had begun with laughter and promise, but now it felt like we were the last two standing on a sinking ship, desperately clinging to the tattered remains of sanity. Behind the façade of glittering dresses and sparkling wine glasses, the theft had shattered the veneer of civility, exposing the raw nerves of ambition and rivalry lurking beneath.

With a deep breath, I pulled back the layers of my thoughts. This wasn't just about the missing technology, a high-stakes piece of innovation worth millions—this was about our families, their legacies entwined like vines strangling a once-flourishing tree. I'd stumbled upon a world far murkier than I'd anticipated, and now, with Nathan's accusation hanging between us, I felt the ground shifting beneath my feet.

"Do you think I'd risk everything for a petty theft?" I asked, forcing myself to meet his gaze, which flickered with uncertainty. "What do you think I am, Nathan?" My voice trembled with the weight of my frustration, and I couldn't hide the hurt beneath the bravado. "I'm not some puppet to be manipulated by our families' greed."

His expression softened, and for a heartbeat, the animosity faded, replaced by something more vulnerable. "Neither am I," he replied, his voice a low rumble, filled with a sincerity that took me by surprise. "But my family's reputation is on the line. If this gets out..." He trailed off, the fear in his eyes belying the bravado he wore like armor.

"I don't want any part of this," I admitted, the admission tasting bitter on my tongue. "But I can't just stand by and let it happen." The words hung in the air, heavy with implications. Whatever was happening, it was bigger than either of us, and as much as I longed to unravel the threads connecting our families, I knew I had to tread carefully. The stakes had escalated beyond mere rivalry; there was a darkness lurking in the shadows that threatened to consume us both.

The gala erupted into a cacophony of voices as the news spread, rumors swirling like leaves caught in a tempest. I caught glimpses of panic on the faces of my parents, the tension visibly tightening around them as they conferred in hushed tones with the other dignitaries. My mother's graceful composure cracked for a moment, revealing a flash of worry that gnawed at my insides. She had always been the pillar of strength, but now she appeared as lost as I felt.

"Whatever's going on, we need to get to the bottom of it," Nathan said, the fire in his eyes reigniting. "I can't trust anyone else, and neither should you." His words felt like a lifeline thrown into turbulent waters, and despite the gravity of our circumstances, I felt the thrill of adventure tugging at my heart.

"Then let's figure this out together," I replied, surprising even myself with my conviction. Trust was a fragile thing, and it was the last thing I expected to extend to him. Yet, as I looked into his eyes, I felt an unexpected alliance forming. Perhaps, just perhaps, we were both tired of playing the roles assigned to us by our families. Maybe we could rewrite our stories together, one unraveling thread at a time.

As we moved away from the prying eyes of the crowd, I felt the weight of our connection deepen. This was not just a collision of worlds; it was the beginning of a partnership fraught with tension and possibility. With every step we took into the unknown, I could feel the stakes rising, the intricate web of lies and truths drawing us deeper into a mystery that would test everything we thought we knew.

With Nathan's piercing gaze boring into me, the rest of the world faded into a muted backdrop. The clinking of champagne glasses and the distant laughter of guests celebrating the evening seemed like echoes from another realm, a stark contrast to the charged atmosphere wrapping around us like a heavy fog. I could practically feel the tension radiating between us, a taut wire ready to snap.

"Do you have any idea what's going to happen if this goes south?" Nathan's voice dropped to a near whisper, the urgency in his tone sending a shiver down my spine. The reality of the situation crept in, gnawing at my resolve. This was not just a theft; it was a crisis that could unravel everything our families had built.

I inhaled deeply, steeling myself. "And what exactly do you think is going to happen? You think I'm going to help you pin this on someone? I'm not some pawn in your family's power play." The heat of my words surprised me, and for a moment, I relished the defiance. But beneath that bravado, a small voice in my head whispered of caution.

He took a step closer, his expression shifting as he dropped the accusation in favor of something that resembled concern. "Look, I know you're not like them, but they won't see it that way. The Graysons have enemies, and they'll try to pin this on anyone they can. You need to be careful." There was an honesty in his tone that tugged at me, making me want to peel back the layers of our animosity and reveal the truth beneath.

"Careful is my middle name," I shot back, half-joking, but the seriousness of the situation hung over us like a looming storm cloud. "But I'm not the one who needs to worry. You're the one who's accusing me."

Before he could respond, a commotion broke out inside the gala, the raucous laughter transforming into a chorus of gasps and raised voices. I turned instinctively, my heart racing as I strained to see what was happening. The crowd had formed a chaotic circle, their faces a tapestry of shock and intrigue.

"Let's get back inside," Nathan urged, taking my elbow and steering me towards the entrance. The warmth of his hand sent an unexpected jolt through me, and I couldn't help but notice how easily we fell into this strange, frantic rhythm together.

As we pushed through the throng, the scene unfolded before us like a dramatic play. A group of attendees, their expensive suits and gowns a stark contrast to the scene, were arguing heatedly. In the center of it all stood my father, a pillar of poise and authority, his expression betraying a crack of vulnerability I had rarely seen.

"Is that—?" I started, but Nathan cut me off with a gentle squeeze on my arm, a silent plea for discretion. We drew closer, the murmurs of the crowd washing over us like waves crashing against a cliff.

"—This isn't just about technology," my father's voice rang out, steady yet edged with emotion. "This is about our integrity as a company. We won't let this define us."

My heart sank as I recognized the look in his eyes—a blend of determination and desperation that was all too familiar. In our world, reputation was everything, and the theft had become a ticking time bomb threatening to obliterate our family's legacy.

"I can't believe you're defending those crooks!" a woman's voice sliced through the chaos, and I recognized her as Mrs. Langley, a prominent investor known for her ruthless approach to business. "Your family has always played dirty, Richard. How do we know this isn't just another stunt to garner sympathy?"

The accusation hung in the air like a foul stench, and I felt the anger bubble within me. "That's enough!" I shouted, surprising even myself. Heads turned, and I could feel Nathan's eyes on me, a mixture of admiration and alarm.

"Who do you think you are?" Mrs. Langley scoffed, her lip curling. "This isn't your place."

"It is my place," I countered, taking a step forward, emboldened by the heat of the moment. "I may be young, but I'm not blind.

You're just here to stir the pot because you can't stand the thought of someone else succeeding."

A tense silence enveloped the room, and for a brief moment, it felt as if the world held its breath. The eyes of the guests flitted between me and my father, anticipation thrumming in the air.

"Enough theatrics, Emma," my father said, his voice a low rumble, but I could see a flicker of pride in his gaze.

"Why don't we focus on the real issue here?" I pressed, my heart racing. "We should be figuring out how to find that technology before it falls into the wrong hands."

"Right," Nathan interjected, stepping up beside me, his presence lending strength to my words. "If this is a ploy, we need to know who benefits from the chaos."

Mrs. Langley shot us both a disdainful glare, but my father's expression shifted from irritation to intrigue. "You're both right. We need to work together to get to the bottom of this," he said, his voice regaining its commanding tone.

Just then, a young intern scurried into the fray, her face flushed with urgency. "Mr. Grayson! I think I found something!" Her eyes darted around the room as if she expected to be swallowed whole by the chaos.

"What is it?" my father asked, his tone sharp and alert.

"An email alert just came through. Someone leaked information about the technology hours before the gala!"

A collective gasp reverberated through the crowd, and I felt a chill creep down my spine. Who would dare betray us like this?

"Let's move," Nathan urged, his voice low, yet imbued with a newfound sense of purpose. I met his gaze, and in that moment, we were no longer adversaries—we were allies, two reluctant players thrust together in a game far larger than either of us had anticipated.

As we followed the intern, adrenaline surged through my veins. The stakes had risen dramatically, and with every passing moment, I could feel the threads of our lives intertwining in ways I had never imagined. This was just the beginning, and together, Nathan and I were determined to unravel the truth.

The intern's face was a canvas of panic as she led us through the swirling chaos of the gala, weaving past clusters of guests who were still grappling with the fallout of the theft. Her heels clicked against the polished floor, a rhythmic echo that underscored the urgency of the moment. Nathan fell into step beside me, his earlier anger replaced by a fierce determination. The familiar scent of his cologne—woodsy with a hint of spice—washed over me, grounding me even as my heart raced with uncertainty.

"Do you think it's someone inside?" I whispered, my mind racing with possibilities. The air was thick with tension, and the flickering candlelight seemed to pulse in time with my pulse. "Someone who knew exactly what to target?"

"Seems likely," Nathan replied, his jaw tightening. "Grayson Industries is always at the top of someone's hit list."

We rounded a corner, and the intern led us to a small conference room that had been hastily converted into a makeshift command center. Screens glowed with data, each filled with frantic graphs and alarmingly colorful alerts. In the midst of it all stood my father, his brow furrowed in concentration as he studied the influx of information.

"Richard," the intern said, breathless, "the email came from an untraceable address. Whoever did this is covering their tracks."

My father looked up, his eyes narrowing as he scanned the room, landing on Nathan and me. "Emma, Nathan. Good, you're here. We need all the minds we can get."

"Seems like you've got quite the mess on your hands," Nathan quipped, a sardonic smile flickering across his lips, cutting through the gravity of the moment.

"Don't get cheeky now," my father shot back, but the hint of a smile tugged at the corners of his mouth, and I knew he appreciated Nathan's levity. "We're facing a potential corporate espionage crisis, and I need to know who's involved and how we can recover our reputation before it gets any worse."

My heart raced as the implications settled over me. Corporate espionage? It felt like something out of a thriller novel, but here I was, tangled in the middle of it, with Nathan standing by my side. "What do we do?" I asked, the weight of the moment pressing down on me.

"We gather intel," Nathan said, his eyes lighting up with that familiar spark of mischief I'd grown to adore. "There are always loose ends. We need to find out who had access to that tech and who might have wanted to take it down."

The gears in my mind began to turn. "There are a few people in the engineering department who would know about it," I suggested, my voice firming with resolve. "They were working on the project for months before the gala."

"That's a start," my father replied, nodding approvingly. "But we'll need more than speculation. We need solid evidence."

Nathan's expression turned serious, his eyes scanning the room before resting on me. "Emma, if we can get a hold of the security footage from the past few days, we might be able to identify anyone acting suspiciously. Someone had to be watching, lurking in the shadows."

"Let's do it," I said, adrenaline coursing through me. "The security office is just down the hall."

As we rushed out of the conference room, I could feel the gravity of the situation shifting. The chaos had been a storm, but now, we were the eye of it, and we had a chance to take back control. Nathan walked beside me, the tension between us coiling tighter with each shared glance. It was almost dizzying, the thrill of the hunt combined with an electric charge that buzzed just beneath the surface of our interactions.

Reaching the security office, we pushed inside, and I could see screens flickering with activity. The head of security, a burly man with a no-nonsense demeanor, looked up as we entered. "What can I do for you?"

"We need access to the security footage from the last week," Nathan stated, his voice firm. "There's been a theft, and we need to see who had access to the tech."

"Standard procedure," the man grunted, but the spark of curiosity ignited in his eyes. "It'll take a moment."

I stood beside Nathan, our shoulders brushing slightly, the contact sending a jolt of awareness through me. "You're handling this better than I expected," I said, attempting to lighten the mood. "I figured you'd be sulking over some vintage car you couldn't buy."

"I might still be sulking later," he replied with a grin, and I couldn't help but smile back. "But for now, I'm all in. Besides, this is way more exciting than a car show."

The security officer pulled up the footage, a mosaic of blurry images and shifting shadows. I leaned closer to the screen, my heart pounding as the images began to play.

"There!" I pointed, my voice rising in excitement. "That's one of the engineers. He was in the lab late one night."

As I leaned forward, Nathan's breath brushed against my ear, causing my skin to prickle. "And he looks shifty as hell," he murmured, his breath warm against my neck, sending another jolt of energy through me.

"Let's see if he interacts with anyone," I suggested, heart racing with anticipation. The video continued, showing the engineer moving through the lab with a furtive glance over his shoulder. "There! He's speaking to someone off-camera."

The security officer fast-forwarded, and suddenly the video jolted. "Wait, wait! Go back!" I urged, and the screen froze, revealing a figure cloaked in shadow, a face hidden beneath the brim of a baseball cap.

"Can you enhance that?" Nathan asked, and the officer adjusted the settings, but the figure remained elusive. It was frustrating, the growing knot of tension coiling tighter in my stomach.

"Come on, come on," I muttered, my frustration mounting as I squinted at the screen. "Who are you?"

As if sensing my growing anxiety, Nathan placed a reassuring hand on my shoulder. "We'll figure this out," he said, his voice low and steady.

Suddenly, the power flickered, plunging us into darkness. The screens blinked out, and the room was engulfed in silence, save for the distant hum of chaos outside. My heart raced, and instinct kicked in—something felt very wrong.

"Stay close," Nathan murmured, gripping my hand. The darkness wrapped around us like a shroud, and I could feel the tension in his body as we stood poised, waiting for something to break the silence.

A loud crash echoed from somewhere outside the security office, and my breath hitched in my throat. "What was that?" I whispered, eyes wide in the dark.

"I don't know, but we're not staying here to find out," he replied, pulling me toward the door. Just as we stepped out into the hallway, a series of panicked screams erupted, the sound reverberating through the building.

"Emma!" Nathan shouted, but before I could respond, a figure emerged from the shadows, lunging toward us with a frantic energy that sent my heart into a frenzy.

Everything moved in slow motion—the flash of movement, the fear coursing through my veins, and the realization that this was no longer just a theft. We were caught in something far more dangerous, and as I turned to Nathan, I felt the ground shift beneath me, the world spiraling into chaos once more.

"Run!" I screamed, adrenaline surging as the figure lunged forward, and in that moment, I knew we were in a fight for our lives.

Chapter 4: A Dangerous Alliance

The dim light of Nathan's office painted sharp shadows on the walls, giving the room an air of clandestine intimacy. It was a far cry from the sprawling chaos outside, where city life pulsed like an angry river. I stood before him, arms crossed, resisting the urge to fidget. The air was thick with the scent of leather and the faintest hint of cedarwood—an oddly comforting combination that contrasted sharply with the nervous energy buzzing between us.

"I'll ask again," Nathan said, leaning back in his chair, his fingers steepled, his gaze piercing. "What do you know about the message?" His voice was smooth, but there was an edge to it, like a knife hidden beneath velvet. It took every ounce of restraint I had not to roll my eyes at his theatrics.

"I don't know anything," I replied, feigning indifference, though my heart raced. The truth was, the moment I had read that cryptic text, a knot of anxiety had formed in my stomach. "Except that it's clearly a setup. A distraction, maybe. Or an invitation."

Nathan's smirk returned, the kind that ignited something both thrilling and infuriating within me. "You're sharper than you look, aren't you?"

"Don't flatter yourself," I shot back, feeling the heat creep into my cheeks. "I'm just not naïve enough to think this is all just coincidence."

He stood, the motion fluid, his tailored suit clinging perfectly to his frame. There was an elegance in his movements, like a predator ready to pounce, and it took all my willpower not to step back, not to give in to the tension that thrummed in the air. "It's never coincidence," he said, his voice low, as if sharing a secret. "Not in our world."

As he paced the room, my gaze followed him, tracing the lines of his jaw, the way his brow furrowed in concentration. I caught glimpses of a vulnerability behind his confident facade, a flicker of something deeper that made my pulse quicken. I was no stranger to the cutthroat world of theft and deceit, yet here I was, pulled into a web spun from equal parts danger and intrigue.

"So, what do we do now?" I asked, my tone less defensive than before.

He paused, turning to me, his eyes narrowing slightly. "We need to work together. I have resources that can help us find the thief, but I won't share them with someone I can't trust."

The challenge in his voice was unmistakable, and it struck a chord deep within me. Trust had always been a fragile currency, especially in our line of work. "And you think I'm just going to roll over and give you the upper hand?"

"Isn't that exactly what you did the last time we faced off?" he replied, that infuriating smirk reappearing. "You handed me the prize without so much as a fight."

"I was saving my energy for a real battle," I retorted, crossing my arms tightly, a futile attempt to shield myself from the onslaught of emotions swirling within me. "And you didn't win, Nathan. You merely found a way to exploit my situation."

"Sounds like you're still bitter," he teased, and I wanted nothing more than to hurl a paperweight at his perfect head.

"Bitter? Hardly." My words dripped with sarcasm, but beneath the surface, I was aware of the truth in his taunt. There was something unsettling about how easily he unnerved me, how his presence seemed to breach the barriers I had built around my heart. "I just refuse to become another pawn in your little game."

"You say that, yet here you are, seeking out my help," he shot back, his expression shifting from playful to serious. "The truth is, we're in this mess together, whether we like it or not. And unless you want to continue playing the victim, you'll have to let me in."

My breath hitched at the weight of his words. The tension in the room morphed, becoming palpable, almost electric. I wanted to argue, to push back against his logic, but there was a part of me that recognized the wisdom in his proposal. We had been competitors for too long, yet now, faced with a common enemy, the lines between us blurred.

"Fine," I finally conceded, the word tasting bitter on my tongue. "But don't think for a second that I'll make it easy for you."

His lips curved into that infuriating smirk again, and for a moment, it disarmed me. "I wouldn't dream of it. This will be more fun with you on the field."

Fun? My stomach twisted at the prospect. There was nothing fun about our situation, but there was a thrilling rush that surged through me as we dove deeper into our investigation, a dance of tension and curiosity.

With every new clue we uncovered, our rivalry transformed, blooming into a partnership that felt undeniably complex. I found myself studying Nathan as he scrolled through files on his sleek laptop, his brow furrowed in concentration. This was a man who thrived on secrets and shadows, but the way he included me in his world felt strangely intimate.

"Have you ever thought about what drives you?" I asked, surprising myself with the question.

He paused, glancing up at me, his eyes revealing a flicker of something vulnerable. "Every day. It's what keeps me alive."

"And what is that?"

He leaned forward, an intensity in his gaze that made me hold my breath. "Control."

"Control?" I echoed, intrigued. "Is that why you're so obsessed with winning?"

"Winning is just a means to an end," he replied, the seriousness in his tone catching me off guard. "It's about staying one step ahead of everyone else."

I couldn't help but wonder if, beneath the bravado, Nathan was just a man grappling with his own demons. As the conversation flowed, I felt the chemistry between us ignite, a slow burn of uncertainty and attraction that I couldn't ignore. Each revelation peeled back layers of his carefully constructed walls, and for the first time, I glimpsed a man fighting his own battles.

In that moment, as we stood on the precipice of something dangerous and exhilarating, I realized I was no longer sure who the real enemy was. The city outside continued to pulse with life, but within these walls, we were trapped in a world of secrets, waiting for the next twist in our tangled tale.

The rhythmic tapping of Nathan's fingers against his laptop filled the silence between us, each keystroke punctuating the electric tension in the air. I leaned against the edge of his polished desk, arms crossed, a carefully crafted wall against the unpredictability of our partnership. The office was a labyrinth of shadows and light, sleek lines and minimalist decor that somehow felt both sterile and inviting. A curious contradiction, much like the man in front of me.

"Are you always this focused, or is it just me?" I quipped, trying to lighten the mood, though the words felt heavier than intended. Nathan's brow furrowed in concentration, but a small grin tugged at his lips, making me question whether I'd gotten through his carefully constructed facade.

"Just you," he replied, his tone teasing yet earnest. "I can't help but be intrigued by the girl who thinks she can outsmart me."

The challenge in his eyes sparked a flame of determination within me. "Intrigued or annoyed?"

"Both," he admitted with a casual shrug, his confidence a shield that both impressed and frustrated me. I was still processing the implications of our unexpected alliance, the way it blurred the lines we had drawn in the sand during our previous encounters.

With a shared purpose that felt as thrilling as it was dangerous, we dove headfirst into the depths of our investigation. The cryptic message on my phone had ignited something fierce and tenacious within me. It wasn't just about uncovering the thief's identity anymore; it was about proving to myself that I could stand toe-to-toe with Nathan and emerge unscathed.

"Let's analyze this message," Nathan suggested, scrolling back through the thread. "What do we know about it?"

I bit my lip, fighting the urge to let the weight of my thoughts spill over. "It hinted at a connection to the recent thefts, but it was vague. Almost like a riddle."

He raised an eyebrow, his interest piqued. "A riddle, you say? What do you think it means?"

I leaned in closer, caught up in the moment. "The phrase 'trust is an illusion' stood out to me. It implies that whoever sent it is toying with us, possibly trying to throw us off the trail."

"Or draw us into a trap," Nathan countered, his expression darkening. The seriousness in his voice reminded me just how high the stakes were. "We need to be careful."

"Since when have you ever been careful?" I shot back, and the corner of his mouth twitched again.

"I like to think of it as calculated risk," he retorted, and I couldn't help but laugh at the absurdity of the statement.

"Calculated? Right. Let's hope it doesn't come back to bite us," I replied, shaking my head at his brashness.

We shared a moment of silence, the gravity of our situation hanging heavily in the air. I was acutely aware of the chemistry between us, a simmering tension that sparked every time our eyes met. Yet it felt dangerous, a fragile thing that could shatter with a single misstep.

As the hours slipped away, our investigation deepened. We combed through files, traced digital footprints, and pieced together fragments of information that felt tantalizingly close to a breakthrough. The more we uncovered, the clearer it became that our thief was not just a petty criminal; they were someone with a plan, a puppet master hiding in the shadows.

"Whoever this is, they know what they're doing," Nathan said, frowning at the screen. "It's not just random thefts; there's a method to their madness."

"More like a twisted game," I muttered, the hairs on the back of my neck prickling with unease. "They want us to play along."

"Which means we can't let them dictate the terms," Nathan replied, his voice steady and confident. "We'll turn the tables."

His determination was infectious, stirring something within me that I hadn't felt in a long time—the thrill of the chase. "Alright, so what's the plan?"

He leaned back in his chair, an inscrutable smile gracing his lips. "We follow the clues, but we do it on our terms. No more waiting for the thief to make the next move. We're taking the initiative."

"Bold move," I remarked, impressed by his audacity. "You're sure you can keep up?"

He shot me a sidelong glance, his eyes sparkling with mischief. "I'm more than capable of keeping up with you. The real question is, can you handle me?"

"Bring it on," I challenged, feeling a rush of adrenaline.

Our banter flowed seamlessly, each quip a thread weaving us closer together in this dangerous dance. Yet, beneath the surface, I sensed the uncertainty that lay coiled, ready to spring at any moment. The stakes had never been higher, and I couldn't ignore the precariousness of our alliance.

Later that night, as the city twinkled like a thousand scattered stars beneath the blanket of darkness, we ventured out together, a partnership forged in secrecy and necessity. The air was thick with anticipation, and I couldn't shake the feeling that we were stepping into a trap laid just for us.

"What's our first move?" I asked as we approached a dimly lit alleyway, the shadows deep and inviting.

"Let's check out the last known location of the stolen items," Nathan suggested, his voice steady. "We might find something the police overlooked."

"Like what? A breadcrumb trail leading us straight to the thief?" I raised an eyebrow, skepticism lacing my tone.

"Or a clue that reveals their true identity," he replied, a hint of excitement creeping into his voice.

The alley smelled of damp concrete and mystery, a place where secrets whispered through the cracks in the walls. With each step, my heart raced, anticipation crackling in the air. Together, we were a team—a precarious alliance navigating the murky waters of betrayal and intrigue.

"Stick close," Nathan said, his expression serious as he pulled his jacket tighter around himself. I nodded, though my thoughts were tangled in the possibilities of what lay ahead.

As we turned a corner, I felt the weight of his gaze on me, a silent acknowledgment of the bond we were forming. The thrill of the chase mingled with the electric tension that simmered beneath our banter, creating a volatile mix of emotions that left me both exhilarated and terrified.

The deeper we ventured into the heart of the city, the more I realized that this alliance, however risky, had become a source of strength. It challenged me in ways I hadn't anticipated, awakening a side of me that longed for adventure, for the unknown. The thought of facing the darkness ahead alongside Nathan was both daunting and undeniably enticing.

We were navigating a dangerous game, but together, we just might have the upper hand.

The alleyway's shadows loomed like dark specters, but they felt oddly comforting, a shroud of anonymity that matched my escalating heart rate. Nathan and I slipped deeper into the labyrinth of back streets, where the neon glow of the city faded into muted tones, and the familiar sounds of life grew distant. The air was thick with the scent of damp earth and secrets, creating an intoxicating mix that stirred my senses.

"I've always wanted to be a detective," I quipped, trying to mask my apprehension with humor. "You know, the kind that solves mysteries in dark alleys with a partner who broods too much."

Nathan's laugh, rich and genuine, sliced through the tension. "So, you're saying I'm broody? You might be onto something." He glanced at me, his expression teasing yet sincere. "But it takes one to know one."

I rolled my eyes but couldn't help but smile back. "Fair enough. Just remember, if we get caught, I'm throwing you under the bus."

"Please, the bus would be a luxury compared to what I have planned for you," he shot back, a wicked grin spreading across his face. "Let's just hope we don't end up in a police station before this is over."

As we ventured further, I couldn't shake the feeling that someone was watching us. The shadows danced just beyond the edges of my vision, and I found myself glancing over my shoulder more often than I cared to admit. Nathan, ever perceptive, seemed to notice, his posture tightening as we approached a deserted storefront.

"What's wrong?" he asked, his tone shifting from playful to serious in an instant.

"I don't know," I admitted, feeling the pulse of adrenaline quicken my heartbeat. "I just have this weird feeling."

He nodded, understanding the weight of unspoken fears. "Stay close. We can't afford any surprises."

We paused before the old storefront, its windows boarded up and covered in grime, but I felt an inexplicable pull. A flicker of light caught my eye from behind the cracks, a beacon beckoning us closer. "What do you think?" I gestured toward the entrance, a twinge of trepidation in my gut.

"Could be nothing, but it could also be everything," Nathan replied, his voice low. "Let's check it out."

With a shared look of resolve, we approached the entrance. The door creaked ominously as Nathan pushed it open, revealing a dimly lit interior that smelled of mold and stale air. The remnants of forgotten merchandise lined the shelves, each item shrouded in dust as if time had conspired to trap them in a state of perpetual neglect.

"Charming place," I murmured sarcastically, taking a cautious step inside. "A real hidden gem."

"Just like us," he quipped back, his eyes scanning the room with an intensity that made my heart race.

As we moved further in, we heard the unmistakable sound of shuffling from the back. My pulse quickened, and I glanced at Nathan, who gestured for silence. The atmosphere thickened with tension as we crept forward, each step deliberate, the floorboards creaking underfoot.

"On the count of three," Nathan whispered, his breath warm against my ear. "One... two..."

Before he could say three, a figure emerged from the shadows, startling both of us. It was a woman, her features obscured by a hood, but the glint of something metallic in her hand caught the light. My breath hitched, and instinct kicked in as I stepped back, ready to bolt.

"Who are you?" Nathan demanded, his tone firm yet cautious, and I felt a surge of protectiveness wash over me.

The woman laughed, a sound that echoed eerily through the empty space. "I'm the one you've been looking for," she said, her voice dripping with a mix of menace and mischief. "The thief. And you two are in way over your heads."

"Great, a thief with a flair for the dramatic," I muttered under my breath, feeling a rush of indignation. "What are you playing at?"

"Playing?" she scoffed, lowering her weapon just enough for me to see the small dagger glinting in her grasp. "This isn't a game. This is survival. You think you can waltz in here, uninvited, and figure everything out? You're wrong."

"Why don't you enlighten us?" Nathan replied, his voice steady, though I could sense the tension coiling in his muscles.

The woman stepped closer, the shadows shifting around her as if they were alive. "You have no idea what you're dealing with. This city is full of secrets, and not all of them are yours to uncover."

"Secrets are what we do best," I shot back, feeling the need to assert myself. "So you can either tell us what we want to know, or we can make this very unpleasant for you."

She studied us, her gaze flicking between Nathan and me, a glimmer of intrigue dancing in her eyes. "You think you're the heroes of this story? Let me assure you, that's not how this ends."

Before I could respond, a noise echoed from outside—heavy footsteps growing closer, followed by the unmistakable sound of sirens wailing in the distance. My heart raced.

"We need to go. Now," Nathan urged, grabbing my arm and pulling me toward the door.

But the woman's laughter echoed through the dimly lit room, a sound that sent chills racing down my spine. "Run all you want, but you can't escape what's coming. You've already made enemies, and they won't forget you."

As we bolted out of the store, adrenaline pumping through our veins, I felt a mix of exhilaration and dread. The streets felt like a living entity, alive with chaos as the lights from police cars flashed ominously, bathing everything in a red and blue hue.

"What do we do?" I asked, breathless as we rounded a corner, desperately seeking a place to hide.

"Head for the alley behind the café," Nathan instructed, his voice low but urgent. "We can regroup there."

We dashed through the backstreets, my lungs burning with the effort. The sirens grew louder, and the world around us became a blur of color and noise. Just as we reached the entrance of the alley, Nathan suddenly stopped, his expression shifting to one of horror.

"Wait!" he shouted, but it was too late.

From the shadows, a figure emerged—tall, imposing, and unmistakably familiar. My heart dropped as I recognized him. It was someone I had never expected to see again, someone whose presence sent a rush of dread cascading through me.

"Fancy meeting you here," he said, a sly smile creeping across his face, and in that moment, the world fell away. All I could see was the danger looming before us, the stakes rising higher than I had ever anticipated.

Chapter 5: The Threat Lurking

The warehouse loomed ahead, its sagging roof and shattered windows giving it an air of forgotten desolation. The city buzzed around us, but this place seemed to exist in a different realm, a sepulcher of secrets waiting to be unearthed. I could almost taste the rust in the air, a bitter reminder of everything that had gone wrong in my life. Nathan, beside me, moved with a confidence that belied the fear coiling in my gut. His dark hair fell over his forehead, catching the faint glow of the streetlights as we approached the entrance. I felt an unexplainable urge to reach for his hand, a spark igniting between us, but the atmosphere crackled with an electric tension that made me hesitate.

As we crept inside, the crunch of debris underfoot echoed in the vast emptiness. Faded graffiti adorned the walls, whispering stories of the past—youthful rebellion, pain, and perhaps a hint of beauty in the decay. My heart pounded in sync with the rhythm of our breaths, and I felt alive in a way I hadn't in ages, a delicious mix of dread and exhilaration. We were intruders in a world we did not belong to, driven by a thirst for answers that had propelled us into the depths of this darkness.

"Over there," Nathan murmured, his voice low and urgent as he pointed toward a flickering light in the distance. We maneuvered through the labyrinth of rusted machinery and old crates, each step echoing our resolve. Just as we rounded a corner, shadows flickered in the dim light, and I felt my heart stutter. A group of masked figures loomed before us, their outlines indistinct but their intentions clear.

"Who goes there?" one of them called, the voice muffled yet menacing, cutting through the stillness. I pressed closer to Nathan, instinctively seeking his strength. His presence enveloped me like a shield, and in that moment, I knew I would follow him into the heart of hell if it meant uncovering the truth.

"Stay back!" Nathan shouted, positioning himself in front of me. The protective instinct radiating from him sent a rush of warmth through my veins, igniting something fierce and undeniable within me. I couldn't help but admire his bravery, the way he faced danger head-on, despite the palpable threat surrounding us. The thrill of danger swirled around us, feeding my own desire to fight back against the shadows of my life.

As the masked figures advanced, I could feel the tension in the air thicken, becoming a living, breathing entity. My pulse quickened, and for the first time, I felt a sense of purpose that transcended my initial quest for family honor. This was no longer just about redemption; it was about standing tall against whatever darkness sought to consume us. Nathan's fierce gaze met mine, and in that instant, a silent understanding passed between us—this was our battle now, and we were in it together.

"Run!" Nathan yelled, breaking the spell that had tethered me to the spot. We bolted through the warehouse, our footsteps pounding against the cold concrete as adrenaline surged through our bodies. I could hear the shouts of the figures behind us, their footsteps echoing like a haunting refrain. Panic clawed at my throat, but there was also an exhilaration, a realization that I was capable of more than I had ever imagined.

We barreled through a back door, plunging into the cool night air, gasping for breath as the shadows receded behind us. Nathan pulled me into a nearby alley, and we pressed ourselves against the damp brick wall, trying to regain our composure. The world outside the warehouse continued to thrum with life, oblivious to the chaos we had narrowly escaped. My heart raced not just from fear, but from the undeniable chemistry crackling between us, the adrenaline of the night amplifying every glance and touch.

"What the hell was that?" I panted, the words tumbling out in a rush. I could see the tension in Nathan's jaw, his brow furrowed in thought.

"I don't know," he replied, his voice steady despite the turmoil in his eyes. "But they're involved in something big, something dangerous. We can't go back there."

"Agreed." My breath came in quick bursts as the realization settled over me. This was bigger than I had anticipated. My family's honor was on the line, but so were our lives. I felt the weight of the world pressing down on my shoulders, and yet, there was an exhilarating sense of purpose that thrummed within me. "But we need to figure out what they're up to."

Nathan studied me, his expression a mix of admiration and concern. "Are you sure? This could get us into deeper trouble than we already are."

"Trouble is my middle name," I quipped, trying to inject humor into the gravity of the situation. He cracked a half-smile, and I felt a rush of warmth bloom in my chest, an unexpected comfort amidst the chaos. "Besides, I didn't come this far to turn back now. We're in this together."

His eyes sparkled with something I couldn't quite place, a mix of respect and something deeper, as if he could sense the transformation taking place within me. We stood there, breathless and exhilarated, two souls standing at the precipice of something far greater than ourselves. In that moment, I understood that this was not just a quest for answers—it was a journey of self-discovery. I was no longer just a girl fighting for her family's name; I was becoming a force to be reckoned with, fueled by a fierce determination to uncover the truth, no matter the cost.

The adrenaline from our narrow escape still coursed through my veins, a wild dance of fear and exhilaration. The cool night air felt electric, swirling around us as we ducked into a secluded corner of the alley. My heart thudded loudly in my chest, each beat echoing the thrill of our confrontation, the intensity of Nathan's fierce protectiveness igniting a fire within me. I glanced sideways at him, trying to gauge what he was feeling. His brow was furrowed, eyes sharp as he surveyed the street, a silent sentinel on guard.

"Are we safe here?" I whispered, my voice barely rising above the hum of the city. The streetlights cast eerie shadows, flickering as if the night itself was holding its breath.

"For now," he replied, though his tone lacked the certainty I craved. "But we need to move. They might come looking for us."

I nodded, suppressing a shiver that had nothing to do with the chill in the air. The encounter with the masked figures had shaken me more than I wanted to admit. I wasn't merely terrified; I was intrigued, hooked by the danger we had stumbled into. It felt like being swept up in a storm, winds swirling around me, and I wasn't sure if I wanted to escape or dive deeper into the chaos.

"Where do we go?" I asked, trying to mask the tremor in my voice. Nathan turned his attention back to me, his features softening as if he could sense my unease.

"Follow me." He took my hand, his grip firm and reassuring, and led me deeper into the shadows. My pulse quickened at the contact, a jolt of warmth spreading through me that clashed with the chill of fear still lingering in the air.

We wound our way through dimly lit streets, weaving past abandoned buildings and flickering neon signs that cast a surreal glow over our path. Each step felt like a leap into the unknown, and with Nathan beside me, I felt a strange sense of security. I had always considered myself a solitary fighter, carrying the weight of my family's honor alone, but with him, I felt emboldened. The idea of sharing this burden, of forging a partnership in the quest for answers, was both terrifying and exhilarating.

As we turned a corner, Nathan stopped suddenly, pulling me behind a dumpster. The metallic scent of refuse mixed with the distant sound of sirens, a reminder of the world we were trying to navigate. He peered out, and I couldn't help but admire the way his jaw clenched in determination.

"Look," he murmured, his voice low. I followed his gaze to a flickering streetlight illuminating a figure standing on the opposite corner. A woman, her silhouette stark against the glow, leaned against a lamppost, fiddling with something in her hands.

"Who is she?" I whispered, squinting to get a better look.

"I don't know, but she looks out of place," Nathan replied, his eyes narrowing. "Let's watch for a moment."

We remained hidden, our breath mingling in the cool air as we observed her. The woman wore a long coat, the collar pulled up against the wind, and her dark hair cascaded over her shoulders like a waterfall of midnight. She shifted nervously, glancing down the street as if waiting for someone. A knot of tension twisted in my stomach.

"Do you think she's part of that group?" I asked, my curiosity battling with instinctual wariness.

"Could be," Nathan replied, his brow furrowing. "But she might also be someone we can trust. We need information, and if she's connected to what we just encountered, she could lead us to it."

I hesitated, uncertainty gnawing at me. "What if she's dangerous?"

"Then we'll be ready." His expression was resolute, igniting a spark of courage within me. He stepped forward, and I followed, my heart racing in anticipation of what lay ahead.

As we approached, the woman's gaze darted to us, her expression unreadable. "You two look like you've been through the wringer," she said, her voice smooth yet laced with an edge of caution. "What are you doing here?"

"We're investigating something," Nathan replied, his tone steady but firm. "We saw a group back at the warehouse. Are you connected to them?"

A flicker of surprise crossed her face before she recovered. "Depends on who you think I am."

I exchanged a glance with Nathan, the tension thickening. "I think you're someone who knows more than she's letting on," I challenged, my voice gaining strength.

Her lips quirked into a half-smile. "Feisty. I like that. But if you're looking for trouble, you're in the right place."

Before I could respond, she stepped closer, lowering her voice as if the shadows themselves were listening. "The people you saw—those masked figures—they're not just thugs. They're part of something much bigger, and it's dangerous. I can help you, but you need to trust me."

Trust. The word hung in the air between us, heavy with implications. My instincts warred within me. This could be a trap, but my gut told me we were at a crossroads, a moment where choices would lead us into uncharted territory.

"What do you know?" Nathan pressed, his gaze unwavering, searching for the truth buried behind her enigmatic demeanor.

She hesitated, weighing her words. "Let's just say I've seen the consequences of their actions, and it's not pretty. There are people in this city who want to keep secrets buried, and anyone who digs too deep..." Her voice trailed off, and I could almost see the unspoken threat lingering in the shadows.

"Anyone who digs too deep what?" I prodded, leaning in, captivated despite myself.

"Anyone who digs too deep... disappears." Her words hung like a dark cloud over us, and I felt a chill crawl up my spine.

"What's the plan then?" I asked, defiance bubbling within me. "You can't expect us to just walk away."

She regarded me for a moment, her gaze piercing. "No, I don't expect that. But I also don't want to see you two become another set of victims. If you're in, you need to be all in. No half-measures."

A surge of adrenaline coursed through me. The stakes had never been higher, and for the first time, I felt the weight of my family's legacy pushing me forward. "We're all in," I declared, locking eyes with Nathan. The resolve in his gaze mirrored my own, igniting a bond that tethered us together in this dangerous dance.

"Alright then," the woman said, a glimmer of approval in her eyes. "Let's get started."

And just like that, the night transformed from a mere escape into a tangled web of intrigue, secrets, and the intoxicating thrill of the chase. Together, we would peel back the layers of deception and uncover the truth, whatever it may cost us.

The woman's expression shifted, a glint of mischief in her eyes as if she relished the idea of dragging us deeper into this murky abyss. "I'll give you the rundown," she said, her voice silky but urgent. "There's a network of power players in this city, all vying for control. The masked figures you encountered are just the tip of the iceberg, pawns in a much larger game. They're working for someone who pulls the strings from the shadows, someone who won't hesitate to silence you if you get too close."

"Silence us?" I echoed, unable to mask the tremor in my voice. "Like, permanently?" The weight of her words pressed heavily against my chest, an anchor threatening to drag me down.

"Precisely," she replied, her tone grave. "This isn't just about your family or whatever vendetta you think you're avenging. This is about survival."

Nathan stepped forward, his brow furrowed in thought. "So what's our next move? We can't just sit around and wait for them to come for us."

The woman chuckled lightly, but it didn't reach her eyes. "You're right. Waiting is for the weak. If you want to make an impact, you need to infiltrate their ranks. Find out who's really behind the masks."

I glanced at Nathan, whose jaw was set in determination, and nodded. "Infiltrate how? We're not exactly trained spies."

"Leave that to me." The woman waved her hand dismissively. "You just need to look the part. I can get you what you need."

"Look the part?" I raised an eyebrow, skepticism bubbling to the surface. "And what exactly does that entail?"

"Let's just say I have a few connections," she replied cryptically. "I can arrange for you to attend one of their underground gatherings. It's an opportunity to blend in, hear what they're plotting, and gather intel without drawing attention to yourselves."

The idea sent a shiver of excitement down my spine. "And how do you plan to get us in?"

"Leave that to me," she said again, this time with a sly smile. "But first, we need to ensure you're prepared. This isn't a tea party; it's a game of wits and cunning."

I glanced at Nathan, whose expression had transformed from apprehension to intrigue. "What do you think?" I asked, gauging his response.

"I think we need to take this seriously," he replied, his voice steady. "If we want to uncover the truth, we have to play the game."

"Then it's settled," I said, my heart racing with the thrill of it all. "But let's make one thing clear: we're not just pawns in their game. We're here to win."

The woman grinned, a spark of approval lighting her features. "Now that's the spirit. But I should warn you—trust is a fragile thing in these circles. Keep your wits about you, and don't take anything at face value."

As we exchanged details, I felt a sense of camaraderie beginning to build, a fragile bond formed through our shared goal. The woman introduced herself as Kira, her eyes glinting with a mix of mischief and mystery. The way she navigated the shadows suggested she was no stranger to danger, and I couldn't help but wonder how many secrets she held.

"Meet me here tomorrow night," Kira instructed, glancing at her watch. "I'll have everything ready for you. Just come prepared to play your roles."

"Roles?" I asked, confusion knitting my brow.

"Yes. You'll need identities. Costumes, if you will. This isn't a masquerade ball, but it might as well be."

"Great. So, we get to dress up and play pretend in a dangerous game," I quipped, trying to lighten the mood despite the tension swirling around us.

"Exactly. It'll be fun, I promise." Kira's smirk was infectious, and I found myself mirroring it despite the gravity of the situation.

As we parted ways, I felt a newfound sense of purpose coursing through me, a heady mix of excitement and fear. "What do you think?" I asked Nathan as we walked away, the city lights casting long shadows on the pavement.

"I think we've opened a door that might lead us somewhere dangerous," he replied, his tone serious. "But I also think we're ready for it. We can't back down now."

I nodded, the thrill of the chase igniting my spirit. "Right. No turning back."

The following day was a blur of anticipation and preparation. I rummaged through my closet, piecing together an outfit that would help me blend in, channeling a sense of cool confidence rather than my usual anxious self. Nathan and I met up later in the day, both of us donning our best disguises, a mix of casual chic and edgy flair that seemed to scream "We belong here."

"You look incredible," Nathan said, his eyes lighting up as they traveled over my outfit. "Very mysterious."

"Right back at you," I shot back with a teasing grin, noticing how he wore his confidence like armor, the perfect balance of casual and commanding. "We could pass for the lead characters in a noir film."

As the evening approached, the anticipation wrapped around me like a warm cloak, but the nervous energy buzzed beneath the surface, a reminder of the danger that lurked just beyond our sight. We met Kira at the designated spot, a hidden entrance at the back of a trendy club where the music thumped like a heartbeat, pulsing through the very walls.

"This is it," Kira said, her excitement infectious as she led us down a narrow corridor lined with graffiti and flickering lights. "Just remember, stick close to me and follow my lead."

We stepped into the dimly lit room beyond, the atmosphere thick with laughter and the clinking of glasses, a mix of revelry and something darker simmering just beneath the surface. The air was heavy with secrets, and I could feel my pulse quicken as I scanned the crowd.

"Looks like a real party," Nathan murmured, eyeing the patrons who danced and mingled, their faces hidden beneath masks that only added to the air of intrigue.

"Remember what I said about trust," Kira reminded us, her voice low and steady. "Keep your ears open and your eyes sharp. We're here for information, not just to enjoy the ambiance."

As we ventured deeper into the throng, I caught snippets of conversations that set my heart racing—discussions of power moves, hidden agendas, and whispered threats. My instincts prickled with anticipation, the realization that we were not just observers but participants in a dangerous game.

Suddenly, I felt a hand on my shoulder. I turned, heart in my throat, to find a tall figure stepping out of the shadows, his presence commanding and intense. "Well, well, what do we have here?" he drawled, his voice smooth like silk but edged with menace.

"Just new faces," Kira replied, her tone cool and collected. "We're here for the fun."

"Fun? In this crowd?" The man laughed softly, a sound that sent a chill down my spine. "You have no idea what you're in for."

As he stepped closer, I felt the temperature in the room drop. The glint in his eyes hinted at knowledge that could unravel everything. I exchanged a worried glance with Nathan, my heart thundering in my chest. This was it. The moment where the facade of fun shattered, revealing the danger lurking just beneath the surface.

And then the lights flickered ominously, plunging us into momentary darkness. A voice boomed from the speakers, slicing through the tension. "Welcome, everyone, to the gathering of the unseen!"

The room erupted in cheers, but my blood ran cold. The thrill of danger twisted into something more sinister as I felt the weight of the man's gaze lingering on me. Whatever we had stepped into, it was far more than we had bargained for.

In that instant, I knew we were no longer mere spectators in this dangerous game; we were now fully immersed players, entangled in a web of deceit and peril from which escape might be impossible.

Chapter 6: Secrets and Confessions

The silence in my apartment felt thicker than the fog outside, wrapping around us like an unwelcome embrace. The glow of the streetlights filtered through the curtains, casting a soft, golden light that barely illuminated the tension in the room. Nathan stood a few paces away, his hands stuffed deep into the pockets of his worn leather jacket. I could see the faintest tremor in his fingers, a telltale sign that this cool facade he maintained was beginning to slip.

"Tell me the truth, Nathan. What are you hiding?" I pressed, my voice firm despite the fluttering uncertainty in my stomach. His blue eyes, which had flickered with playful mischief just hours ago, now darkened with shadows of guilt and fear. For a moment, I regretted my harsh tone, but the urgency of our situation demanded answers.

He took a deep breath, the kind that filled his chest but seemed to deflate the bravado that had wrapped around him like armor. "It's not as simple as you think," he began, his voice low and steady. "My family... they're involved in things you wouldn't believe. I didn't choose this, Emily. It was handed to me like a curse."

I shifted, feeling the weight of his words sink into the space between us. "What kind of things?" My curiosity pricked at the edges of my apprehension. I wanted to trust him, to understand the man who had both baffled and intrigued me from the moment we met. But secrets, especially dangerous ones, had a way of corrupting everything they touched.

Nathan stepped closer, his expression earnest, almost desperate. "You have to know—I'm not like them. I never wanted any part of it." His voice cracked slightly, revealing the burden he carried. "When I found out about the tech theft, it was like a switch flipped. I didn't want to believe my family could be involved in something so... vile. I thought I could ignore it, bury it under layers of denial. But then, when I saw you..."

"Me?" I interrupted, surprised by the weight of his admission. "What do I have to do with this?"

He ran a hand through his tousled hair, the gesture revealing a vulnerability that made my heart race. "Everything. You're the first person I've connected with in ages. You see me, not just the facade. I don't want to drag you into this mess, but..." He hesitated, as if weighing his next words against the possible fallout.

"But?" I prompted, stepping closer, my heart pounding in my chest.

"I need you to trust me. This isn't just about my family. There are people out there who would use you to get to me." The gravity of his words landed heavily between us, and I instinctively moved closer, drawn in by the magnetic pull of his intensity.

"I already trust you," I admitted, the admission spilling out before I could catch it. "But how can I help if I don't know the whole story?"

He glanced around my modest living room, the small details—the mismatched furniture, the stack of books teetering precariously on the coffee table, the half-finished bottle of wine from our earlier impromptu dinner—offering a stark contrast to the chaos swirling just outside our door. "There's a network of people who are as ruthless as my family, and they're searching for something they believe I have. They'll stop at nothing to get it."

"Something?" I echoed, my mind racing. "What could possibly be worth all of this?"

His gaze bore into mine, and for a moment, the world outside faded into nothingness. "A project. Something my father and his associates were developing before it got out of hand. I was supposed to be a part of it, a pawn in their game, but I can't be that anymore. I won't."

The resolve in his voice sent a shiver down my spine, but there was something deeper at play. "So you're just going to run? Is that your plan?" I asked, crossing my arms in defiance.

"I'm not running," he countered, frustration lacing his tone. "I'm trying to make things right. But I can't do it alone, and that's why you have to stay with me. We need to figure out what's going on before it's too late."

I felt a rush of warmth at the thought of standing by his side, the idea igniting a spark of courage within me. "Then we figure it out together," I said, determination igniting in my chest.

His lips twitched into a hesitant smile, one that illuminated his features and turned the tension in the air into something softer, more tangible. "Together," he echoed, as if the word itself was a promise.

As we stood there, the walls between us began to shift and dissolve, revealing the raw truths beneath the bravado. The air hummed with unspoken confessions, and I felt a connection with Nathan that I had never expected.

Just then, a loud crash from outside shattered the fragile moment. My heart raced as I instinctively moved closer to Nathan, our shoulders brushing. "What was that?" I whispered, my pulse quickening.

He shifted, alert and tense, every muscle in his body attuned to the encroaching danger. "I don't know, but we need to check it out."

He grabbed my hand, and together we crept toward the door, my heart thundering in my ears. Whatever secrets lay ahead, whatever truths were waiting to be uncovered, we were in this together now, bound by the tension of the moment and the promise of something deeper.

The moment we stepped outside, the air was thick with a kind of electricity that felt both exhilarating and foreboding. The night was alive with distant sirens, the hum of city life juxtaposed against the unease that lingered in my chest. Nathan's grip on my hand was

DANGEROUS ALLIANCES 59

firm, grounding me in the chaos that seemed to envelop us. As we navigated the dimly lit streets, I felt the weight of our shared secrets and unspoken fears.

"Do you always find trouble in the middle of the night?" I quipped, trying to lighten the mood. A wry smile flickered on his lips, the tension in his shoulders easing ever so slightly.

"It seems to be a recurring theme when I'm around you," he shot back, his voice a low rumble. The banter, familiar yet charged with unacknowledged feelings, created a strange sense of normalcy amidst the turmoil.

We turned a corner, the streetlights casting elongated shadows that danced along the pavement. My heart raced, not just from the fear of the unknown lurking in the shadows, but from the intoxicating realization that we were in this together, two reluctant allies in a twisted game we barely understood. "So, what's the plan?" I asked, feeling the need to grasp something solid in a world that had turned suddenly chaotic.

Nathan paused, his brow furrowing as he surveyed the street. "We need to figure out who's after me, and why they want whatever it is my family's been involved with. But first, we should find a safe place to regroup."

I nodded, mentally flipping through the map of our surroundings. "There's a café not far from here. It's open late, and I know the owner. We can lay low there."

With a quick nod, Nathan began to lead the way. As we walked, I couldn't help but steal glances at him, each one revealing something new—his jawline shadowed in the soft light, the determination etched into his features. This man was more than just the sum of his family's misdeeds; he was an enigma I yearned to solve.

The café appeared just around the bend, a quaint little spot tucked between a bookshop and an antique store. The neon sign flickered softly, casting a welcoming glow that contrasted sharply with the anxiety roiling within me. As we entered, the rich aroma of coffee mingled with the scent of baked goods, momentarily distracting me from our dire circumstances. The café was almost empty, save for a couple of night owls hunched over laptops and a small group at the back, engaged in animated conversation.

"Over there," I gestured toward a secluded table in the corner, hoping the shadows would grant us some semblance of privacy. We slid into the booth, the vinyl seat cool against my skin.

Nathan leaned back, exhaling a long, weary breath. "I didn't think we'd end up here tonight," he admitted, running a hand through his hair. "I figured I'd just be dealing with family drama. Now, I'm dodging who knows what."

"Welcome to my world," I replied with a teasing lilt, the tension between us softening momentarily. "This is just another Tuesday for me."

He laughed, the sound a rich note that rang through the air, providing a brief escape from our reality. "Right, because everyone's life involves tech heists and shady family secrets."

"Hey, I like to keep it interesting," I shot back, then paused, allowing the weight of the moment to settle in again. "But seriously, what did your family get involved in? It sounds like something out of a spy novel."

Nathan's expression darkened, the humor fading like the last light of day. "They were working on advanced technology. Something that could change how we interact with the digital world. But it was never meant for good. I didn't realize it until it was too late."

"Too late?" I leaned forward, my curiosity piqued. "What happened?"

He hesitated, searching for the right words, his eyes narrowing as he reflected on the past. "I was meant to take over the project. My father wanted me to be the face of it. But when I started to dig deeper, I found out about the ethical breaches, the people they were stepping on to get ahead. I knew I had to walk away, but they don't take kindly to betrayal in our family."

A chill skittered down my spine at his revelation. "So now you're being hunted because you chose to do the right thing?"

"Something like that." He leaned closer, his voice dropping to a conspiratorial whisper. "And now that I'm out, they think I know something that could expose them. They'll stop at nothing to get it back."

The gravity of his situation wrapped around me like a vise. "What do you think they're looking for?"

"I don't know," he replied, frustration creeping into his tone. "Maybe the plans or the prototypes. They've always been a step ahead, but I can't let them win this time."

The barista approached our table, breaking the tension as he set down two steaming mugs of coffee, the dark liquid swirling like the chaos of our conversation. I thanked him, savoring the warmth that radiated from the cup as I cradled it in my hands.

"What about you?" Nathan asked, his gaze steady. "How do you fit into all of this? Why do you care so much?"

I took a moment to collect my thoughts, the vulnerability of the moment weaving an unexpected thread between us. "Honestly? I've always been the quiet observer. I'd watch my friends dive headfirst into drama, and I'd just sit back and shake my head. But something about you—your passion, your determination—made me want to break free of my own patterns."

He raised an eyebrow, a playful smirk tugging at the corner of his mouth. "So, you're saying I'm your bad influence?"

"More like the catalyst I didn't know I needed," I corrected, feeling the heat rise in my cheeks.

His eyes sparkled with amusement, but the moment was fleeting, overshadowed by the reality outside those café walls. The weight of our circumstances pressed in, reminding us both that our time was limited.

"Whatever happens next," Nathan said, his voice low and serious, "I want you to promise me that you'll stay close. I don't know what I'd do if anything happened to you."

I swallowed hard, the sincerity in his tone wrapping around me like a security blanket. "I promise. But let's hope it doesn't come to that."

Just as we began to delve deeper into our plans, the café door swung open with a jingle, a gust of cold air sweeping in, carrying with it the unsettling sound of hurried footsteps. My heart raced as I turned to see a figure enter, their eyes scanning the room with a predatory focus.

Nathan's grip tightened around his mug, and I felt the tension in the air shift. We were no longer just two people discussing secrets; we were potential targets, and I realized then that our game of cat and mouse had only just begun.

The figure at the door was tall, cloaked in shadows, with an air of predatory confidence that made my pulse quicken. They stood there for a moment, scanning the café, their gaze landing on Nathan and me like a spotlight on an unsuspecting prey. My heart thudded heavily in my chest as I instinctively shifted closer to him, the connection between us becoming a lifeline in the face of an impending storm.

"Do you know them?" I whispered, trying to keep my voice steady, though my stomach twisted in knots.

Nathan's brow furrowed, his body tense beside me. "No, but they don't look friendly."

The newcomer stepped further inside, shaking off the chill of the night, their eyes sharp and glinting like a hawk spotting its next meal. I felt exposed, vulnerable in this cozy little café that suddenly felt too small, too open. As the figure approached the counter, the barista, oblivious to the tension crackling in the air, greeted them with a warm smile.

"Can I get you something?" the barista asked, but the stranger barely acknowledged him. Instead, they continued to survey the room, their expression a mixture of irritation and determination.

"What's the play here?" I asked, leaning in closer to Nathan, my voice barely above a whisper. "Should we leave?"

He glanced around, his jaw tight. "Let's wait a moment. If they're looking for me, they might leave if they don't see me."

My instinct was to bolt, to escape the brewing confrontation before it escalated, but something in Nathan's expression held me in place. He was trying to remain calm, and I felt a strange comfort in his presence, even as my nerves screamed at me to flee.

The stranger finally turned away from the counter, a steaming cup of coffee in hand, and with deliberate slowness, they made their way toward our table. Panic surged through me as I contemplated the various ways this encounter could go wrong. I couldn't shake the feeling that whatever secrets Nathan held were about to be laid bare under this newcomer's scrutiny.

"Nice place," the stranger said, their voice smooth and dripping with an unsettling charm. "Too bad it's about to get a little more... exciting."

Nathan's eyes narrowed. "Who are you?"

"Just someone looking for answers," the stranger replied, taking a leisurely sip from their cup, seemingly unfazed by the tension they had just introduced. "I'm here to help. Or to make things very difficult for you, depending on how you respond."

"Help?" I echoed incredulously. "What kind of help involves stalking us in a café?"

The stranger chuckled, an amused sound that didn't reach their eyes. "Stalking? How dramatic. Let's just say I prefer to observe before making introductions." They leaned in, eyes locking onto

Nathan's. "You've stirred the pot, and it's boiling over. Your family has quite the reputation, Nathan. Care to explain why I shouldn't bring it all crashing down?"

I felt the air grow thick with unspoken threats, and I glanced at Nathan, who seemed to have gone still, the bravado slipping from his face. "You don't know what you're talking about," he said, voice low but steady, though I could see the tension in his clenched jaw.

"Of course I do. And so do you. Let's cut to the chase. You've got something I need, and it's time we talked."

The weight of those words hung heavily in the air, and I could see Nathan's mind racing, processing the implications of this sudden encounter. "And what makes you think I'd give you anything?"

The stranger smirked, a calculated expression that suggested they relished this game of cat and mouse. "Because you're not as clever as you think, and you know deep down you can't keep running. I can help you navigate this chaos, but you'll have to be willing to share a little something in return."

"What kind of chaos?" I interjected, feeling like I was intruding on a conversation I didn't fully understand. "And what exactly are you after?"

"Just the truth," they replied, their gaze sharp, as if they were slicing through the layers of our defenses with each word. "The truth about your family's little project and where it might lead. You don't even know what you're dealing with, do you?"

Nathan's fingers tightened around his coffee cup, the tension in the air thickening with every beat of silence that followed. "I know enough," he said finally, his voice even but carrying an undertone of steel.

"Enough? Is that what you tell yourself to sleep at night? You've bitten off more than you can chew, and if you're not careful, it'll swallow you whole."

Just as Nathan opened his mouth to respond, a loud crash erupted from outside, the sound reverberating through the café like a thunderclap. The stranger's expression shifted, a flicker of concern flashing across their features before they masked it with feigned nonchalance.

"Seems like the chaos has arrived," they said, rising from the table. "Consider this a warning, Nathan. You're running out of time."

"What do you mean?" I blurted, instinctively moving closer to Nathan, whose posture had become defensive.

Before the stranger could respond, the door to the café swung open again, and a group of figures spilled inside, their faces obscured by hoods and masks. My heart dropped as I recognized the telltale signs of trouble—their eyes darting around the room like predators scenting their prey.

"Time's up," the stranger muttered, their demeanor shifting from laid-back to alert in an instant. "You need to go—now."

Nathan grabbed my hand, and together we bolted from the table, adrenaline surging as we raced toward the back exit. The clatter of chairs echoed behind us, the chaotic scene unfolding with a terrifying urgency. I felt a surge of panic as we reached the door, and just as Nathan yanked it open, I glanced back to see the masked figures advancing, their intentions as clear as the moonlight spilling through the windows.

"Run!" Nathan urged, his voice urgent and sharp. We darted into the alley behind the café, the cool night air hitting me like a wave as we stumbled into the darkness.

But as we rounded the corner, I couldn't shake the feeling that this was just the beginning. Whatever tangled web Nathan's family had woven was tightening around us, and with every frantic heartbeat, I sensed the danger drawing closer.

We ran, the echoes of chaos behind us urging us forward into the unknown, where even the shadows felt alive and waiting, and a chilling realization gripped my heart—some secrets were far more dangerous than I had ever imagined.

Chapter 7: Crossing Boundaries

The soft light of the setting sun spilled through the window, casting warm golden hues across the small living room where we had made our makeshift office. Papers were strewn across the coffee table like the remnants of a battle, each one a testament to the late nights and long discussions that had bound us together. I was acutely aware of the gentle hum of the city outside, a rhythm that matched the quickening beat of my heart as Nathan leaned closer, his presence both comforting and electrifying.

The room was filled with the rich scent of brewed coffee, its warmth mingling with the faint hint of lavender from the candles flickering in the corners. Each flicker reminded me of the pulse of tension between us, as though the very air was charged with possibility. I stole a glance at Nathan, whose brow furrowed in concentration as he rifled through the documents, his fingers grazing the pages with an effortless grace that was utterly captivating. His shirt, rolled up to his elbows, revealed muscular forearms that seemed to speak of long hours spent working hard and a life lived with purpose.

When our fingers brushed, the world around us melted away. That singular moment felt like the softest ignition, a spark in a darkened room that set off an inferno in the pit of my stomach. I looked up, meeting his gaze, a mix of surprise and something deeper—something that whispered of all the things we hadn't said but both felt. "We should probably keep this professional," he murmured, a playful smirk tugging at the corners of his mouth. His tone was teasing, yet the huskiness in his voice wrapped around my senses, leaving me momentarily speechless.

"Professional? Is that what you want?" I countered, my voice softer than I intended, the challenge hanging in the air between us like a taut wire ready to snap. His laughter was low, deep, resonating in the space between us, and I felt a heady thrill at the thought that we were dancing on the edge of something wildly unpredictable.

"I don't know, perhaps I'm just trying to keep my sanity intact," he replied, leaning back slightly, a gesture that was both defensive and inviting. "You're a distraction I didn't see coming."

"Good distractions can be a blessing," I said, a playful glint in my eyes. The corners of his mouth twitched upward, and for a moment, I was lost in the depths of his gaze, a dark blue that felt like a tempest brewing. The warmth of his body radiated against mine, the tiny space between us pulsating with an energy that seemed to vibrate off the walls.

Before I could overthink it, I leaned closer, emboldened by a rush of adrenaline. "What if I don't want to be professional right now?" My heart raced, and I saw the surprise flash across his face, quickly replaced by a burning intensity that matched my own.

"Then what do you want?" he asked, his voice barely a whisper, filled with intrigue and challenge. My breath hitched as the distance between us evaporated, leaving only an electric connection that had us both teetering on the precipice of what could be. I opened my mouth, then closed it, not trusting myself to speak.

"Maybe," I said finally, leaning even closer, "I want to know what this could be." The words hung between us, thick and heavy with anticipation.

Before I could second-guess myself, I reached out, my hand brushing against his cheek, feeling the rough stubble beneath my fingertips. He hesitated for a heartbeat, and in that instant, every worry about the consequences washed away. With a mutual understanding that we were both crossing a threshold we might never return from, I closed the gap.

Our lips met, softly at first, a gentle collision that sent a shockwave through my body. As our kiss deepened, it felt as if time had suspended itself, the chaos of our lives quieting into a perfect silence where nothing else mattered. His hands found their way to my waist, pulling me closer as if he wanted to etch this moment into his memory.

The kiss ignited something deep within me, a heat that coursed through my veins and turned my insides to molten lava. I had imagined this moment a thousand times, but none of those fantasies could compare to the reality of being wrapped in his arms, tasting the warmth of his lips, feeling the raw energy of our connection.

We pulled apart, breathless and dazed, our foreheads resting against one another as we tried to grasp the enormity of what had just happened. I could see the confusion swirling in his eyes, mingled with desire, a cocktail of emotions I had never witnessed before. "What do we do now?" he asked, his voice a mixture of vulnerability and bravado.

"Maybe we should figure that out," I replied, my heart still racing, the thrill of the unknown igniting every fiber of my being. The line between professional and personal had blurred irrevocably, and the exhilaration of it sent shivers down my spine.

But before we could delve into the implications of our kiss, the shrill sound of my phone shattered the moment, echoing off the walls and cutting through the charged atmosphere like a knife. The ringtone—an obnoxious pop song—seemed almost disrespectful to the intimacy we had just shared. Nathan sighed, running a hand through his hair in a gesture of frustration that made my heart flutter.

"Always the timing, isn't it?" he muttered, breaking the spell that had enveloped us. I laughed, the sound light and airy, a buoy in the turbulent sea of emotions swirling around us. I could feel the tension returning, the fragile thread of our newfound intimacy stretching as I reached for my phone, reluctantly stepping back into reality.

As I answered the call, I felt the weight of Nathan's gaze on me, a mix of curiosity and something more profound lurking beneath the surface. The moment had passed, but the fire between us still flickered, waiting for the right spark to ignite it once more.

The call I answered was from my mother, her voice a cheerful lilt against the backdrop of my swirling thoughts. "Hey, sweetie! How's that project of yours going? Any sign of a breakthrough?" I tried to focus on her words, forcing myself to smile even as Nathan remained just a breath away, his presence a distracting heat that lingered in the air like the scent of summer rain.

"Just busy with the usual," I replied, the sound of my own voice feeling far too light and breezy compared to the weight of the moment we had just shared. Nathan busied himself with the documents, pretending to read while I could feel his gaze darting back to me, curiosity etched into his features. I bit my lip, fighting the urge to smile like a giddy schoolgirl while I tried to maintain an air of professionalism.

"Well, don't work too hard! You know I worry about you." My mother's words pulled me back, reminding me that beneath the whirlwind of emotions and new beginnings, there was still a life outside my apartment—a life full of obligations and expectations. "And don't forget, your aunt is coming over for dinner this weekend. I expect you to be here!"

"Of course, I'll be there," I replied, my tone lightening as I imagined my mother bustling around the kitchen, her laughter echoing as she whipped up one of her famous pasta dishes. "Tell her I'll make dessert."

"Great! I'll let her know. I can't wait to see you, honey!" With that, we exchanged our usual farewells, and I hung up the phone, the weight of reality settling back onto my shoulders.

Nathan's expression shifted as I set my phone down, his brow furrowing in that way that made my heart flutter with an unexpected rush of affection. "You okay?" he asked, concern threading through his voice.

"Just my mom, you know," I replied, waving a dismissive hand. "A family dinner this weekend. The usual chaos."

"Sounds fun," he said, though his tone suggested he was less than convinced. "Big family gatherings can be intense."

"Only if you let them," I quipped, a smile creeping onto my face. "You learn to navigate the storm or you get swept away. Besides, the food is usually worth the fuss."

He chuckled, the sound warm and rich, sending a thrill of delight through me. "Food always wins. That's a universal truth."

The atmosphere shifted as our conversation took on a more casual tone, the weight of our earlier moment lingering like an unspoken promise. But soon, the serious nature of our project came rushing back. "So," I said, adjusting the papers on the table, "back to the grind. We've got deadlines to meet and a report to finish."

As we dove back into the work, the air between us crackled with an unacknowledged tension. Each time our shoulders brushed or our hands neared each other again, it sent jolts of excitement through my veins. I wondered how long we could dance around this uncharted territory, knowing full well that every shared smile and fleeting touch was a step closer to something inevitable.

The next few days turned into a whirlwind of late-night brainstorming sessions and caffeine-fueled debates. Each hour spent together pulled us deeper into the gravity of our connection. It was exhilarating and terrifying all at once, like standing on the edge of a cliff, ready to jump.

One particularly late evening, we found ourselves entrenched in a discussion about our project's direction. Nathan leaned back against the couch, his fingers running through his hair, frustration evident on his handsome face. "What do you think? Should we approach this from a statistical angle or focus more on the narrative?"

I considered his question, tapping my pen against my chin. "Narrative can pull the reader in, but if we don't back it up with solid data, it could fall flat," I replied, my tone serious yet lightened by a teasing smile. "Unless you want to throw in some dramatic flair about how the numbers alone will change the world."

He shot me a playful glare. "Dramatic flair? I'm not sure my heart can take that kind of intensity."

"Heart? What's that?" I countered, feigning ignorance. "I thought you just operated on caffeine and spreadsheets."

"Touché," he laughed, a sound that reverberated through the space, breaking the tension that had woven itself between us like a tight-knit fabric. "Let's go with both—some storytelling laced with solid statistics. The perfect recipe for success."

We both leaned forward, diving back into the documents, the energy in the room shifting as we collaborated. But just as I began to lose myself in the work, the doorbell chimed, startling us both.

I frowned, glancing at the clock. "Who could that be?"

"I'll get it," Nathan said, standing up with a grace that made me momentarily forget the interruption. He made his way to the door, leaving me with a swirl of unease. I couldn't shake the feeling that this was a moment where our fragile balance could be disrupted.

He opened the door, revealing a tall figure shrouded in a long coat, the sharp outline hinting at someone with purpose. "Can I help you?" Nathan asked, his voice steady but laced with a hint of caution.

I stood, curiosity and concern mixing in my gut as I edged closer, straining to hear the conversation. "I'm looking for Rachel," the figure said, the voice smooth yet chilling.

I stiffened at the sound of my name, and Nathan shot me a questioning glance. "I'm Rachel," I said, stepping into view, my pulse racing.

"Perfect," the figure said, a sly smile curling on their lips. "I have a message for you."

The air thickened with tension, my instincts screaming that this was not the ordinary visitor I had expected. Nathan's protective stance shifted, subtly placing himself between me and the stranger. "What kind of message?" he asked, his voice firm and steady.

The stranger's gaze flickered between us, amusement dancing in their eyes. "You'll want to hear this. It's about your family."

A wave of dread washed over me, the words cutting deeper than I could have anticipated. The fragile world we had been crafting around our project now felt precarious, the comfortable cocoon of our connection fraying as uncertainty loomed. I looked at Nathan, searching his face for reassurance, but he appeared just as tense, the protective fire in his eyes a fierce reminder that whatever was happening now was beyond our control.

I felt the gravity of that moment shift, as if the foundations of my life were trembling beneath me. The boundaries I thought we had carefully navigated had just been thrust wide open, and the real world had intruded with all its unpredictability.

The figure at the door, cloaked in shadows and mystery, stepped into the light with an air of authority that sent a shiver of apprehension through me. My heart pounded, the atmosphere thickening as curiosity and fear intertwined like the tangled strands of my thoughts. Nathan stood resolute, his body a protective barrier, every muscle taut as if ready to spring into action. "What's this about my family?" I asked, my voice steadier than I felt, though a tremor betrayed my concern.

The stranger's smile widened, revealing an unsettling confidence that did little to ease my unease. "You have something that belongs to us," they replied, their tone deceptively smooth. "And it's time we had a little chat about it."

"Us?" Nathan echoed, his voice sharp as a knife's edge. "Who are you exactly?"

"Names are a bit overrated," the figure said, waving a dismissive hand. "Let's just say I'm a friend of the family. And I bring a warning."

A warning? My mind raced as I exchanged a glance with Nathan. I could feel the heat of his body close to mine, a silent reassurance amid the rising tension. "What kind of warning?" I pressed, my gut churning with unease.

"Your family's history isn't what you think it is," the figure replied, stepping closer. The light revealed a face that was both captivating and unsettling, sharp features shadowed by the weight of secrets. "You're on a path that could lead to dangerous places."

"Dangerous places?" I scoffed, masking my growing dread with bravado. "What does that even mean?"

"Oh, you'll find out soon enough," they said cryptically, tilting their head in a way that felt far too knowing. "But first, you need to understand the truth about your heritage. The past is clawing its way back, and it has its sights set on you."

The air around us crackled with an unsettling energy, the weight of their words pressing down like a heavy fog. My heart raced, not only with fear but with a rising tide of confusion. I had always believed my family was ordinary, rooted in the mundane like so many others, yet this stranger hinted at something deeper, something darker.

"Look," Nathan interjected, his voice firm but calm. "We're not interested in whatever game you're playing. If you have something to say, say it clearly, or get out."

I marveled at his confidence, the way he stood unwavering, shielding me as if I were made of glass. I wished I shared his certainty. "Yes," I added, taking a small step forward, my voice trembling but resolute. "If you're here to threaten us or play mind games, you can leave."

The stranger's laughter rang out, a sound that was both melodic and chilling. "You think you can just dismiss me? You're in deeper than you realize." They pointed a finger at me, a smile playing on their lips. "You're the key, Rachel. And they will come for you."

Before I could respond, Nathan stepped closer, his hand reaching for mine, a protective instinct radiating from him. "You need to leave now," he stated, authority lacing his words. "I don't know who you think you are, but you're not welcome here."

The figure regarded us for a moment, their expression shifting from amusement to something more serious. "You'll regret this. The past never stays buried." With that, they turned on their heel, striding out of my apartment and leaving us in stunned silence.

I exhaled slowly, as if the air had been knocked from my lungs. The tension in the room was palpable, thick enough to cut with a knife. Nathan released my hand, though I could still feel the warmth of his touch lingering on my skin. "What was that about?" he asked, his brows furrowed, concern etched in his features.

"I have no idea," I confessed, trying to process the whirlwind of emotions spiraling within me. "But they knew something. Something about my family."

Nathan's gaze softened, and I could see the wheels turning in his mind, trying to piece together the fragments of this unsettling encounter. "Then we need to figure out what they meant. We can't just let this hang over us."

"Right," I replied, determination rising within me. "But where do we even start? I don't know anything about my family's past—at least, nothing that would indicate we're anything but ordinary."

"Maybe we need to dig a little deeper," Nathan suggested, his eyes alight with purpose. "Your family history might be more accessible than you think. Old records, family trees, anything that could give us a clue."

I nodded, feeling a spark of resolve flicker to life. "I can talk to my mom. She might have some old photos or documents stored away. If there's a history, she'll know."

"Good. We'll tackle this together," he said, a reassuring smile breaking through the remnants of our earlier tension. "No digging through old family albums alone. I'll come with you."

Just then, my phone buzzed on the table, the screen lighting up with a new message. I snatched it up, heart racing as I read the words on the screen. It was from my mother, and it sent a chill racing down my spine: "Rachel, I need you to come home. There's something we need to discuss. It's about our family."

The air thickened with a sense of impending dread, the kind that settles heavily in your chest, pushing down on your lungs. "I think my mom knows something," I whispered, my fingers trembling slightly.

Nathan stepped closer, a protective fire igniting in his eyes. "Let's go, then. We'll figure this out."

Just as I reached for my jacket, the door swung open again, this time revealing a second figure, this one distinctly familiar yet equally alarming. My heart dropped as I recognized the face—someone I hadn't seen in years, but whose reappearance in this moment felt like an omen of chaos to come.

"Rachel," they said, their voice a mixture of relief and fear. "I came as soon as I heard. You need to listen to me."

The room spun, the sense of reality twisting into something surreal, and just like that, the world I thought I knew began to unravel. The shadows deepened, and in that moment, I realized this was only the beginning of something much more complicated and dangerous than I had ever imagined.

Chapter 8: Shadows of the Past

The moon hung low in the sky, a pale orb casting a silver glow over the garden. The scent of night-blooming jasmine wafted through the air, mingling with the crispness of autumn leaves underfoot. I leaned against the wrought iron fence, the cool metal pressing into my palms, as I watched Nathan pace back and forth like a caged animal. His silhouette danced in the soft light, a powerful figure burdened by unseen weights, and I could feel the tension radiating off him in waves.

"Cleo, I can't keep you in the dark about this any longer," he said, his voice gravelly, laced with the exhaustion of someone who had been fighting a war for far too long. There was an urgency in his eyes, a flicker of something dark that sent a chill down my spine. "It's about my brother, Liam. He's back in town."

At the mention of Liam, a name I had heard but never met, my heart sank. Nathan's family was a tightly woven tapestry of love and pain, and Liam was the frayed thread that had once threatened to unravel everything. "I thought he was gone for good. Isn't that what you told me?" I crossed my arms, trying to shield myself from the storm brewing between us.

"I thought so too," Nathan replied, raking a hand through his tousled hair, the frustration evident in his movements. "But he's involved in something dangerous. I don't know all the details, but he's tangled with people I'd rather forget." His eyes held mine, and for a moment, I glimpsed the turmoil hidden behind his stoic facade—a whirlpool of loyalty and fear.

A breeze picked up, rustling the leaves overhead and filling the silence that enveloped us. I took a step closer, my heart thumping against my ribs like a trapped bird. "What kind of danger, Nathan? If it involves you, I need to know. I can't just stand by while you deal with this alone."

He shook his head vehemently, the sharpness of his gesture almost causing me to recoil. "You don't understand, Cleo. This isn't just some petty crime. Liam's involved in things that could get him—and anyone close to him—hurt. I can't drag you into this mess. You have no idea what these people are capable of." His voice dropped to a whisper, heavy with unshed emotions, and I felt the sting of rejection.

"But you're already dragging me into it," I countered, my voice firm despite the tremor beneath the surface. "Every moment we spend together, I feel the shadows lurking. I can't be part of your life without knowing what's really going on. I refuse to be some innocent bystander." The challenge hung between us, thick and palpable, like the air before a summer storm.

Nathan's gaze softened for a fleeting moment, the warmth of his regard nearly dispelling the chill that had settled over us. "I wish it were that simple, but you don't understand the stakes," he murmured, his expression pained. "Liam's made enemies, and they're not the type to walk away quietly. If they find out I'm involved with you, they could use you against me. I won't let that happen."

The weight of his words settled like a stone in my stomach. I had always known that Nathan was a good man caught in a bad situation, but now the edges of his world were creeping closer to mine, threatening to engulf me. "You think I'm weak? You think I can't handle the truth?" The hurt seeped into my voice, twisting it, and I took a deep breath to steady myself. "I care about you, Nathan. That means being in this together."

He hesitated, his expression a tumult of indecision. The moonlight illuminated the sharp lines of his jaw, and I wanted to reach out, to bridge the distance between us, but the walls he had built felt insurmountable. "You deserve better than this," he finally said, his voice low and thick with emotion.

"Maybe what I deserve is to choose my own path," I replied, my heart racing as I pressed on. "You're not some burden I have to carry; you're the person I care about. If your brother is causing you this much pain, I want to help. You're not alone in this fight, Nathan. I refuse to let you push me away." I took another step closer, feeling the heat radiating from him, desperate to breach the chasm of uncertainty that had formed between us.

He looked away, his brow furrowed in thought. "If you only knew what you were getting into..." His words trailed off, and the gravity of our situation weighed heavily upon us both. I could sense the shadows of his past whispering between us, threatening to disrupt the fragile connection we were forging.

As the tension hung in the air, a figure emerged from the shadows, the soft crunch of footsteps breaking our fragile bubble. A woman, tall and striking, stepped into the light, her presence imposing. I felt Nathan's body tense beside me, the change in his demeanor sending a jolt of apprehension through my veins. "Liam," he murmured under his breath, an unmistakable tremor lacing his tone.

"Thought you could keep this all to yourself, Nathan?" she said, her voice dripping with sarcasm. "How noble of you." The challenge in her eyes was unmistakable, and I felt the familiar rush of adrenaline as the confrontation unfolded before us.

I glanced at Nathan, searching for a cue, a hint of what this unexpected visitor's arrival meant for us. His jaw clenched, and I could see the conflict roiling just beneath the surface, a tempest brewing as he faced the specter of his past. The air thickened with the tension between them, and my heart raced, caught in the crossfire of loyalty and the dangerous pull of the unknown.

"Why are you here, Eliza?" Nathan asked, his voice steady despite the turmoil I could feel emanating from him. "I thought you were done with this life."

Eliza laughed, a sound tinged with bitterness. "You should know by now, Nathan, you can never truly leave. And neither can your brother." The stakes had risen, and suddenly, our intimate moment shattered like glass, replaced by the cold grip of reality.

I glanced at Nathan, whose eyes darkened with concern, and in that fleeting moment, I realized the shadows were not just remnants of his past but the very fabric of our present.

Eliza's presence loomed in the air, as thick and suffocating as a summer fog. Her dark hair framed a face that was both beautiful and sharp, the kind that could cut glass with a single glance. Nathan's entire demeanor shifted, tension rippling through him like an electric current. I sensed that this woman was not merely a remnant of his past; she was an undeniable storm that had returned to wreak havoc.

"Still playing the hero, are we?" she said, tilting her head, her lips curling into a smirk that danced dangerously between admiration and contempt. "How quaint."

The sarcasm dripped from her words, and I felt a sharp pang of protectiveness for Nathan. "What do you want, Eliza?" he shot back, his voice steady but low, as if he were holding back a tide of emotions that threatened to crash over him.

"I came to see how my favorite brother is doing." She stepped closer, the light revealing a glint of mischief in her eyes. "And to remind him of the family he's so desperate to escape. You can't outrun us, Nathan. Not now."

I crossed my arms tightly against my chest, feeling like an intruder in a play that had been set long before I ever arrived. "If you're so concerned about family, maybe you should keep your distance," I interjected, my voice sharper than I intended, but I couldn't stand by as Nathan appeared to shrink under Eliza's scrutiny.

She raised an eyebrow, a look of genuine surprise mingled with amusement crossing her features. "And who might you be? The new girlfriend playing the savior? How charming."

The weight of her words settled over me like a heavy cloak, and I bristled at the implication. "I'm not playing anything," I replied, unwilling to let her take control of the conversation. "I'm here for Nathan, whether you like it or not."

Nathan's eyes flickered between us, and in that moment, I saw a flash of something—perhaps pride, or maybe admiration—swimming behind his concern. "Cleo's not a game to me," he said firmly, stepping a fraction closer to me, as if to shield me from whatever tempest Eliza had unleashed.

"Is that so?" Eliza's voice turned sultry, dangerous. "You're not the same boy I used to know, Nathan. The one who used to fear the dark. You've been playing with fire, and I'm here to tell you it's going to burn."

"Stop it," Nathan snapped, the tension in his voice cracking like a whip. "You don't know anything about her. You're here to stir up trouble, and I won't let you do that."

Eliza took a step back, feigning innocence. "Oh, darling, I'm just a messenger. You're the one who's been reckless."

"Reckless?" I echoed incredulously, feeling my cheeks heat with indignation. "You're the one who shows up uninvited, ready to unleash chaos. What's your angle?"

She smiled, but there was a coldness to it that made my skin crawl. "My angle? I'm simply reminding Nathan of his obligations."

A muscle twitched in Nathan's jaw as he glanced at me, his expression torn. "I'm not obligated to anything that endangers Cleo," he said, his voice resolute.

Eliza stepped back, crossing her arms in mock contemplation. "Is that so? How noble, really. But let's face facts, Nathan. Your brother is back, and whatever he's involved in, you can bet it's not just a friendly reunion. You're not a knight in shining armor. You're just one more player in this game, and Cleo's your greatest weakness."

The air thickened, and I could feel the very fabric of the moment stretching taut, ready to snap. "What do you know about Liam's return?" Nathan demanded, his voice tight, a man cornered.

Eliza leaned closer, her voice a conspiratorial whisper that sent chills racing down my spine. "I know he's in trouble, and he'll come crawling back to you. He always does." She paused, letting the silence hang heavy. "And when he does, you'll have to choose between your past and your future."

"Stop playing mind games," Nathan shot back, but the tremor in his voice revealed how close he was to breaking.

Eliza simply shrugged, her demeanor unfazed. "I'm just laying out the facts. You can ignore them if you like, but it won't change the reality."

Feeling the gravity of the situation crushing down on me, I stepped forward, determination replacing uncertainty. "Nathan, you can't let her manipulate you. We'll face whatever comes together, right?" I glanced at him, hoping my conviction would cut through the fog of doubt surrounding us.

He looked at me then, really looked, and in that brief moment, I saw the fear that had been hidden beneath layers of bravado. "I want to keep you safe," he said, the vulnerability in his tone like a crack in a dam, threatening to let everything pour out.

"I don't need you to keep me safe by shutting me out," I countered, frustration mingling with affection. "I'm not some damsel in distress, Nathan. I'm here because I want to be here. Let me in."

Eliza's lips curled into a smile that was far too knowing, her amusement cutting through the tension like a knife. "Oh, this is delightful. The two of you against the world. How romantic."

Ignoring her, I focused entirely on Nathan, trying to draw him back from the brink of whatever darkness Eliza had conjured. "You can't let your past dictate your future," I urged, my heart pounding with urgency. "We can handle this together, no matter what comes our way."

Nathan's gaze flickered back to Eliza, then settled on me, a war raging in his eyes. "You don't understand," he murmured, his voice a low rumble filled with conflict. "This isn't just about Liam. It's bigger than that. There are things I can't explain, things I can't let you get tangled in."

"Then show me," I pressed, my voice firm and unwavering. "Don't let fear win. I want to know what we're up against. If we're truly in this together, I deserve to know everything."

The world around us felt like it had slowed, the shadows of our pasts encroaching ever closer, but in that moment, something shifted in Nathan's expression. He took a deep breath, the resolve slowly hardening in his gaze. "Alright," he said finally, "but you need to be ready for the truth. It might change everything."

Eliza laughed softly, the sound like a dark melody. "Oh, it will change everything, Nathan. Just wait and see."

As the tension hung in the air, I took Nathan's hand, squeezing it tightly. I could feel the pulse of uncertainty between us, but I was determined to face whatever lay ahead. Together.

The air crackled with tension as Nathan wrestled with the enormity of Eliza's words. I could see the gears turning in his mind, each thought a new weight pressing down on his shoulders. "You need to leave," he said, his voice strained as he turned to Eliza, who stood with a smirk, as if she were enjoying every moment of our turmoil.

"Oh, Nathan, you're adorable when you're trying to assert yourself," she purred, leaning against the wrought iron fence with a casual air that belied the chaos swirling around us. "But let's face it, you don't get to make the rules here anymore."

I felt my patience wear thin, her taunts cutting through my resolve. "What is it you really want?" I asked, my voice steady despite the tempest brewing inside me. "This isn't just a family reunion. You have an agenda, and I want to know what it is."

Nathan's eyes flickered with gratitude, but the tension in the air was suffocating. "Cleo," he began, but I cut him off, unwilling to back down.

"Eliza, if you have something to say, just say it. You're here, clearly you want to stir the pot. Why don't you just dive right in?" I challenged, crossing my arms defiantly, willing my voice not to tremble.

The corner of Eliza's mouth quirked upward, a glimmer of amusement lighting her eyes. "You're feisty. I like that," she said, her tone dripping with condescension. "But this isn't a game you can play. My brother's life is in jeopardy, and Nathan's too busy playing the part of the gallant knight to see the bigger picture."

Nathan stepped forward, determination radiating off him like heat from a flame. "You don't know what you're talking about. Liam made his choices, and I won't let him drag me back into that life."

"And what if those choices put you both in danger?" Eliza shot back, her eyes narrowing. "You think you can just walk away? You can't escape the mess he's made. It's only a matter of time before it finds you."

The atmosphere shifted, an unsettling chill creeping in around us. I turned to Nathan, searching his face for any sign of what he was feeling, and saw a flicker of fear mixed with resolve. "I won't let anything happen to you," he said softly, his voice raw, but I could see doubt clouding his gaze.

"Is that so?" Eliza chimed in, her tone mocking. "You're sweet to think that. But this is not just about you protecting her, Nathan.

It's about family. Blood always runs thicker than water, even if it's muddied."

I felt a wave of frustration wash over me. "What is your deal, Eliza? You act like you're doing this for him, but it sounds like you're just stirring the pot because you enjoy the chaos."

Eliza chuckled, the sound dark and hollow. "And what if I am? This isn't just a social call, darling. This is a warning." She straightened, her expression shifting to one of seriousness. "Liam has made some very powerful enemies. He's in deeper than you can imagine, and you've both just caught their attention."

My heart raced as her words sank in. "What kind of enemies?" I asked, my voice barely above a whisper.

"People who don't take kindly to being crossed. They don't play by the rules, and they don't care who gets hurt in the process." She glanced at Nathan, a gleam of something dangerous in her eye. "You really want to get involved with him, Cleo? You'd be wise to cut ties now before it's too late."

"Not a chance," I said, shaking my head firmly. "I'm not going anywhere. If this is dangerous for Nathan, then it's dangerous for me too. I refuse to be afraid."

Nathan's hand found mine, squeezing tightly, and I could feel the warmth of his determination coursing through me. "We'll figure it out together," he said, his voice steadying me against the whirlwind of uncertainty.

Eliza's expression hardened, and I could see the calculation behind her eyes. "Very noble, but that's not how this world works. You think you can just stand there, all lovey-dovey, and pretend everything will be fine? It won't be. You're not just putting yourself at risk; you're putting Nathan's family at risk."

"And whose fault is that?" I shot back, my resolve hardening. "You're the one who waltzed in here like some harbinger of doom, waving your threats around like confetti. If you care so much about your family, maybe you should be doing something to help them instead of trying to drive us apart."

Her laughter rang out, harsh and jarring. "Ah, the fiery spirit! But the truth is, you don't know what's coming. This isn't just a little spat between brothers. There are consequences for every choice we make."

Nathan's jaw clenched as he turned to me, and in that brief moment, I saw the depth of his struggle. "Cleo, I want to protect you," he murmured, his voice a mix of frustration and yearning. "But if this goes south, it could get really messy."

"I can handle messy," I replied, my heart pounding in my chest. "I'm already in the deep end with you. I'm not about to turn back now."

Eliza stepped forward, her gaze piercing through the air. "Then prepare yourself, because the storm is coming, and it's not going to spare anyone. Liam may think he can hide, but he's a beacon in the dark. And you, sweet Cleo, are a very bright target."

Suddenly, the sound of gravel crunching underfoot drew our attention. We turned as a shadow loomed at the edge of the garden, an unfamiliar figure emerging from the dark, his presence instantly unsettling.

"Looks like I'm not the only one interested in family reunions," Eliza said with a smile that didn't reach her eyes.

Nathan's grip tightened around my hand as he stepped protectively in front of me, eyes narrowing in suspicion. "Who the hell are you?" he demanded, his voice low and threatening.

The stranger's lips curled into a smirk, and he took a deliberate step closer. "Just a friend of Liam's, here to discuss some... unfinished business."

Eliza's laughter rang out again, but this time it sounded hollow, and I felt a creeping sense of dread settle over us like a thick fog. "I think we're going to have a very interesting evening, don't you?"

In that moment, with the air heavy with threat and uncertainty, I realized we had crossed a threshold from which there was no turning back. The darkness was closing in, and the shadows of the past had come to claim their due.

Chapter 9: Echoes of Betrayal

Nathan and I stood in the dimly lit library, the air thick with the scent of aged leather and the musty embrace of forgotten secrets. The mahogany shelves loomed around us like guardians of the past, holding stories that had long since faded into whispers. I had been searching for answers, sifting through stacks of papers, when I stumbled upon a document that felt like a thunderclap in my chest. The words blurred for a moment as disbelief clouded my mind, but then the reality settled in, sharp and unforgiving.

"They've been playing us like pawns!" I shouted, the echo of my voice bouncing off the walls, mingling with the dust motes dancing in the feeble light. My heart raced, a wild drumbeat that drowned out the surrounding silence. Nathan's expression morphed from confusion to shock as he leaned closer, his eyes narrowing as he grasped the weight of the situation. I had shared secrets with him, poured out my heart, and now it felt like those moments were woven into a tapestry of betrayal that was unraveling before us.

"What do you mean?" he demanded, his voice a low growl that belied the chaos swirling within him. I could see the conflict etched across his features, the handsome lines of his jaw tightening as if he were holding back a storm.

I thrust the document toward him, my fingers trembling slightly. "Look at this! It details a collaboration between our families. A covert project, Nathan. Something sinister."

He took it, his gaze darting over the printed words, brows furrowing deeper with every line. The room felt smaller, the shadows closing in, as we both absorbed the implications of what we had uncovered.

"What does this even mean?" he murmured, half to himself. "Why would they do this?" The confusion in his eyes twisted my stomach in knots.

"I don't know, but it means everything we thought we were fighting for..." I paused, the truth slicing through me like ice. "It was all a game to them. We were never meant to be enemies, Nathan. We were just pawns in their chess match."

A tense silence fell between us, thick with unspoken thoughts and tangled emotions. Betrayal isn't just a word; it's a visceral sensation that lodges itself in your chest, making it hard to breathe. I felt it coursing through my veins, mingling with the flickering remnants of the feelings I had for him. Nathan, who had become my confidant, my partner in this chaotic investigation, was now the embodiment of everything I thought I had known—complicated, beautiful, and painfully human.

His voice was barely above a whisper, laden with disbelief. "You think they've been manipulating us all along? All those late-night talks, all the moments we thought we were discovering something real...?" His words trailed off, and I could see the gears turning in his mind, processing the betrayal that had woven itself into our lives.

I nodded, the weight of my realization settling heavily on my shoulders. "Yes! They set us against each other while they conducted their little secret project. What if... what if this rivalry was just a cover for whatever they were planning? What if they wanted us to hate each other?"

Nathan's brow furrowed deeper, and I could see the wheels of his mind spinning, the raw emotions wrestling beneath his surface. "This can't be how it ends for us," he said, determination rising in his voice. "We need to find out what they're really up to."

My heart warmed at his words, a flicker of hope igniting in the darkness. "You're right. If they've been plotting behind our backs, then we have to uncover the truth. Together."

The promise lingered in the air, a fragile thread weaving our fates back together even as the ground shifted beneath us. In that moment, our alliance solidified, and the burgeoning feelings I had tried to suppress surged to the forefront, complicated and tangled with the chaos of our lives.

"Let's dig deeper," I said, the fire of determination igniting in my chest. "There has to be more information out there. We need to figure out what this project is and how it involves our families."

Nathan met my gaze, a fierce glint igniting in his emerald eyes. "Agreed. We'll follow this wherever it leads us." His voice was steady, a stark contrast to the turmoil whirling inside me. Yet, there was something comforting in the strength he offered—a quiet assurance that we could face this together.

As we began to formulate a plan, I could feel the heat of our earlier conversation still simmering between us, a delicate tension that was both exhilarating and terrifying. The shadows of the library seemed to creep closer, but I pushed the anxiety aside, focusing on Nathan's presence beside me. He was here, a constant in the midst of uncertainty, and together we were determined to unearth the truths buried beneath layers of deception.

Time slipped away as we plotted our next steps, adrenaline coursing through my veins. The boundaries between love and loyalty blurred, thickening the atmosphere around us. I caught Nathan's gaze, and for a heartbeat, I was reminded of the countless moments we had shared—the laughter, the whispered secrets in the dark, the way he made my heart race just by being near.

But now, those moments felt fragile, like glass teetering on the edge of a precipice. Would we emerge from this tangled web of deceit unscathed, or would the very foundation of our feelings be shattered by the truth we sought?

The uncertainty loomed, a specter hovering just beyond the edges of our awareness. Yet, as I stood shoulder to shoulder with Nathan, I felt an undeniable urge to confront whatever lay ahead. We were two souls entwined in a game that had begun long before us, and I refused to let our families' manipulations dictate the course of our lives any longer. Together, we would rewrite our story.

The library, with its towering shelves and muted light, felt like a sanctuary for our secret discussions. I had always relished this quiet corner of the world, a place where books breathed life into my imagination. But now, the air crackled with tension, and the shadows seemed to leer at us, the weight of our discoveries pressing down with an almost palpable force.

Nathan leaned against the edge of the desk, the document still clutched in his hand as if it were a ticking time bomb. I watched his brow furrow, the tension in his shoulders coiling tighter as the implications of our findings took root. "You really think they've been setting us up? All those late-night phone calls, all the sneaky looks across the dinner table—it was all part of their plan?"

I could only nod, the sense of betrayal mingling with something heavier in my chest, an emotion I couldn't quite name. The familiar warmth I felt in Nathan's presence was now tangled with suspicion and hurt. "It makes sense, doesn't it? They've always been so competitive, and we were the perfect distraction. But why?"

He dropped the document onto the desk, frustration sparking in his eyes. "Because they wanted us to fight. To distract us from whatever it is they were really working on. Maybe they were too busy with their own ambitions to care about us."

I chewed on my bottom lip, the taste of metal rising as I felt anger bubble up. "Ambitions? Or something darker? We have to figure this out, Nathan. If they think they can control us, they're dead wrong."

The determination in my voice was a welcome reprieve from the whirlwind of emotions that had threatened to drown me moments before. Nathan's gaze met mine, and for a fleeting moment, the world outside faded. "What do we do now?" he asked, his voice steady, as if he were my anchor in a turbulent sea.

"Now? We dig deeper." The thrill of the chase ignited something within me, a spark that had dimmed under the weight of our families' manipulations. "We need to uncover what this project is and how we can expose them. They can't keep pulling the strings."

"Right," he agreed, the flicker of hope returning to his eyes. "But how do we do that without drawing their attention? We can't let them know we're onto them."

I grinned, the thrill of mischief dancing through my veins. "I have a few ideas up my sleeve. We can act like everything's normal. We keep attending those family dinners and pretending everything is fine. It's the perfect cover."

"Dinner with your parents? You really think that's a good idea?" He chuckled, shaking his head. "I can already see your mother's suspicious glare. She'd smell the betrayal a mile away."

"True," I admitted, rolling my eyes at the thought. "But if we play it cool, they'll never suspect we're onto them. And besides, I've been wanting to sneak into my father's office. He always leaves the door ajar, and I swear I heard him talking about the project last week. If we can get in there and find something concrete..."

"Then we can turn this whole thing around," Nathan finished for me, excitement lacing his words. "Let's do it."

The plan felt audacious, even reckless, but that only added to the thrill. We exchanged a conspiratorial smile, and in that moment, we were no longer just pawns in our families' games; we were players, ready to make our move.

As the evening wore on, we crafted our strategy, leaning against the desk, surrounded by the scent of aging paper and polished wood. My heart raced, not just from the rush of plotting against our parents, but from the subtle warmth of Nathan's presence beside me. The air was thick with unspoken words, a connection that had shifted from simple camaraderie to something far more intimate.

"Hey, what if we staged a little distraction?" Nathan suggested, his voice dropping to a conspiratorial whisper. "You know, something to keep the adults occupied while we snoop around?"

I raised an eyebrow, intrigued. "You mean like a family game night? Because you know how much my family loves those."

"Exactly!" He laughed, the sound echoing warmly in the stillness. "We can throw in some board games, maybe some friendly competition. It'll keep them busy and give us the perfect cover to slip away."

A smile crept onto my face as I imagined my parents huddled around the dining table, overly competitive and loud. "They won't even notice us gone," I said, excitement bubbling inside me. "Let's do it. We can grab dinner and then make our move while they're yelling at each other over Monopoly."

"Perfect. But, you know, I'll probably win, right?" Nathan teased, his eyes glinting with playful mischief.

"Not if I have anything to say about it," I shot back, laughing. "Prepare to be dethroned!"

As the banter flowed easily between us, I felt the weight of our earlier conversation lifting, replaced by a shared sense of purpose. The warmth of his laughter was intoxicating, drawing me closer to the edge of the line we had been dancing around.

Later, when I returned home, the house felt unusually quiet. The faint sounds of my parents arguing drifted through the walls, reminding me of how deeply entwined their ambitions were with our lives. I made my way to my room, the shadows stretching across the floor, and plopped onto my bed, staring up at the ceiling as I replayed the night's events in my mind.

Would they ever understand the chaos they had sown? Did they even care about the fallout from their actions? I shivered at the thought, unwilling to let their choices dictate my life any longer.

The plan was set, and with it came a spark of rebellion. If Nathan and I could uncover the truth, we could break free from the chains our families had forged. And as my heart fluttered at the thought of working alongside him, a different kind of uncertainty wrapped around me—this one deliciously tempting.

But the question lingered in the back of my mind like a persistent itch: What would happen when the dust settled? When we peeled back the layers of deception, would we emerge stronger, or would the very foundation of our relationship crumble under the weight of our families' secrets?

With that thought swirling in my mind, I closed my eyes, letting the night envelop me, a restless sleep teasing the edges of my dreams. Tomorrow, we would set our plan in motion, and I had to be ready for whatever surprises lay ahead. The game had only just begun.

The day arrived with a mix of trepidation and excitement thrumming through me, like the gentle hum of a violin string just before a concert. Nathan and I had spent hours plotting, discussing the family game night that would serve as our perfect distraction, and now it was time to put our plan into action. I stood in front of the mirror, adjusting my hair, my stomach a tight knot of nerves.

As I headed downstairs, the familiar chaos of my family greeted me. My parents were already squabbling over the choice of game, their voices rising and falling in a symphony of playful rivalry that felt almost comforting. I found it amusing how this competitive spirit dominated our household, yet here we were, on the precipice of a much darker game.

"Hey, you're just in time!" my mom called out, her eyes bright with enthusiasm. "We decided on Scrabble. Your father thinks he can finally beat me this time." She shot him a teasing smile that felt genuine, an illusion of normalcy I was desperate to hold onto.

"I always win, sweetheart. You just don't know how to handle defeat," Dad quipped, puffing out his chest. I rolled my eyes, the banter almost soothing in its familiarity.

I forced a smile, but inside, my thoughts were elsewhere. Nathan would arrive soon, and I could already feel the weight of what we were about to attempt. "Great. I'll grab some snacks," I said, slipping into the kitchen to distract myself. The sound of potato chips crinkling in their bag was like a tiny reassurance, a reminder that this was just one step in a much larger game.

Minutes later, the doorbell chimed, and my heart leaped. Nathan stepped inside, his usual casual attire complimented by a slightly nervous grin. "Ready to get our game faces on?" he asked, trying to mask his own tension with a bright demeanor.

"Always," I replied, letting the thrill of the moment take over. The sight of him made the chaotic rhythm of my family seem less daunting. We exchanged a quick glance, a silent understanding passing between us. We were both in this together.

As we settled around the dining table, my parents welcomed Nathan as if he were one of the family. "We could use a little extra competition," Dad declared, grinning at Nathan. "Maybe you can finally teach my daughter how to play properly."

"Oh, I'd love that," Nathan replied with mock seriousness. "I'm sure it will be a learning experience for all of us." The playful banter filled the air, but beneath it, I could sense our shared urgency simmering just below the surface.

The game began, and as my father struggled to form a word that would trump my mother's earlier points, I caught Nathan's eye from across the table. He nodded slightly, a silent cue that it was time for us to make our move. My heart pounded as I excused myself to the kitchen, signaling Nathan to follow.

Once we were out of earshot, the lightness of the atmosphere shifted into something more serious. "You sure about this?" Nathan asked, concern etched in his features.

"More than ever," I said, feeling the weight of my resolve. "Let's check my dad's office. If we find anything about the project, we'll know what we're really up against."

We tiptoed down the hallway, the floorboards creaking under our weight like the quiet anticipation building within me. I could feel my pulse quickening, every step towards the office both thrilling and terrifying. The door was slightly ajar, a narrow beam of light spilling into the dim corridor, illuminating the dust motes swirling in the air.

With a quick glance back to ensure my parents were still occupied, I pushed the door open. The office smelled of leather and old books, a sanctuary of knowledge that felt forbidden and enticing. Bookshelves lined the walls, laden with volumes that spoke of history, ambition, and family secrets.

Nathan's fingers brushed against the spines as he stepped deeper into the room. "If we're going to find something, it's probably hidden here," he said, moving to the desk. I watched as he rifled through papers, his brow furrowed in concentration.

I scanned the room, my eyes landing on a framed photograph on the wall. It was a picture of our families together, beaming smiles frozen in time, oblivious to the fractures brewing beneath the surface. But it was the cabinet in the corner that caught my attention—a heavy wooden structure with intricate carvings that hinted at its age and importance.

"Over here," I whispered, nodding toward the cabinet. "Maybe there's something inside."

Nathan approached cautiously, opening the doors with a creak that echoed ominously in the quiet room. Inside were various papers, files, and books stacked haphazardly. He began to sift through them, his fingers delicately brushing against the paper.

"Anything?" I asked, my heart thudding loudly in my chest.

"Just a bunch of old correspondence... wait." Nathan's expression changed as he pulled out a folder labeled with a date that sent a chill down my spine. "This is dated two weeks before we found that document. It looks like a summary of some kind."

He began to read aloud, his voice steady but low. "The collaboration has progressed well, with both parties eager to see the project come to fruition. All data points to a successful outcome, but continued secrecy is paramount. The consequences of exposure could be... dire."

"Dire?" I echoed, dread pooling in my stomach. "What the hell are they planning?"

Just then, a noise from the hallway caused us both to freeze. I held my breath, my heart racing. It was the sound of footsteps, firm and deliberate, growing closer. Nathan quickly shoved the folder back into the cabinet and closed the doors, and we exchanged panicked glances.

"Get ready to act normal," Nathan whispered, moving slightly in front of me as if he could shield me from whatever storm was about to burst through the door.

The footsteps approached, and I barely had time to steady my breathing before the door swung open, revealing my mother's familiar silhouette. She wore an expression that swung between curiosity and suspicion, her gaze darting around the room before landing on us. "What are you two doing in here?" she asked, arching an eyebrow.

"Oh, just checking out Dad's office," I replied too quickly, forcing a smile. "You know how much I love the smell of old books."

Nathan chimed in, "We were just admiring the—uh—decor."

Mom narrowed her eyes, and the air thickened with tension. I could feel Nathan stiffen beside me, the weight of our deception heavy between us. "You shouldn't be in here without your father's permission. He's been working on something important."

"Important?" The word echoed in my mind, ringing with implications. Had she sensed that we were onto something?

"Yes, important. It's a project he's been working on with your father." Her voice was calm but carried an edge that suggested there was more beneath the surface. "You really shouldn't pry."

We exchanged a fleeting glance, our minds racing as we realized we were standing on a precipice of danger. The tension hung thick in the air, a palpable force as my heart threatened to leap out of my chest.

"I promise we weren't trying to snoop," I managed to say, my throat dry. "We'll just head back to the game."

But as I turned to leave, my mother's voice stopped me in my tracks. "I hope you both understand the importance of loyalty."

In that moment, I knew that whatever game we had just stumbled into was far more intricate and dangerous than I had ever imagined. And as Nathan and I stepped out of the office, the weight of our families' secrets felt heavier than ever, an unseen chain binding us to a fate we were desperately trying to escape.

Just as we reached the door, a sudden loud crash echoed from somewhere in the house—a sound so jarring it made my heart skip a beat. What had just happened? The night was turning darker, and whatever secrets were hidden in the shadows were beginning to reveal themselves.

Chapter 10: Shadows and Whispers

The grand estate loomed before us, its silhouette dark against the twilight sky, the light from the windows spilling like liquid gold onto the manicured lawns. Nathan and I slipped through the wrought iron gates, our hearts pounding in rhythm with the distant music of the soirée inside. The air was thick with the sweet scent of jasmine, mingling with the crispness of impending night. I could feel the soft grass beneath my feet, a comforting contrast to the concrete reality of what we were about to do.

With Nathan at my side, his presence both reassuring and electric, we navigated the estate's perimeter, the sound of laughter and clinking glasses resonating from within. A crowd of well-dressed guests swirled around the expansive ballroom, their voices a symphony of wealth and privilege. I could make out snippets of conversation, the way people leaned in, their faces illuminated by the flickering light of chandeliers overhead, eager to share secrets wrapped in glittering smiles.

"Are you sure this is a good idea?" Nathan whispered, his voice a low murmur that barely rose above the gentle hum of the evening. His dark hair fell into his eyes, and I could see the uncertainty etched on his handsome features, a handsome mask often worn by those who knew too much and yet not enough.

"It's the only idea we have," I replied, my voice steadying as determination coiled within me. The truth was out there, swirling like the smoke from the cigars the guests puffed on the patio. I could almost taste it, tangy and electric, pulling me closer to the secrets hidden beneath the estate's gilded facade.

As we crept closer to a window partially obscured by heavy drapes, I felt a jolt of adrenaline. The room beyond was dimly lit, the rich hues of mahogany and deep emerald enveloping the guests in a luxurious embrace. We crouched low, peering through the fabric that rustled softly in the evening breeze, our breaths mingling in the cool air.

Inside, the atmosphere was thick with tension. The voices of Nathan's father, a formidable figure in the world of finance, and a man I recognized as the city's most influential developer, were laced with animosity. "We cannot afford to falter," Nathan's father said, his voice commanding, yet there was a tremor beneath the surface. "If this deal goes south, everything we've built will crumble. You understand that, don't you?"

"Trust me, Arthur," the developer replied, leaning forward, his expression shadowed. "This is just a minor setback. The plan is still viable, and the city is ripe for what we're proposing. But we need to deal with the interference. You know how the Marshalls are when they get wind of something."

The mention of my family sent a cold shiver racing down my spine, echoing in the depths of my gut. It was as if the air had thickened, and I felt Nathan's presence beside me, solid and unwavering. "Did you hear that?" he breathed, his voice barely a whisper. The spark of fear ignited in his eyes mirrored my own.

I nodded, the implications of their words clawing at me. "They're planning something against us. We need to—" But my thoughts were abruptly cut short by the sudden movement in the room.

A figure emerged from the shadows at the far end, a presence cloaked in mystery, with eyes that glinted like shards of ice in the dim light. The newcomer moved with a predatory grace, and I instinctively held my breath, an urge to flee flooding through me. This wasn't just a meeting about business; it was a confluence of danger and deceit, and we had wandered right into the heart of it.

"Who's that?" I murmured, feeling Nathan's muscles tense beside me as he followed my gaze.

"I don't know," he replied, brows furrowing in concern. "But I don't like it."

Before we could make a decision on what to do next, the figure stepped into the light, revealing a familiar face—the cold, calculating smile of Julian, Nathan's cousin. A wave of confusion swept over me, thickening the air around us. Julian was known for his charm and wit, but I had always sensed a darkness lurking beneath his polished exterior. He was trouble wrapped in designer clothing, and now he was here, watching the meeting unfold.

"Arthur, we need to talk," Julian said smoothly, his voice low and conspiratorial, the glint in his eyes betraying a hidden agenda. "The stakes are higher than you realize. It's not just the Marshalls who are a concern."

"Julian," Nathan hissed under his breath, an edge of annoyance creeping into his tone. "This is not the time."

But Julian merely waved a hand, dismissing Nathan's protest with an airy gesture. "You're both in deeper than you know," he continued, his gaze sweeping over us as if sensing our presence, even hidden behind the curtains. "The future of our families depends on how we navigate the treachery ahead. You must choose your alliances carefully."

A chill settled over me, making the hairs on the back of my neck stand on end. His words wrapped around me like a vice, igniting a fire of dread that spread through my veins. My instincts screamed for us to leave, to retreat into the safety of the night, but the thrill of the chase, the intoxicating promise of truth, kept me rooted in place.

As Nathan and I exchanged wary glances, a mix of fear and excitement coursed through me. We were teetering on the brink of something monumental, and the thrill of it surged like electricity in the air. I felt the weight of secrets pressing down on us, each heartbeat reverberating with the tension of what lay ahead. In that moment, I knew we were standing on the edge of a precipice, where shadows danced with whispers, and the truth was a tantalizing lure, waiting to be uncovered.

The tension in the air was palpable, a fine mist of dread settling over the gathering as Julian continued to speak, his words dripping with something sinister that I couldn't quite place. Nathan shifted beside me, his body taut, radiating a mix of concern and indignation. It was as if he were a coiled spring, ready to snap. I could sense the wheels turning in his mind, his thoughts a tempest of loyalty and familial betrayal. I wanted to reach out, to steady him, but my own instincts screamed that we needed to keep our heads down and our ears open.

"Julian, I don't see how any of this concerns you," Nathan finally said, his voice a low growl. "This is a family matter."

"Oh, darling cousin," Julian replied, his tone syrupy sweet yet laced with mockery. "Everything is a family matter when the family is at risk. And right now, you're too close to the fire. I'm merely trying to save you from getting burned."

The way Julian leaned in, his dark eyes sparkling with amusement, made my skin crawl. There was a flicker of something in Nathan's expression, a shadow of doubt that I hoped he wouldn't entertain. Julian was slippery, and I wasn't ready to trust him—not now, when so much was at stake.

I leaned in, whispering to Nathan, "We have to find out what he knows. If there's a threat against us, we can't just sit back and let them plot."

Nathan's jaw tightened, but he nodded, his eyes darting back toward the conversation in the room. The flickering candlelight cast dancing shadows on their faces, emphasizing the gravity of their discussion. I strained to catch every word, my heart racing in tandem with the flicker of hope that we might uncover a way to protect our families.

"Look, all I'm saying is that the Marshalls are not the only players in this game," Julian continued, and I leaned in closer, my breath hitching in my throat. "There are those who would see us all fall, and I can guarantee you, they're already in motion."

"Who?" Nathan demanded, his voice rising with barely contained frustration.

Julian held up a finger, silencing the room with an almost theatrical flourish. "That's for me to know and for you to find out. But trust me, it involves a certain degree of discretion."

Discretion. The word hung in the air like a poisoned gift, and I felt a shiver run down my spine. I couldn't shake the feeling that Julian was playing a game far beyond our understanding. There was something darker lurking beneath his polished exterior, a glimmer of malevolence that I couldn't ignore.

As I exchanged glances with Nathan, a wave of determination surged through me. We couldn't let fear dictate our actions. The very thought of sitting idle while our families danced on the precipice of danger was unbearable. I couldn't fathom a world where betrayal thrived unchecked.

"We need a distraction," I whispered to Nathan, my voice barely more than a breath. "Something to draw attention away from us."

His brow furrowed as he considered my suggestion, and then a spark of mischief lit his eyes. "I might know just the thing."

Before I could ask what he had in mind, Nathan slipped away from our hiding spot, blending into the crowd as effortlessly as smoke curling through the air. My heart raced as I held my breath, torn between wanting to stay put and the undeniable pull of adventure that tugged at my core.

It didn't take long before the opulent ballroom was filled with laughter and commotion, an audible wave that swelled around me. I peered through the drapes, straining to see what Nathan was up to. I caught a glimpse of him as he approached the bar, his demeanor casual yet purposeful. He leaned in, whispering to the bartender, who nodded with a knowing smile.

Suddenly, a loud crash echoed through the room, drawing every eye toward the entrance. A stack of ornate champagne glasses toppled over, sending bubbles cascading across the marble floor like sparkling rain. Laughter erupted, and in that moment of distraction, Nathan slipped back to my side, a triumphant grin on his face.

"Now's our chance," he whispered, eyes gleaming with excitement.

We moved like shadows through the crowd, our hearts pounding with the thrill of the chase. The chaos provided us cover, and as we crept deeper into the mansion, the sound of muffled voices guided us through winding hallways lined with portraits of stern ancestors, their gazes following us with unyielding scrutiny.

The deeper we ventured, the more the atmosphere shifted, the air growing heavy with unspoken secrets and whispers of old grievances. We stopped outside a door marked with the Rowen family crest, the intricate design catching the dim light. Nathan glanced at me, his expression serious, yet there was a flicker of mischief beneath the surface.

"Ready for this?" he asked, a playful smile tugging at his lips.

I grinned back, feeling emboldened by his confidence. "Absolutely. Let's uncover some secrets."

With a quick glance over our shoulders, Nathan turned the knob, and the door creaked open, revealing a dimly lit study lined with shelves of books and documents. The scent of aged paper and polished wood filled the air, and as we stepped inside, the door clicked shut behind us, sealing our fate.

We moved cautiously, searching for anything that might shed light on the impending threat. Papers lay scattered across the desk, some half-opened, others marked with ominous red ink. Nathan picked one up, skimming over the text before his brow furrowed in confusion.

"What does it say?" I asked, my voice barely a whisper.

"Plans for a development... but there's something here about 'eliminating obstacles.'" His eyes narrowed, and I felt a chill run down my spine as the implications sank in.

Before I could respond, the door swung open, and we froze, hearts hammering in our chests. A figure stepped into the room, silhouetted against the light spilling in from the hallway, and I felt my breath catch in my throat. Nathan's expression morphed from curiosity to horror in a heartbeat.

Julian stood in the doorway, a sly smile playing on his lips, a predator who had just cornered his prey. "Well, well, what do we have here?" he purred, stepping into the room with an unsettling ease that sent ripples of dread through my veins.

"What do you want, Julian?" Nathan shot back, his voice steady despite the tension crackling in the air.

"Oh, just checking on my dear cousins." Julian's gaze flicked between us, eyes glinting with mischief. "And it seems you've stumbled upon something rather interesting."

In that moment, I knew we were standing on a precipice—between uncovering the truth and being consumed by the very darkness we sought to expose. The room felt alive with the weight of secrets, and I braced myself, knowing that whatever happened next would change everything.

Julian stepped into the room with an unsettling confidence, the glimmer in his eyes reminiscent of a cat toying with its prey. I could feel the tension crackling in the air like static electricity, the atmosphere thick with unspoken challenges. Nathan's posture stiffened beside me, his bravado flickering like a candle caught in a gust of wind.

"What are you doing here, Julian?" Nathan demanded, his voice firm but laced with an undercurrent of urgency.

Julian smirked, that infuriatingly charming smile playing on his lips. "Oh, just making sure my favorite cousins are playing nice."

His gaze danced over the scattered papers on the desk, a mixture of curiosity and glee reflected in his expression. "But it seems you've found something rather juicy."

"We're not here for a family reunion," I interjected, stepping forward, my heart racing. "What do you know about the threats against us?"

"Threats?" Julian feigned innocence, raising an eyebrow. "Such a strong word. I prefer to think of it as... strategic maneuvering." He leaned against the doorframe, arms crossed, an image of casual menace.

Nathan stepped between us, his protective instincts kicking in. "You're playing a dangerous game, Julian. If there's a threat to our families, we need to confront it, not dance around it."

"Oh, Nathan," Julian sighed dramatically, pushing himself off the frame with a theatrical roll of his eyes. "Always the noble one. But you're too close to the fire. Sometimes, it's best to let the flames burn themselves out."

"What does that even mean?" I snapped, frustration bubbling to the surface. "If there's a danger to our families, you need to tell us."

Julian chuckled, a low, sardonic sound that sent shivers racing down my spine. "You really think I'm going to spill my secrets to you? My dear cousins, you're like moths flitting toward the flame, and I'm not ready to watch you get burned."

The weight of his words pressed heavily in the room, and the implications coiled around my thoughts like a serpent, tightening with each breath. I glanced at Nathan, who looked ready to launch himself at Julian, the determination radiating from him palpable. But before I could suggest we make a hasty retreat, Julian's expression shifted from playful to serious, the gravity of the situation settling in.

"However," he continued, his voice dropping to a conspiratorial whisper, "I do have some interesting information that could keep you from being singed."

I held my breath, my pulse racing in my ears. "What do you know?"

Julian stepped closer, his gaze darting toward the door before he leaned in, the scent of his expensive cologne mingling with the musty smell of the study. "It's not about what I know; it's about what I can offer." He paused, a calculating look crossing his features. "If you want the truth, you need to be prepared to play the game."

I felt a wave of nausea at his words, the realization that this was no simple family affair. Whatever was unfolding was rooted in a much darker play of power and manipulation. Nathan and I exchanged a glance, and in that silent moment, we understood the stakes had just risen significantly.

"Game?" Nathan echoed, incredulous. "What are you talking about?"

"Look, I can't just hand you everything on a silver platter," Julian said, shrugging nonchalantly. "There are rules. But if you want to survive what's coming, you need to be willing to make deals, to bend the rules yourself."

"Bend the rules?" I repeated incredulously, my voice rising. "You mean we should sink to your level?"

"Let's call it a necessary evil," Julian replied smoothly. "The world we live in isn't as black and white as you wish it were. There are shades of gray, my dear cousins."

"And you're the king of gray?" I shot back, unable to hide my disdain.

Julian grinned, unperturbed by my sarcasm. "I prefer to think of myself as a strategist. Knowledge is power, and right now, you're sitting on a mountain of it. All you need is a little guidance to leverage it."

Nathan, still wary, crossed his arms over his chest, the protective stance sending a message that he wasn't buying Julian's act. "What's your angle, Julian? You've never been this generous."

Julian's expression darkened for a split second, revealing a flicker of vulnerability beneath his facade. "Let's just say my interests align with yours—at least for now. We're all in danger, and I have no intention of letting our family legacy burn to ashes."

"Your 'interests' usually come with a price," I countered, my skepticism evident. "What's the catch?"

He stepped back, letting out a low chuckle. "Ah, you're sharp, I'll give you that. But for now, let's keep things simple. I'll give you information, but you owe me a favor in return."

Before I could respond, the atmosphere shifted again, a palpable sense of foreboding washing over us. Footsteps echoed in the hallway outside the study, heavy and purposeful. Julian's gaze snapped to the door, his playful demeanor vanishing like smoke.

"Someone's coming," he hissed, eyes wide with an urgency that was hard to ignore. "You need to get out of here—now."

Panic surged through me as I turned to Nathan, my mind racing. We couldn't get caught here, not when we were so close to understanding the danger threatening our families.

"Let's go," Nathan said, grabbing my arm, pulling me toward the back exit I had spotted earlier.

"No," Julian interjected, stepping closer, a frown creasing his forehead. "If you go out that way, you'll run into whoever's coming. You need to leave through the front. They'll think you're just guests."

I hesitated, torn between the impulse to trust Julian and the instinct to run from him. "Why would you help us?"

"Because," he replied, a ghost of a smile playing on his lips, "you're far more entertaining alive."

With a glance at Nathan, who nodded in reluctant agreement, I took a breath and steeled myself. "Fine. We'll take the front."

We moved swiftly, ducking through the study and slipping into the hallway just as the footsteps grew louder. The ornate decor blurred around us, the gilded frames and plush carpeting contrasting sharply with the unease swirling in my gut.

Julian lingered behind, a devilish grin on his face, as if he reveled in our risk. "Good luck, cousins! I'll be watching."

I shot him one last wary glance, but Nathan was already pulling me forward, urgency pushing us toward the grand entrance. The sounds of laughter and chatter from the party faded into a distant murmur as we made our way down the corridor.

As we reached the massive oak doors, a thought struck me. "Nathan, if Julian's right, then the danger isn't just coming for us. It's coming for everyone here."

"I know," he said, his expression grim. "That's why we need to warn them. But first, we need to get out."

I nodded, adrenaline coursing through my veins, pushing me to act. We reached for the door handle together, pushing against the heavy wood. Just as the door began to swing open, a voice echoed from behind us—sharp, commanding, and dangerously familiar.

"Where do you think you're going?"

I froze, the color draining from my face as I turned slowly to see Nathan's father standing in the hallway, flanked by two imposing figures. A predatory glint in his eyes mirrored the threat hanging in the air, and in that moment, I realized our escape was just the beginning of a far darker game.

Chapter 11: A Heart Divided

The night air was thick with tension as we slipped away from the estate, the shadows of the trees stretching like fingers across the ground, trying to pull us back into the darkness we had just escaped. The moon hung low, casting a silvery glow that illuminated Nathan's determined face. I could see the turmoil brewing behind his dark eyes, a tempest of fear and resolve battling for supremacy. The moment felt electric, charged with unspoken words and the weight of decisions yet to be made.

"Are you sure about this?" he asked, his voice low and gravelly, as we paused at the edge of the woods. I could hear the faint rustle of leaves, the distant call of a nightbird—a soothing reminder that the world continued beyond our strife. But I was far from calm; my heart raced as I considered the depth of our predicament.

"I've never been more sure about anything in my life," I replied, the words tumbling out in a rush. My stomach twisted with uncertainty, yet a fire ignited within me, urging me to take a stand. "You're not facing this alone, Nathan. Whatever this is—whatever your family is capable of—I'm right there with you."

He shook his head, frustration creeping into his features. "You don't understand the lengths they'll go to. They will use anything—anyone—to protect their secrets." His breath hitched, and I saw the weight of his family's legacy pressing down on him like a physical burden. The very idea that he would choose to shield me, to cast me aside for my own safety, sent a shiver down my spine. I wasn't some fragile thing to be protected; I was strong, determined, and ready to fight for what felt right.

"I know they're dangerous, Nathan. But they don't get to dictate our lives. Not anymore." My words hung in the air, thick with resolve. I stepped closer, narrowing the space between us. "If I'm going to lose someone I care about, it won't be because I stood by while you faced this nightmare alone."

His gaze softened for a fleeting moment before the hard edges returned. "You think it's easy for me? You think I want to bring you into this mess?" His voice trembled with a mix of anger and something deeper—an emotion I couldn't quite place. "I didn't choose this. I didn't ask for any of this."

"No one asked for this!" I shot back, exasperated. "But here we are, stuck in the middle of a situation that threatens everything we hold dear. If we're going to get through this, we need to confront our families, expose the truth, whatever it takes."

There was a flicker of doubt in his eyes, but it was quickly masked by a hardened resolve. "Fine," he relented, crossing his arms over his chest as if to shield himself from my insistence. "But you need to promise me you'll stay close. I can't lose you, not like this."

I nodded, though uncertainty clawed at my insides. The idea of facing our families—of unveiling the tangled web of secrets that had ensnared us both—felt like standing on the precipice of an abyss. But I wouldn't let fear dictate my choices. I would confront the darkness head-on.

The next morning dawned gray and foreboding, the sun hidden behind a blanket of clouds as if nature itself mourned our plight. My family's estate loomed before me, its grand façade now feeling more like a prison than a home. The vastness of the hallways echoed with silence, a stark contrast to the tempest that brewed within me. Every room seemed to whisper of secrets untold, of laughter that had long since faded.

I could sense Nathan's presence behind me, his silent support a balm to my fraying nerves. "Are you ready?" he asked, his voice barely above a whisper, yet it carried the weight of the moment.

"Ready as I'll ever be," I replied, my heart hammering against my ribs. I straightened my shoulders, determined to walk into the lion's den with my head held high. We stepped through the doors, the opulence of the foyer pressing in on us like a reminder of all that was at stake.

Moments later, we found ourselves face-to-face with my family. Their expressions varied from surprise to confusion, but all shared a sense of foreboding that hung in the air like smoke. "What is the meaning of this?" my father boomed, his authoritative voice echoing against the high ceilings.

"We need to talk," I declared, surprising even myself with the strength of my words. The air crackled with tension as I glanced at Nathan, who stood beside me, unwavering.

"About what?" my mother asked, her brow furrowed in concern. "What could possibly be so urgent that you would summon us here?"

"About the Rowen legacy," Nathan interjected, his voice steady. "About the truth you've kept hidden."

A heavy silence fell over the room, thick enough to slice through. My family exchanged glances, their unspoken thoughts swirling like a storm. I felt the urge to retreat, to turn and run back to the safety of the woods, but I stood firm.

"If we don't confront this now, it will consume us," I continued, my voice rising with conviction. "The lies, the secrets—they'll tear us apart from the inside. We deserve to know what we're up against."

My father stepped forward, his eyes narrowing. "And what makes you think you're ready for the truth?"

"I don't know if I'm ready," I admitted, feeling the weight of my own words. "But I can't stand by while everything falls apart. Not when it could change the course of our lives."

The air crackled with the tension of unspoken words, and I could see my mother's jaw clench, her fingers tightening around the armrest of her chair. Nathan shifted beside me, a reassuring presence in the storm.

"We're not just here to expose secrets," he added. "We're here to forge a new path. A way to reclaim our lives from the chains of the past."

The room was silent, save for the sound of our breaths mingling with the palpable tension. I held my breath, hoping my words would break through the fortress of silence.

And then, as if on cue, the clouds outside parted, sending a shaft of sunlight cascading through the grand windows, illuminating the room in a warm glow. It felt like a sign, a moment of clarity amid the chaos, urging us to face what lay ahead.

Finally, my father took a deep breath, his gaze shifting from me to Nathan. "Very well," he said, his voice steady but edged with caution. "Let's discuss this, but know that the truth can be a double-edged sword."

I exchanged a glance with Nathan, a shared understanding sparking between us. The path ahead was fraught with danger, but for the first time, I felt a glimmer of hope amidst the uncertainty. Together, we would navigate the labyrinth of secrets that had ensnared us, ready to confront the heart of the storm.

The tension in the room felt palpable, a living entity swirling around us as we sat across from my parents, their expressions a mixture of disbelief and concern. My father, with his dark eyebrows knitted together, scrutinized Nathan as if he were a puzzle waiting to be solved. "You have no idea what you're asking for," he stated, his voice a low rumble that seemed to vibrate through the ornate wooden furniture. My mother, usually the voice of reason, remained silent, her gaze flicking between me and Nathan with an expression that was all too familiar—protective, yet tinged with the fear of what the truth could unravel.

"Maybe it's time we all face the reality of this situation," Nathan said, his tone surprisingly calm despite the storm raging in the room. "What's hidden won't stay buried forever. You're putting your family at risk by keeping these secrets." I admired his bravery, even as my heart pounded in response to the weight of his words.

"Risk?" my father echoed, incredulity sparking in his voice. "You think this is just a game? Our family's legacy isn't something to toy with." There was an edge to his tone, a sharpness that made it clear he would protect our lineage at all costs, even if that meant shrouding us in lies.

"And yet, that's exactly what we're doing—playing games with our lives." My own voice surprised me, carrying a fierce determination I didn't know I possessed. "What good is a legacy if it's built on fear and deception? I'm tired of feeling like a pawn in your game."

Nathan's hand brushed against mine under the table, the gentle warmth of his touch sending a surge of courage through me. I turned to him, finding his expression a blend of admiration and apprehension, as if he were trying to gauge my resolve. Together, we stood on the brink of a precipice, one that could either plunge us into chaos or lead us toward freedom.

A tense silence settled over us as my parents exchanged glances. My mother finally leaned forward, her expression softening ever so slightly. "We only want to protect you," she said, her voice tinged with an urgency that struck a chord in my heart. "There are things about our family's past that—"

"Things that could change everything," Nathan interjected, his voice sharp, but a glimmer of understanding passed between him and my mother. "If you truly want to protect her, then you need to trust her. We can face this together."

"Trust is a delicate thing, Nathan," my father said, his voice dropping to a whisper that felt heavy in the air. "You're asking us to trust someone from a family that has been at odds with ours for generations."

"Trust me, then." I leaned forward, desperation clawing at my throat. "I don't want to live in fear of what might happen. If there's a chance to break this cycle, to bring our families together instead of tearing them apart, we owe it to ourselves to explore it."

"Exploring it could lead to consequences neither of you are prepared for," my mother warned, her gaze piercing as she studied my face. "You think you know what's at stake, but you're still young, and this world can be unforgiving."

"Then let us be young and foolish together," Nathan replied with a wry smile, attempting to lighten the mood, yet the underlying tension remained.

I couldn't help but laugh a little, even as my heart raced. "Right, because nothing screams youthful folly like confronting family legacies over dinner."

The corners of my mother's lips twitched, and for a brief moment, I saw a flicker of warmth behind her stern exterior. "This isn't a joke, you know. You may think it's all romantic and dramatic, but there are real stakes involved."

Nathan and I shared a glance, a silent understanding passing between us. The path ahead might be riddled with danger, but there was no turning back. We were on this journey together, bound by our shared resolve and the burgeoning connection that had formed amidst the chaos.

As we continued to discuss the intricacies of our families' histories, I felt the tide of determination rising within me. It was as if I had stepped into a role I had never auditioned for, one where the stakes were far too high for me to remain passive. The history of our families lay before us like a tapestry, intricate and frayed, each thread representing a choice that had led us to this moment.

But the conversation took an unexpected turn when my father suddenly stood, the chair scraping against the polished wood of the floor. "Enough!" His voice thundered, cutting through our dialogue like a knife. "If you want to know the truth, then be prepared for what comes next. There are sacrifices involved. The past will not let us go without a fight."

The gravity of his words settled over us like a thick fog. I exchanged a glance with Nathan, and I could see the uncertainty shadowing his features. "What do you mean by sacrifices?" he asked, his voice cautious, as if he were probing a live wire.

My father hesitated, the tension in the air thickening. "There are things that we've hidden, truths that are better left buried. But if you wish to uncover them, you must be ready to face the consequences. The Rowen family has always carried a burden, and revealing that burden may bring forth shadows that we're not prepared to confront."

"I can handle shadows," I insisted, adrenaline surging through my veins. "Whatever it takes, I want to know the truth."

"I don't think you understand," my father replied, his eyes narrowing. "The shadows you're willing to face might not just threaten you but everyone you care about."

"And that's a risk I'm willing to take," I declared, the weight of my words echoing against the ornate walls.

My mother's expression shifted to one of concern. "Are you certain? Once the door is opened, there's no closing it again."

"I'm sure." My heart thudded in my chest, the finality of my words ringing with a clarity I had never felt before.

Nathan squeezed my hand beneath the table, his grip firm and reassuring. "Then let's open that door together," he said, his voice steady.

My father let out a slow breath, resignation washing over his features as he seemed to come to terms with our resolve. "Very well. But know this: you will be embarking on a journey that could shatter everything you believe about your families. Are you truly ready for that?"

I met Nathan's gaze, and in that moment, the world around us faded. The weight of our pasts loomed large, but so did the promise of what lay ahead. "We are," I said, my voice steady, unwavering.

The air shifted, charged with an energy that made the hairs on my arms stand on end. Together, we stood at the brink of the unknown, ready to face the shadows and the secrets that had long haunted our families, united in our pursuit of the truth.

As the tension in the room began to shift, I could feel the air grow thick with unspoken words. My father's brow remained furrowed, an unyielding fortress of skepticism. "You both understand that the truth has consequences. Our families are entwined in ways you can't even begin to fathom," he cautioned, his voice laced with a seriousness that made my heart pound.

Nathan and I exchanged another determined glance, our resolve strengthening in the face of his father's warning. "Let's just say we're ready to do what it takes," Nathan replied, his tone defiant. "And we're not backing down."

"Ah, youthful bravado," my father scoffed, but there was a flicker of something in his eyes—perhaps a begrudging respect or an acknowledgment of our courage. "But you must understand that knowledge can be both a gift and a curse. What you seek to uncover may put you at greater risk than you realize."

"If we don't uncover it, we're already at risk," I countered, my voice steady despite the tremor of uncertainty that lingered beneath. "Isn't it better to face the unknown than to live in the shadow of your fears?"

"I admire your spirit," my mother finally chimed in, her gaze softening as she leaned forward, resting her chin on her hands. "But you must tread carefully. The truth has a way of revealing more than we intend, and not all shadows can be trusted."

A ripple of apprehension ran through me at her words. The weight of our conversation settled heavily, and I knew she spoke from experience.

"What are we really up against?" Nathan asked, breaking the silence that hung like a dense fog.

My father sighed, his shoulders sagging as if the very mention of our family's past was a burden too great to bear. "It's not just the Rowens we have to worry about. There are forces at play that extend beyond our understanding—old grudges, ancient rivalries that have festered through generations. Secrets that, if unearthed, could unleash chaos on both families."

A shiver ran down my spine. "What kind of chaos?" I whispered, my curiosity battling my instinct to retreat.

"Chaos that could threaten not just your lives but the very fabric of what we've built," my father replied, his voice heavy with foreboding. "The last thing we want is for you two to be caught in the crossfire."

"Then we have to be the ones to set things right," Nathan interjected, determination etched across his features. "We can't let the past dictate our future."

My father's eyes flicked to my mother, seeking her support. "And if you're serious about this... then we must ensure your safety first and foremost. There are places we can go for answers, hidden within our family history."

"Where?" I asked, my heart racing with a mix of fear and excitement.

"There's a vault in the estate," he said, his tone shifting to something conspiratorial. "A place where our ancestors kept records—accounts of the past that may shed light on the current state of affairs between our families. But it's heavily protected, and getting there won't be easy."

"Nothing worth knowing ever is," Nathan quipped, a smirk tugging at his lips. "Lead the way, then."

My father regarded us for a moment, his expression a blend of pride and concern. "If you're willing to risk it, then so be it. But I need you both to promise me something: you will not let your emotions cloud your judgment. What you discover may shake your faith in everything you hold dear."

"Nothing can shake my faith in Nathan," I stated firmly, glancing sideways at him. His smile widened, a flicker of hope in his otherwise troubled expression.

"Your optimism is refreshing," my father said, shaking his head slightly. "But it's also naïve. Just remember, the truth doesn't come without sacrifice. Are you prepared for that?"

"I'm prepared for anything," I assured him, feeling the weight of his scrutiny.

We gathered our courage and prepared to leave the room, the tension still thick but tempered with the promise of discovery. I could sense the gravity of our mission hanging over us like a storm cloud, and the air crackled with anticipation.

As we stepped into the dimly lit hallway, Nathan and I shared a look of resolve. "Ready to unlock some family secrets?" he asked, his voice teasing yet serious.

"Only if you promise not to let me fall into a vault full of skeletons," I replied, unable to suppress a grin.

"Deal," he said, and we exchanged a fleeting smile, a reminder of the connection that kept us anchored amid the uncertainty.

The corridor stretched before us, the elegant wallpaper and ornate décor whispering tales of generations long past. Each step echoed in the silence, the weight of history pressing upon us as we moved toward the hidden vault. The scent of aged wood and lingering dust filled the air, a reminder of the stories waiting to be unearthed.

As we reached the heavy wooden door leading to the vault, my heart raced in anticipation. "So, how do we get in?" I asked, glancing at my father, who stepped forward to examine the lock.

"Simple," he said, pulling a small key from his pocket. "I've kept this safe for years, hoping we'd never have to use it. But it seems today is that day."

With a deft twist, he unlocked the door, the hinges creaking as it swung open to reveal a darkened space within. The dim glow of lanterns flickered to life, illuminating shelves lined with dusty tomes and forgotten relics. The air felt charged, alive with the secrets held within these walls.

"Wow," I whispered, stepping into the room, the sheer weight of the atmosphere enveloping me. The musty scent of parchment and leather mingled with the excitement of what we might find.

"Be careful what you touch," my father warned, glancing around the room. "Not everything here is safe."

I nodded, glancing at Nathan, who stood beside me, his expression a mixture of awe and trepidation. "I guess we should start looking for answers," I suggested, my voice barely above a whisper.

As we began to sift through the volumes, my fingers brushed against a particularly ornate book. The cover was embossed with intricate designs that seemed to dance in the flickering light. I hesitated, a strange pull urging me to explore further.

"Wait, check this out," Nathan said, drawing my attention. He held up a fragile-looking scroll, its edges frayed and yellowed with age. "It looks like an old family tree."

My heart raced at the thought of uncovering our interconnected histories. "Let's see it!"

As Nathan carefully unrolled the scroll, a shadow flickered in the corner of my eye. I turned quickly, my breath hitching as I caught a glimpse of movement beyond the door. The darkness seemed to ripple as if something unseen lingered just out of sight.

"Nathan?" I said, a tremor of fear creeping into my voice. "Did you see that?"

He looked up, his brow furrowing. "See what?"

Before I could respond, a low growl echoed through the room, reverberating off the walls like a warning bell. My heart raced as dread pooled in my stomach.

"Did you hear that?" I whispered urgently, the gravity of the moment sinking in.

Nathan's eyes widened as he turned to face the entrance, his protective instincts kicking in. "We should—"

Before he could finish his thought, the door slammed shut with a deafening thud, plunging us into darkness. The lanterns flickered violently, casting eerie shadows that danced along the walls.

"Get back!" Nathan shouted, instinctively pulling me behind him as we heard the unmistakable sound of footsteps approaching, slow and deliberate, echoing through the vault like a death knell.

My heart raced, pounding against my chest as fear gripped me. "What do we do?" I gasped, desperately searching for a way out.

Nathan's grip tightened around my arm, his eyes scanning the darkness. "We fight or we find a way to escape. But either way, we're not backing down now."

Just then, a figure emerged from the shadows, cloaked and menacing, their face obscured. The growl rumbled again, low and threatening, and I felt a chill run down my spine.

"Who dares to disturb the secrets of the past?" the figure intoned, their voice smooth yet laced with danger, sending tremors of fear coursing through my veins.

I clutched Nathan's arm tighter, my pulse racing as the reality of our situation washed over me. Whatever truths we sought to uncover, it was clear that we had awakened something far more sinister, and now we would have to confront the shadows that lurked in the vault, and perhaps, the very darkness within ourselves.

Chapter 12: The Dark Truth

The air inside the diner was thick with a mix of stale coffee and the faint scent of grease, creating a cloying atmosphere that seemed to seep into the very fabric of my being. I sat across from Nathan in a booth tucked away in a shadowy corner, the vinyl seats worn and cracked, yet oddly comforting. His fingers laced through mine, a small anchor amidst the rising tide of uncertainty that threatened to drown us both. The flickering neon sign outside cast an eerie glow through the window, intermittently illuminating the lines of worry etched across Nathan's brow.

Our informant—a wiry man with an unkempt beard and a nervous twitch—shifted in his seat, eyes darting to the door as if expecting the shadows themselves to come alive. His name was Felix, and he had a reputation for walking the line between truth and deceit, a tightrope act that left many, including us, uncertain of what to believe. "You two shouldn't be here," he said, his voice barely above a whisper, thick with trepidation. "What you're involved in…it's bigger than you think."

Nathan squeezed my hand tighter, his thumb brushing over my knuckles, as though trying to soothe the storm brewing within me. "We've come this far, Felix. We need to know what's happening. Why our families are being targeted."

Felix hesitated, his eyes darting to the door once more before he pulled a worn folder from his jacket, the edges frayed and curling as if it had been hidden away for far too long. "This," he said, sliding it across the table with a shaky hand, "is just the tip of the iceberg. Your families are entangled in something dangerous—something that goes back years. I don't know all the details, but I've pieced together enough to know that the theft was just a distraction. They want something else entirely."

The folder felt heavy as I picked it up, my heart racing with anticipation and fear. Inside were photographs and documents, a tangled web of connections that made my stomach twist. I glanced at Nathan, whose expression mirrored my own—a mix of determination and dread. "We have to expose this," I said, my voice firmer than I felt. "Whatever it takes, we can't let this go any further."

Felix leaned in, his voice dropping even lower. "There are people in high places who don't want this to come out. If you're going to do this, you have to be smart. They won't hesitate to silence anyone who gets in their way."

The weight of his words hung heavily in the air, wrapping around us like a shroud. I thought of my family, the risks they faced, and the innocence they would lose if this conspiracy continued to fester in the dark corners of our lives. Nathan's hand was warm and reassuring, grounding me as I flipped through the contents of the folder. There were names, dates, and locations, all intertwining like a sickly vine creeping through the cracks of a crumbling wall.

As I absorbed the information, one name stood out—a name that sent a chill racing down my spine. "This can't be right," I whispered, my pulse quickening. "It can't be connected to my father."

Nathan leaned closer, his brow furrowing. "What is it?"

"Here," I said, pointing to a photograph of a man with sharp features and cold eyes. "This guy... he was at our family's charity gala last year. He's close to my father. They were talking... I thought it was just business, but—"

Nathan's eyes widened as he processed the implications. "If he's involved, then we need to tread carefully. This is getting deeper than we imagined."

The world outside the diner seemed to fade away, the neon lights reflecting the urgency that pulsed through my veins. My resolve hardened, solidifying into something unyielding. "We need a plan. We can't just wait for someone to make the next move." I leaned forward, a fire igniting within me. "What if we confront him? If he's involved, maybe he knows more than he's letting on."

Nathan shook his head slowly, concern etched into his features. "That's a dangerous game, and we can't afford to be reckless. We need more information first."

But something inside me—something primal—was screaming to take action. I had spent too long being passive, too long allowing others to dictate my fate. Now, with this truth laid bare before me, I felt the weight of my choices pressing down like a shroud. "What if we gather evidence first? Maybe we can find out what he's planning. We could bug his office or something," I suggested, my voice barely concealing my excitement.

"Are you insane?" Nathan chuckled, a nervous smile breaking through the tension. "You think we can just waltz in and plant a bug like it's a scene from a movie?"

I grinned, my heart racing with the thrill of the idea. "Maybe not waltz in, but we could find a way. We're not helpless in this."

His gaze softened as he considered my words. "You really want to do this, don't you?"

"More than anything. I won't let them take our families down without a fight."

Felix cleared his throat, drawing our attention back to him. "If you're serious about this, you'll need allies. You can't do it alone."

A million thoughts raced through my mind, possibilities unfurling like petals in bloom. Allies. We needed the right ones—people we could trust to stand alongside us in this escalating storm. "What do you suggest?"

"The right allies will have access to resources and information you'll need. Start with your closest connections—anyone who has something to gain or lose. They'll want to protect their interests," he replied, his eyes narrowing as he leaned back. "But be careful. Trust is a luxury you can't afford right now."

As we left the diner, the world outside felt different, charged with a sense of purpose. The danger was real, palpable, and creeping closer with every tick of the clock. I looked at Nathan, his resolve matching my own, and together we stepped into the uncertain night, ready to unearth the dark truth that had entangled our families in a sinister web of conspiracy.

The chill of the night air wrapped around us like a thick blanket as we stepped out of the diner, the sound of the door creaking shut behind us fading into the distant hum of the city. My heart thrummed in my chest, each beat echoing the gravity of what lay ahead. The neon lights, once a source of false comfort, now felt like warning signals flashing ominously in my peripheral vision. I could sense the dangers lurking in the shadows, eyes watching from the corners, ready to pounce.

Nathan took a deep breath beside me, his presence steadying, yet I could see the storm brewing in his hazel eyes. "So, what's the plan?" he asked, running a hand through his tousled hair, a nervous habit that made him appear boyish and earnest all at once. "Because I'm not exactly keen on diving headfirst into a conspiracy without a solid strategy."

I let out a small laugh, the tension in my shoulders easing slightly. "Right. Because last time I checked, being reckless is still on your 'to-do' list." I nudged him playfully, though my stomach churned with uncertainty. "How about we start with the people we can trust? Your brother might be able to help, and I can reach out to my dad's assistant. She knows the ins and outs of his business dealings."

"Sounds good," Nathan replied, his expression serious once more. "But we need to be careful. If this guy we saw in the folder is involved, we could be walking straight into a trap."

"True. But I can't just sit back and let them manipulate our families. We need to take the initiative." My resolve strengthened as I spoke, the sense of purpose flooding back. "Let's head to your place. It'll be easier to brainstorm there without prying eyes."

The streets glimmered under the dim glow of streetlights, and the city felt alive around us. As we walked, I couldn't shake the sensation that we were being followed. The occasional sound of footsteps echoed behind us, but every time I turned, the street remained empty. It was likely paranoia, yet it gnawed at the edges of my confidence.

"Do you ever feel like we're in a movie?" Nathan mused, breaking the silence as we rounded a corner. "You know, the kind where the protagonists rush headlong into danger, thinking they're invincible?"

"Sure, but I'd rather be the one with a plan than the one who gets cornered in an alley," I replied, giving him a sidelong glance. "Not all movie heroes survive, you know."

"Touché." He smirked, the tension easing as we reached his apartment complex. The building loomed ahead, a brick structure with a hint of charm, though it was desperately in need of a fresh coat of paint. Inside, the familiar scent of his mother's lavender candles filled the air, instantly relaxing me.

"Home sweet home," Nathan announced, and I couldn't help but smile. He tossed his jacket onto the nearby chair and moved to the kitchen, the clinking of dishes breaking the comfortable silence. "Want some tea? It might help calm your nerves."

"Tea sounds great," I said, settling onto the couch and glancing around. The walls were lined with family photographs, moments captured in time—smiling faces, candid laughs, all while oblivious to the darkness that would soon ensnare us. It felt so normal, so cozy, and yet it was about to collide with the chaos of our lives.

As Nathan prepared the tea, I took out the folder Felix had given us, spreading the documents on the coffee table. "Let's go over this again," I suggested, sorting through the pages. "We need to connect the dots. If we can figure out who's behind this, we might be able to anticipate their next move."

"Right." Nathan leaned closer, his brow furrowed as he examined the photographs and notes. "This looks like a web of corruption that stretches from the local businesses to some influential players. The question is—why us? Why now?"

I traced a finger over a name, feeling a jolt of recognition. "This guy, Gerald Thornton, he's not just anyone. He's a financial advisor for some of the wealthiest families in the city. If he's involved, it could mean our parents are tangled in something far worse than we realized."

Nathan's expression darkened, and he leaned back, running a hand through his hair. "We need to confront my brother. He works closely with Gerald, and if anyone knows what's happening, it's him."

"Let's hope he's not too far gone," I replied, knowing their sibling dynamic could be fraught with tension. "I mean, who knows what secrets he's been keeping?"

"Exactly." Nathan's eyes held mine, a silent agreement passing between us. "But first, let's get some tea, and then we'll strategize."

As he brought the steaming mugs to the table, I couldn't help but feel a sense of comfort in this ordinary moment, the warmth of the tea and the coziness of the space contrasting sharply with the treacherous world we were stepping into. We sipped in silence for a moment, the steam curling upwards like wisps of our thoughts, swirling and mingling.

"I've been thinking," Nathan said, breaking the silence. "If we're going to do this, we need to be prepared for anything. It might not just be about uncovering the truth; we might end up facing some serious consequences."

"Consequences," I echoed, letting the word linger. "But isn't that the point? To protect our families? We can't let fear dictate our choices."

"I admire your spirit, really." He leaned forward, a hint of admiration in his voice. "Just promise me we'll stay on the same page. If we start going off on wild tangents, we could end up in serious trouble."

"Deal. But let's be real—if we get caught, I'm blaming you for dragging me into this." I grinned, attempting to lighten the mood even as the gravity of our situation pressed down on us.

"Fair enough." Nathan chuckled, but the laughter faded quickly as the weight of our reality settled back in. "I'll text my brother. If we can get him to meet us somewhere private, we might have a chance to get some answers."

He reached for his phone, and as he typed, a sudden crash echoed from outside. It was loud enough to rattle the windows, an unexpected intrusion that made us both jump. We exchanged startled glances, our hearts racing in synchrony.

"What was that?" I whispered, my instincts kicking into high gear.

"Let me check." Nathan rose cautiously, moving toward the window. I followed closely, peering out into the darkened street below. The scene that unfolded sent a shiver down my spine. A group of men stood clustered near a car, shadows twisting under the harsh glare of the streetlight. Their movements were agitated, and I could sense the tension crackling in the air.

"Those guys… they look familiar," Nathan murmured, narrowing his eyes. "I think they're connected to the people in the folder."

Before I could respond, one of the men turned sharply, glancing up at the building as if sensing our gaze. Our eyes locked for an instant, and I felt a chill skitter down my spine. In that moment, I realized the danger was closer than we had ever imagined.

The tension in the room was palpable, almost tangible in the air between us. Nathan and I stood at the window, our eyes locked on the group outside, adrenaline coursing through our veins like wildfire. The man who had spotted us shifted slightly, his posture rigid as he gestured animatedly to his companions. Their collective energy crackled with hostility, the kind that ignited alarm bells in my mind.

"Do you think they've seen us?" I whispered, my voice barely above a breath.

"I can't tell. But we should definitely not stick around to find out." Nathan's face was set in grim determination. He stepped away from the window, pulling me back with him as he scanned the room for our next move. "We need to get out of here. Fast."

I nodded, the reality of our situation settling like lead in my stomach. We had jumped headfirst into a dangerous game, and now the stakes felt terrifyingly high. "But how? We can't just walk out the front door. They'll be waiting."

He paused, considering our options, and I could see the gears turning in his mind. "The fire escape." It was a plan born from desperation, but it was the best we had. "We can slip out the back and down the stairs. If we're quick, they won't even know we're gone."

"Lead the way," I replied, the thrill of fear mingling with the pulse of excitement. There was something almost exhilarating about the prospect of escaping through the unknown, fueled by the adrenaline that was steadily mounting.

With one last glance at the window, I followed Nathan as he made his way to the door that led to the stairwell. Each step felt heavy with urgency, my heart racing as we pushed through the door. The narrow hallway was dimly lit, but we moved swiftly, the sound of our footsteps muffled against the worn carpet.

As we descended the stairs, the quietness around us amplified the thudding of my heart. Every creak of the metal framework seemed to echo our fears. "Do you think they'll really follow us?" I asked, my voice low.

"I wouldn't put it past them. We have to be smart about this," Nathan replied, his brow furrowed in concentration. "If they're tied to the theft, they'll definitely want to find us."

We reached the bottom and slipped out onto the landing, where the back exit awaited us. The night air was cool and refreshing as we pushed through the door, but the safety it promised was still distant. I stepped outside, scanning the darkened alley for any signs of the men from before.

The alley was lined with refuse bins and graffiti-covered walls, the remnants of a city that thrived on secrets and shadows. "Okay, what now?" I whispered, trying to keep my voice steady.

"We need to make it to my car. It's parked a few blocks away." Nathan's grip on my hand tightened as he led the way down the alley, glancing around to ensure we weren't being followed.

"Let's hope it's not surrounded by thugs," I murmured, trying to inject some levity into the moment.

"Funny you should say that," Nathan shot back, a glimmer of amusement in his eyes despite the tension. "I was thinking the same thing. Just our luck, right?"

The alley opened up onto a street, and we quickly ducked behind a parked car, peering around the edge. The night was thick with unease, but the street appeared deserted. "Now or never," he urged, and we bolted across the road, hearts racing as we approached his car, an unassuming sedan that blended in with the mundane traffic.

As we reached it, I fumbled for my keys, my fingers trembling slightly. "You drive," Nathan urged, and I nodded, sliding into the driver's seat while he settled into the passenger side, scanning our surroundings.

"Let's hope we're not being watched," I said, trying to project confidence despite my anxiety. I inserted the key and turned the ignition, the engine humming to life with a reassuring growl.

"Okay, now get us out of here." His voice was steady, yet I could hear the undercurrent of urgency.

I shifted into gear and pulled away from the curb, glancing in the rearview mirror. The street seemed clear, but my instincts screamed that we were not yet safe. "Where to?" I asked, maintaining a steady gaze on the road ahead.

"Let's head to the warehouse district. It's quieter, and we can figure out our next move without prying eyes," Nathan suggested, his voice low.

"Right. The warehouse district it is." I took a left turn, my palms slick against the steering wheel, the shadows of the night stretching around us as we drove deeper into the unknown.

We navigated through the labyrinth of streets, each corner we turned felt like a step further into a hidden world. The thrill of danger electrified the air, but the gravity of our predicament loomed over us like a dark cloud.

As we approached the warehouse district, the buildings grew larger and more foreboding, their silhouettes looming like sentinels against the night sky. The quietness was unnerving, broken only by the occasional distant siren or the rustling of leaves. "We should find a place to park and lay low for a bit," Nathan suggested, scanning the area for an ideal spot.

"Agreed. I just hope we can keep our heads down long enough to figure out what to do next." I turned into a secluded lot behind one of the warehouses, parking in the shadows. The headlights flickered off, plunging us into near darkness.

"Now what?" I asked, the anticipation crackling between us.

"Let's take another look at that folder. We need to start connecting the dots, and see if we can find any leads," he said, digging through his bag as I turned off the car's engine.

As Nathan pulled out the folder, we leaned closer together, the intimacy of the moment lending an unexpected comfort amidst the chaos. I flicked on the overhead light, illuminating the documents as he spread them across his lap.

Just then, the sound of footsteps echoed outside, a sharp reminder that we were not alone. I froze, my heart pounding against my ribcage as I glanced up.

"Did you hear that?" I whispered, panic creeping in.

"Yeah, and it's coming closer." Nathan's eyes widened, his voice a low hiss.

I held my breath, listening intently as the footsteps grew louder, resonating against the pavement. "We need to hide. Now."

In an instant, Nathan dove into the backseat, urging me to follow. We ducked low, hearts racing, as the door swung open.

"Stay quiet," Nathan breathed, our eyes wide with fear.

The figure stepped inside, silhouetted by the faint light spilling from the street, the outline of a man—a face obscured in shadow, yet I felt a chill that hinted at familiarity.

"Nathan?" the figure called out, voice low and threatening.

My heart plummeted as recognition dawned. "It can't be..." I whispered, my breath hitching in my throat.

But it was too late for second guesses. The truth was about to unravel before us, and in that moment, everything changed.

Chapter 13: A Dance of Deceit

The Winter Gala unfurled before us like an opulent tapestry, rich in hues of emerald and gold, the kind that glittered even under the soft glow of the chandeliers. Every surface sparkled, reflecting the laughter and chatter that wove through the air like a shimmering thread of silk. Guests flitted about, their laughter ringing out like music, but beneath the surface, I sensed an undercurrent of tension—an electric charge that made the hairs on my arms stand at attention.

I stepped into the ballroom, a swirl of icy air following me as I crossed the threshold. The scent of pine mingled with the sweetness of spiced cider wafting from a nearby table, creating an intoxicating aroma that both warmed and invigorated me. I'd donned a gown that clung to my frame in a way that felt like armor—a deep crimson that contrasted sharply with my pale skin, giving me the appearance of someone daring enough to challenge the norms that surrounded me. I could almost feel the weight of the conspiracy pressing down on my shoulders, but the fabric swishing around my legs offered a sense of empowerment, a reminder that I was more than just a pawn in a game far beyond my control.

As Nathan arrived by my side, I couldn't help but notice how his tailored suit emphasized his broad shoulders and the way he carried himself with an effortless grace that belied the tension I knew lay beneath his calm exterior. His blue eyes sparkled with mischief, a hint of a smile playing on his lips as he leaned closer, murmuring something just for me. "Ready to set the ballroom ablaze?" The warmth of his breath sent a shiver down my spine, and for a moment, the world faded away, leaving just the two of us suspended in our private bubble.

"Only if you promise not to step on my toes," I shot back, raising an eyebrow. The playful banter felt like a necessary release, a way to disguise the intensity of our mission beneath layers of flirtation. It was a dance as much as it was a strategy, one that required both deft footwork and sharp wit.

The music swelled, and Nathan grasped my hand, leading me onto the dance floor where couples twirled gracefully, lost in the rhythm. The first notes of a waltz enveloped us, wrapping us in a warm embrace. As we began to move, I couldn't help but lose myself in the moment, the music pulling me along in a current of emotion. With each turn, our bodies brushed together, igniting an energy between us that was impossible to ignore. I felt invincible, caught between exhilaration and the thrill of our conspiracy.

As we spun around, the prying eyes of our families loomed large, a storm waiting to break. I caught sight of my mother across the ballroom, her perfectly coiffed hair glinting in the soft light. She was in her element, charming guests with practiced ease, her smile a mask that hid the determination beneath. Just beyond her, Nathan's father stood, his presence imposing even amidst the glittering chaos, discussing business with another guest. The air around him felt thick with unspoken agendas, a palpable tension that whispered of the looming confrontation we both dreaded.

"Do you think they suspect anything?" Nathan's voice was low, his brow furrowed in concern as we twirled in a gentle arc, avoiding the couples swirling around us.

"Not yet," I replied, forcing a casualness I didn't quite feel. "But they will soon enough. This charade can't last forever." I took a deep breath, savoring the moment but also feeling the weight of our shared secret. The stakes were high, and we were risking everything to gather the evidence we needed to expose the conspiracy that threatened both our families.

The melody shifted, turning from light and airy to something darker, more foreboding. I leaned in closer, our cheeks brushing as I whispered, "We need to find a way to get them alone, away from prying eyes." The heat of Nathan's body sent sparks through me, but I pushed those feelings aside, focusing instead on the task at hand.

"Follow my lead," he said, his voice steady, exuding the confidence I so desperately needed. "We'll create a diversion. Once we have them cornered, we'll make our move."

Just as the music reached a crescendo, the atmosphere shifted. A figure from the shadows emerged—a cousin of Nathan's, who had always been an untrustworthy presence in our family. His gaze roamed the room, a smirk curling at the edges of his mouth as he caught sight of us. The air thickened, the weight of his scrutiny wrapping around us like a noose.

"Looks like we have company," I murmured, my heart racing as I recognized the threat he posed. "What do we do now?"

Nathan's jaw tightened, and the flicker of uncertainty in his eyes made my pulse quicken. "Just keep dancing," he urged, a hint of steel creeping into his tone. "Let him think we're oblivious."

I forced a smile, but inside I was churning with unease. We were balancing on a knife's edge, and one misstep could plunge us into chaos. The music swelled again, and as we glided through the dance, I felt the tension seep into my bones. With each turn, I scanned the room, searching for allies, for a way to turn this gala from a mere spectacle into an arena of revelation. The dance of deceit was just beginning, and I was determined to lead us to victory, no matter the cost.

The music swelled, drawing us deeper into the heart of the gala, where elegance danced with the undercurrents of secrecy. The floor was a patchwork of brilliant colors—silk gowns that billowed like petals in the wind, suits that gleamed under the chandeliers like polished stone. Couples moved gracefully, but as I twirled with Nathan, the real dance was unfolding in our minds—a delicate choreography of intrigue and betrayal.

"Look over there," Nathan said, tilting his head discreetly toward the far side of the ballroom. My gaze followed his, landing on a small cluster of our parents, their faces taut with a mixture of false cheer and hidden agendas. "They're planning something. I can feel it."

I adjusted my grip on his hand, the warmth of his skin grounding me amidst the chaos. "What if we don't confront them just yet? Let's gather a little more intel first." My heart raced with both excitement and apprehension. The weight of our secret was heavy, and every passing moment heightened the stakes.

"Intel? Is that what we're calling it now?" His smile was teasing, but I could see the seriousness lurking behind those twinkling eyes. "I thought we were on the verge of some grand, dramatic reveal. I was ready for the red carpet and the spotlight, not just whispering behind the potted ferns."

"Right, because nothing says gala glamour like standing behind a fern." I shot back, unable to suppress a laugh. "If we're going to turn this night around, we need a strategy, and you know that means being smart about it."

Nathan chuckled, and for a moment, the weight of the world lightened between us. It was as if the swirling skirts and laughter faded, leaving just us—the world was a stage, and we were playing our roles. But reality crept back in, tugging at my heart as I glanced at our families. Their masks of joy concealed an array of motives, and I knew the truth could explode at any moment, shattering the fragile façade.

Just then, a sudden commotion drew my attention. A group of young socialites had gathered near the fountain at the center of the ballroom, their voices rising in excitement. "What's going on over there?" I asked, tilting my head. Nathan followed my gaze, curiosity sparking in his expression.

"I don't know, but it looks like the kind of distraction we could use." With a swift motion, he led me away from our anxious circle of family and into the throng of onlookers. We maneuvered through the crowd, our bodies moving instinctively in sync, the chemistry between us palpable.

When we finally reached the front, I peered over the heads of the other guests. A young man, clearly tipsy, had climbed onto the fountain's edge, his laughter echoing through the ballroom. "Ladies and gentlemen, gather 'round! I'm about to reveal the greatest secret of the night!" His proclamation hung in the air, drawing gasps and giggles.

"Should we be worried about his secrets?" Nathan muttered, his voice laced with amusement. "Or should we just prepare for an embarrassing fall?"

"Both," I replied, grinning. "But this could be the perfect diversion. While everyone is captivated by his antics, we can eavesdrop on the parents."

As the crowd's laughter erupted, I tugged Nathan away from the fountain, leading him to a nearby alcove framed with lush greenery. Hidden from view, we could still hear the commotion while keeping our eyes on the unfolding drama. I leaned against the cool stone wall, adrenaline coursing through me, ready to make our move.

"Now, let's listen," I whispered, pressing my ear against the foliage, which rustled softly in the gentle draft. Just then, a voice cut through the laughter—the unmistakable tone of Nathan's father, resonant and authoritative.

"—we can't allow any more slip-ups. This is our chance to secure everything we've worked for. We must keep the details under wraps."

My heart raced. This was it—the words that could unspool the conspiracy we suspected was festering beneath the surface. Nathan's hand tightened around mine, a mix of excitement and fear lighting up his expression.

"What do you think he means?" Nathan asked, his voice barely above a whisper.

"I don't know, but it sounds serious," I replied, adrenaline sparking in my veins. "We need to find out what they're planning. If we're going to confront them, we can't just barge in blind."

"Agreed. Let's see if we can catch more of the conversation."

We leaned in closer, the whispers of the party fading into the background as we tuned into our parents' discussion.

"—the gala is merely a cover. We move forward with the acquisition next week. Once we have the land, we can implement our plans without opposition." The gravity of the statement sent a chill down my spine.

"Acquisition? Land?" Nathan murmured, incredulous. "What land? What plans?"

"I don't know, but we need to get evidence," I said, urgency sharpening my tone. "We need to know what's at stake here."

As we huddled, I caught snippets of their plotting, each revelation drawing us deeper into the murky waters of deceit. The parents' voices rose and fell like a sinister melody, revealing their intentions cloaked in well-practiced charm. My mind raced, connecting the dots—the land, the acquisition, the conspiracy that had cast a shadow over our lives.

Then suddenly, a piercing cry shattered the moment. The young man on the fountain, now waving his arms wildly, lost his balance and tumbled backward into the fountain with a spectacular splash. Laughter erupted, and the crowd roared with delight, completely oblivious to the gravity of what was unfolding just a few feet away from them.

"Perfect timing," Nathan said, grinning as he pulled away from the alcove. "That's our moment. Let's make a move before they notice we've been eavesdropping."

As we stepped back into the crowd, the jubilant atmosphere wrapped around us like a comforting blanket, but underneath, my heart hammered with anticipation. Our plan was precarious, but as

Nathan's eyes met mine, a spark of determination ignited within me. We were in this together, and no matter what secrets lay ahead, I was ready to confront the shadows that threatened to engulf us both.

The laughter echoed like a spell, weaving its way through the crowd, yet it felt oddly discordant against the backdrop of our burgeoning plot. I could still hear the splashes from the fountain where the young man had fallen, water droplets dancing in the air, sparkling like shards of glass. It was a moment of sheer chaos that turned the ballroom into a stage for the absurd, and yet it provided the perfect distraction. Nathan and I moved through the throng, our hearts racing as we searched for an opening to confront our parents without raising suspicion.

"Think they're busy contemplating their next move, or just enjoying the spectacle?" Nathan quipped, casting a sidelong glance at the crowd. I could see the familiar glint of mischief in his eyes, a reminder that even in moments of crisis, he maintained a sense of humor that both irritated and delighted me.

"I'd wager they're too caught up in their self-importance to notice the floor is about to drop out from under them," I replied, arching an eyebrow. "But let's not test that theory too much. I'd prefer to confront them without a sudden trip to the fountain ourselves."

As we navigated the dance floor, I couldn't help but catch snippets of conversation around us. The chatter floated like bubbles, bright and cheerful, masking the heavier undercurrents swirling just beneath the surface. It was an odd juxtaposition, this cheerful gathering, when the fate of our families lay hidden behind their forced smiles.

We found ourselves on the edge of the ballroom, near an ornate side door leading to a small balcony overlooking the grounds. With a glance to ensure no one was watching, Nathan took my hand and pulled me through the doorway, the cool night air greeting us like an old friend. I inhaled deeply, savoring the contrast of fresh air against the cloying perfume of the gala.

"What now?" I asked, shivering slightly as the chill nipped at my skin. Nathan leaned against the railing, his posture relaxed yet alert, the moonlight casting a silver sheen on his features.

"Now we wait," he said, his voice low. "They're bound to step outside for some fresh air, and when they do, we'll have our chance."

I nodded, the thrill of anticipation building within me. We stood close, the night wrapping around us like a cloak. I could hear the distant hum of music, a haunting waltz that seemed to echo my own racing heart. The stars twinkled above, a scattering of diamonds against a velvet sky, while below us, the snow-dusted grounds glimmered in the moonlight.

"You know," I ventured, breaking the charged silence, "I never pictured us sneaking around like this. If someone had told me a year ago that I'd be standing outside a gala with you, plotting to expose our parents' conspiracies, I might have laughed."

"Laughter would've been a suitable response," he said, smirking. "Who would've thought we'd be the ones unraveling the family secrets instead of dancing the night away like every other couple?"

"True, but I think I'd prefer to be at a regular dance, twirling around with no care in the world."

"Don't underestimate the thrill of espionage. It has a certain... edge to it," he teased, and I could see the playful glint in his eye.

Just as I was about to retort, the door behind us creaked open, and we both froze, pressing ourselves against the cool stone wall. I peered around Nathan to see my mother step onto the balcony, followed closely by Nathan's father. Their voices were low but clear, their conversation dripping with the kind of tension that made my stomach churn.

"—you need to understand the stakes here. We cannot afford any mistakes," my mother said, her voice firm and unwavering. "The

DANGEROUS ALLIANCES

acquisition must go smoothly, or we risk everything. The partnership depends on our discretion."

Nathan's father nodded, his expression serious. "You know that I will handle it, but we have to be cautious. The moment they catch wind of our plans..." He paused, glancing around, as if sensing an unseen threat.

I exchanged a quick glance with Nathan, our eyes wide. The pieces were falling into place, but the magnitude of what lay before us sent a shiver down my spine. This was more than just a secret; it was a ticking time bomb.

"Let's move closer," Nathan whispered urgently, pulling me just a few steps forward. We remained hidden behind a pillar, our hearts thudding in sync as we strained to catch more of the conversation.

"—there are rumors," my mother continued, her voice low, almost conspiratorial. "We can't let them interfere. This is too important, too valuable. We have to make sure we're the only players in this game."

"Agreed. But if they find out what we're doing—"

"Then we'll do what needs to be done," she cut him off sharply, the steel in her tone sending a chill through me. "We have to protect our interests. No one can be trusted outside our families. Not even them."

My pulse raced at her words, the implication hanging in the air like a noxious cloud. "Them"—the outsiders, whoever they were—could threaten everything we knew.

"What do we do?" I breathed, glancing at Nathan, who was as pale as the snow outside.

"Gather evidence. We need to find something solid before we confront them. They're dangerous, and they're playing for keeps."

Just then, my mother turned abruptly, her gaze scanning the balcony as if sensing our presence. I ducked instinctively, my heart pounding in my chest as I pressed against the wall.

"Did you hear that?" Nathan asked, his voice barely a whisper. "It sounded like—"

"Someone's out there!" my mother exclaimed, her voice sharp and commanding.

The door swung wide open, and I felt my stomach drop. We had been discovered. Nathan's hand tightened around mine, panic flaring in his eyes.

"Run," he said urgently, pulling me back toward the edge of the balcony. I didn't need to be told twice. We dashed back inside, weaving through the crowd, adrenaline surging as I glanced over my shoulder.

But the gala felt like a labyrinth, each path twisting and turning away from our escape. We needed to find a way out, and fast. Just then, the laughter faded into a muffled roar, and my heart raced even faster as I felt eyes boring into my back.

"Over here!" Nathan pointed toward a set of double doors at the far end of the ballroom, the exit to the staff corridor that led to the service entrance. We darted toward it, desperate to evade our pursuers.

Just as we reached the doors, a hand shot out, grabbing my wrist. I turned to see Nathan's cousin, his expression a mix of confusion and amusement. "What are you two up to?"

"Let go!" I shouted, but the grip was unyielding.

Nathan stepped forward, his eyes fierce. "You need to move. We don't have time for games, Julian!"

Before we could react, the door to the ballroom swung open again, revealing my mother, her expression a storm of fury. "There you are!" she barked, her eyes narrowing as they fell on us.

In that moment, the world fell silent, every sound drowned by the roar of my pulse in my ears. The mask of the gala had slipped, and the dance of deceit had only just begun.

Chapter 14: The Unraveling

The gala shimmered like a mirage, a sprawling sea of silk and laughter under the crystal chandeliers that hung like stars above the glistening dance floor. Music wafted through the air, a melodic tide that ebbed and flowed, yet beneath the surface, a tempest brewed. As I twirled among the elegantly dressed guests, my heart raced not from the intoxicating atmosphere but from the weight of the truth threatening to surface like a dark shadow, poised to disrupt the fragile harmony of the evening.

It was Nathan's touch on my arm that drew my attention, his fingers cool and steady, a lifeline amidst the swirling chaos of emotions. I caught his gaze, and in his deep brown eyes, I saw a reflection of my own turmoil—a shared understanding that we were on the brink of something explosive. "Are you okay?" he murmured, his voice barely audible over the clinking of glasses and distant chatter. I nodded, though I felt the unshakeable knot tightening in my stomach.

Moments later, the music swelled and faded, and the air crackled with anticipation. My mother stepped onto the makeshift stage, her presence commanding, as always. Dressed in a stunning emerald gown that flowed like water, she was a picture of poise. But the moment she began to speak, a wave of unease washed over me. "Thank you all for joining us tonight," she said, her voice smooth, her smile disarming. "Tonight marks a significant step forward in our families' alliances, a celebration of unity."

Unity. The word hung in the air like a whispered lie. I could feel Nathan tense beside me, the muscles in his jaw clenching as if he, too, sensed the storm approaching. It wasn't long before the first cracks in the facade began to show. The chatter around us grew hushed as my mother continued, weaving her words into a tapestry of promises and plans. But I couldn't shake the feeling that we were merely pawns in a game far more sinister than I had ever imagined.

Then came the revelation, sharp as a knife slicing through silk. "Our families have worked together for generations, and it is time to solidify our position," she declared, her eyes sweeping over the crowd, landing on us with a steely gaze. In that moment, everything changed. The weight of betrayal crashed over me like an avalanche. "We will not only secure our legacies but also ensure our future. We will use all means necessary to maintain our power."

Anger surged within me, a molten tide threatening to overflow. "You let us fight while you played your own game!" I shouted, unable to contain the fury bubbling to the surface. The room froze, every head turning to witness the unfolding drama. A ripple of surprise passed through the guests, the shimmering laughter replaced by a tense silence that hummed like a live wire.

"Darling, please," my mother began, her tone unyielding but laced with condescension. "You don't understand—"

"No, you don't understand!" I cut her off, my voice echoing in the stunned silence. "You've manipulated us, sacrificed our futures for your own ambitions. Do you even care what this has done to us?"

Beside me, Nathan's expression mirrored my outrage. "We won't let you manipulate us anymore," he declared, stepping forward as if to stand between me and the world that had just shifted beneath our feet. His words hung in the air, a declaration of independence that felt like a vow. In that instant, our united front shattered the illusion of family loyalty, leaving nothing but raw emotion in its wake.

My mother's face shifted from surprise to a mask of irritation, her patience clearly wearing thin. "This is not the time for rebellion. This is for your own good."

"For our good?" I scoffed, incredulous. "Or for your convenience? You want to keep us in the dark while you pull the strings, don't you?" I could feel the heat rising in my cheeks, the anger transforming into something more vulnerable—fear of the truths I had yet to uncover.

As whispers filled the room, a sense of impending doom loomed. Friends turned into spectators, their eyes darting between my mother and me, as if waiting for a dramatic resolution. The laughter of the evening had morphed into a taut silence, the tension palpable, thick enough to cut through the air. I could sense the shifting alliances, the re-evaluating of loyalties among our guests, who had once danced and mingled without a care in the world.

The moment felt monumental, electric, yet I was painfully aware of how fragile it all was. The stakes had never been higher, and I couldn't back down now. With every ounce of strength I possessed, I stepped deeper into the fray, refusing to let my voice be silenced by the very people who had promised to protect me. "We deserve the truth!" I yelled, my voice trembling but unwavering.

In that charged silence, my mother's expression hardened, her cool facade beginning to crack. "You think you know what's best for you, but you're wrong." Her words were sharp, each syllable cutting deeper than the last. "You'll thank me one day for keeping you safe."

"Safe from what? The truth?" I shot back, the bitterness on my tongue a familiar taste. "Maybe it's time we took control of our lives."

The murmurs in the room grew louder, fueled by curiosity and disbelief. Nathan stepped beside me, a silent partner in my defiance, grounding me with his presence. The heat of the moment surged, igniting something deep within me—a resolve that I wouldn't be a pawn in their game any longer.

"Your game ends here," Nathan added, his voice steady and strong, mirroring my own determination. The fire in his gaze lit something within me, an understanding that we were in this together. Whatever the consequences, we would face them side by side.

The air was thick with unresolved tensions and shifting allegiances, and as the echoes of our rebellion lingered in the air, I felt a profound sense of liberation. It was a moment of reckoning, not just for us but for everyone in that room. The truth was a powerful weapon, and we were ready to wield it, no matter the cost.

The silence in the room stretched like a taut string, vibrating with the weight of my accusation. My heart thundered in my chest, the rhythm a fierce drumbeat urging me onward. I had crossed a line, yes, but it felt like the only line worth crossing. I could see the shock ripple across the faces of our guests, the aristocracy of our small town, their masks of sophistication slipping, revealing the anxiety and discomfort lurking beneath. It was a potent reminder that underneath the polished surface of wealth and power lay a world of deception and manipulation.

"Is this really how you want to play it, darling?" my mother's voice broke through the stillness, smooth yet laced with an icy edge. The dispassionate tone reminded me of a serpent, coiled and ready to strike. "You're not equipped to understand the intricacies of our dealings. This is not just a game; it's survival."

"Survival?" I echoed, incredulous. "Is that what you call using your children as leverage? Is that how you sleep at night?" The sting of betrayal twisted like a knife, and for a moment, I felt small, like a child again caught in my mother's manipulative web. Yet, standing beside Nathan, I felt a surge of strength. This was no longer just my battle; it was ours, and I wouldn't falter.

"Look around, Mother," Nathan said, his voice firm, a grounding presence beside me. "Everyone here is just as complicit. This isn't survival; it's exploitation. You've pitted us against one another for your own gain."

A flicker of something—fear, perhaps?—crossed my mother's face, but it was quickly masked by her practiced composure. "You think you can undermine everything I've built? You are merely pawns in a much larger game, and you will learn your place."

"Then it's time we took the game back," I challenged, my voice steady despite the tempest raging within me. The room held its breath, and I could almost hear the gears turning in the minds of our audience, weighing their loyalties, calculating their next moves.

Before my mother could respond, the large doors at the back of the ballroom swung open with a thunderous bang, startling everyone into silence. A figure stepped inside, silhouetted against the dim light, a striking contrast to the glittering affair. It was Lucas, my estranged cousin, looking as though he had just sprinted a marathon. His hair was tousled, and the breath he drew in was shaky, but his expression was fierce, resolute.

"Enough!" Lucas's voice rang out, silencing the murmurs that had begun to rise again. "Enough of this charade. I've had it with the lies and the manipulation. We are not your pawns!"

"Lucas, this isn't your—" my mother began, but he cut her off with a sharp glare.

"I know this is your event, but let's be honest. You've turned this gala into a circus. Everyone here knows it's about more than just celebrating family. You're playing us all against each other, and I won't stand for it." His eyes swept the crowd, seeking allies among the elite who had once seemed so untouchable.

I watched, breathless, as the tension in the room shifted yet again. Lucas had always been the wild card of our family—a charming rogue who reveled in stirring up trouble. The guests exchanged glances, and I could see the seeds of doubt taking root in their minds.

"Lucas, please," my mother implored, her voice losing its authority, her facade cracking ever so slightly. "This is not the time."

"The time was years ago when you started this mess!" he shot back. "You've turned us into a family of strangers, and I won't let you destroy any more of us."

His words hung in the air, and I felt the spark of rebellion ignite within me, a flame fanned by the passion of the moment. Lucas was right; we had all become mere pieces on a chessboard, shuffled around for our parents' amusement.

And then, just as the tension reached its peak, a shrill voice broke through. "This is unacceptable!" It was Veronica, a socialite known for her razor-sharp tongue and penchant for stirring drama. "I didn't come here to witness a family feud. This is supposed to be a gala, not a soap opera."

"Isn't that what you all signed up for?" I snapped back, surprising even myself with the vehemence of my response. "If you don't want to see the truth, then perhaps you should have thought twice before attending."

Laughter erupted from a corner of the room, a couple of guests clearly entertained by the spectacle. It was as if the atmosphere had finally cracked, and the air was filled with the electric thrill of potential chaos.

"Look, we can either stand here and pretend that everything is fine, or we can confront the reality of what's happening," Nathan said, his voice cutting through the commotion. "We deserve the truth, not the convenient lies that have kept us in the dark for too long."

At that moment, the swirling emotions in the room shifted yet again. The whispers grew louder, and I caught sight of a few heads nodding in agreement, a few guests stepping forward as if to support our stand against the tyranny of secrecy.

"Maybe it's time for a little honesty," Lucas suggested, his eyes gleaming with mischief. "Let's air the dirty laundry while we're at it. Who knows? Maybe we'll even find a few skeletons in the family closet that might make this night even more interesting."

Before my mother could regain her composure, Nathan leaned in closer to me, his voice low but urgent. "What if we actually let them have it? What if we expose everything?"

The thought sent a thrill of fear mixed with exhilaration through me. To lay bare the secrets that had bound us for so long—to unleash the truth, regardless of the consequences. The temptation was intoxicating.

As I scanned the room, I felt the tension shift, a palpable undercurrent of rebellion rising among the guests. This was no longer just about us; it was about everyone who had been swept into this intricate web of deceit. For the first time, I sensed that we might have the power to change the narrative, to break free from the constraints of our families' machinations.

"Yes, let's do it," I said, the conviction in my voice surprising even me. "Let's pull back the curtain and let the world see who we really are—no more facades, no more secrets."

And with that, as laughter and murmurs swelled around us, a new chapter unfolded, one where we would rewrite the rules of engagement, reclaim our agency, and confront the shadows that had lurked in our lives for too long.

The charged atmosphere thrummed with tension, a palpable energy that crackled through the ballroom as I locked eyes with my mother. The pristine chandeliers, once so glamorous, now felt like judgmental eyes surveying the scene. Guests whispered among themselves, their expressions shifting from shock to intrigue, and I could practically feel the scales tipping in our favor. The game, however twisted, had taken a new turn, and I couldn't help but revel in the delicious thrill of it all.

Lucas, emboldened by our audacious stand, stepped forward. "If we're really family, then we should be able to discuss the truth without fear. Or are we only supposed to keep pretending?" He addressed the assembly, his voice steady yet simmering with indignation.

His words resonated, and a murmur of agreement rippled through the crowd. "That's right!" someone called out, a brave voice from the back, emboldened by the turmoil. "We deserve the truth! No more secrets!"

I turned to Nathan, whose expression mirrored my own shock and exhilaration. "Did you hear that? They're with us!" I whispered, unable to hide my disbelief. The notion that we could be more than just pawns had ignited a fire within me, a fierce desire to dismantle the oppressive facade our families had constructed over the years.

My mother's expression morphed, revealing an unexpected blend of anger and vulnerability. "You're all being foolish!" she snapped, her voice rising above the murmurs. "You think you can just challenge the foundation of our family's legacy? You have no idea what you're meddling with!"

"Maybe that's the problem," I shot back, feeling the courage swell within me. "We've been kept in the dark, playing roles in a script we never signed up for."

The guests seemed torn between a desire for entertainment and the palpable fear of what this revelation might mean for their own standing. I could see glances exchanged, alliances recalibrating as they reconsidered the implications of what was unfolding before them. My heart raced with the thrill of the unknown, but beneath it all lurked a nagging uncertainty—what would this mean for us once the truth came to light?

"Enough!" My mother's voice boomed, silencing the room once again. "You're being reckless. If you expose these truths, you'll destroy everything we've built."

"Isn't that what we're trying to do?" Nathan asked, his tone sharp. "It's time to tear down the walls you've built. Maybe then we can rebuild something honest."

Just as the words hung in the air, a different kind of tension shifted the atmosphere. The doors swung open once more, and in strode a figure that had everyone's eyes widening in surprise—Sebastian, my estranged uncle, dressed impeccably in a tailored suit that accentuated his imposing stature. His presence, usually a harbinger of authority, now felt ominous.

"What's going on here?" he demanded, his gaze sweeping over the gathering. The air crackled with his authority, and I felt my heart race with an uneasy mixture of fear and defiance.

"We're taking a stand," I replied, summoning all my courage. "It's time to confront the lies, Uncle."

Sebastian's brow furrowed as he absorbed the tension and my words. "You think you can just—"

"I don't care what you think," I interrupted, emboldened by the fire burning within me. "This isn't just about our families anymore. It's about us. It's about breaking free from the manipulation that has controlled our lives for too long."

He stepped closer, his expression darkening. "You're playing a dangerous game, my dear. You may want to think twice before you burn bridges you can't cross back over."

With his words hanging heavy in the air, an unexpected wave of support surged through the crowd. People were rising to their feet, encouraged by our boldness, as if we were the spark igniting a long-festering discontent. I felt the tide shifting beneath us, an uprising brewing that threatened to unseat the very foundations of our families' power.

"Enough with the threats, Sebastian!" a voice cut through the tension. It was Veronica again, her eyes flashing defiantly. "You may be family, but this is our moment. Let them speak!"

"I can't believe what I'm hearing," he growled, visibly shaken. "You think you can just unravel decades of tradition in one evening?"

"Tradition is just another word for oppression," I countered, fueled by the newfound strength coursing through me. "We deserve the chance to define our own paths, not just follow in your footsteps."

With each word, the ballroom pulsed with a rhythm of rebellion, the whispers growing louder, each voice a strand in the fabric of this spontaneous insurrection. For once, we were all on the same page, the invisible chains of expectation rattling around us, ready to be broken.

But just when it felt as if we were on the brink of something monumental, Sebastian's face twisted with rage, and he stepped back, calculating. "You'll regret this. All of you," he warned, his voice low and ominous, sending a chill down my spine. "You have no idea what you're up against."

As if on cue, the lights flickered ominously, plunging the room into shadows, a haunting reminder of the dark corners of our family's past. Gasps echoed, and for a fleeting moment, I felt the weight of our actions crashing down around us. The air was thick with an unnameable tension, and I could almost hear the collective heartbeat of the crowd quicken, thrumming with uncertainty.

Then, without warning, the grand chandelier above us began to sway, a slow, menacing arc that caught everyone's attention. Panic rippled through the guests, their expressions morphing from defiance to fear as if they sensed the brewing storm within the walls of our family's legacy. I could feel Nathan stiffen beside me, his grip tightening on my arm, a silent acknowledgment that whatever came next would change everything.

"Something's wrong," Nathan whispered urgently, his gaze darting around as if searching for the source of the disturbance.

Before I could respond, a deafening crash echoed through the ballroom, reverberating off the marble walls. The chandelier, once a symbol of opulence, began to plummet, its crystal shards glinting in the dim light as it broke free from its moorings, careening toward the center of the room where we stood.

Time slowed as I watched the shards glitter like a rain of stars, suspended in the air for a brief heartbeat before the chaos erupted. My heart raced, adrenaline surging as I pulled Nathan down with me, instinctively shielding him from the falling debris. But as we hit the ground, a realization struck—a primal fear that this was no mere accident, that the unraveling had only just begun, and the real game was only about to be revealed.

With the world around us descending into chaos, I caught a glimpse of Sebastian's face, twisted in rage and something else—something darker. As the room erupted into screams, I understood that the truth was no longer just a weapon but a force that could shatter everything.

Chapter 15: Fire and Ice

The air was thick with tension, a swirling tempest of emotions that clung to me like a second skin. I could feel the pulse of the world around us, a chaotic symphony of muted voices and the distant clatter of dishes. Yet here, in the soft cocoon of Nathan's embrace, it was as if we had created our own universe—one where the outside noise faded into nothingness, and all that mattered was the heat radiating between us.

We sat together in his family's sprawling estate, a place that had seen its fair share of grandeur and heartbreak. Ornate chandeliers dangled from the ceiling, casting flickering shadows that danced across the walls, a reminder of the opulence that now felt tainted by the aftermath of the gala. Every glimmer of light seemed to whisper secrets, taunting us with the knowledge of our precarious situation. Outside, the storm raged, mirroring the turmoil brewing in our hearts.

"I can't believe we're actually doing this," I murmured, pulling back slightly to search Nathan's eyes for reassurance. His gaze was steady, unwavering, a dark ocean that promised both safety and the unknown.

"Neither can I," he replied, his voice low, a soft rumble that sent shivers down my spine. "But I wouldn't want to be anywhere else."

His thumb traced the line of my jaw, a simple gesture that ignited a wildfire of longing within me. I leaned into his touch, craving the comfort it brought. But beneath that comfort lay an urgency, a desperation that pulled us closer, our breaths mingling in the space between us. It was exhilarating and terrifying all at once—a dance on the razor's edge of desire and danger.

We had spent countless nights like this, wrapped in each other's warmth as the world outside continued to unravel. Each moment felt stolen, as if we were characters in a grand romance, hidden away from the prying eyes of family and foes. I reveled in the quiet intimacy, yet I was all too aware of the shadows lurking just beyond our sanctuary. The stakes were rising, and with each whispered confession, the line between safety and chaos blurred further.

"What do you think will happen next?" I asked, trying to tether myself to the reality of our situation. The vulnerability of the question hung heavy in the air.

Nathan sighed, his expression shifting, shadows passing over his face like clouds obscuring the sun. "I wish I knew. But with our families at each other's throats, I can't shake the feeling that this isn't just about us anymore. It's like we're pawns in a game we never agreed to play."

I nodded, feeling the weight of his words. Our relationship had ignited a fierce battle not only within our hearts but within our families. Whispers of betrayal swirled around us like autumn leaves caught in a gust of wind, threatening to expose the truth we were so desperately trying to protect.

"Do you think they'll come for us?" I asked, my voice barely a whisper, fear creeping into my chest like ice settling in my veins.

"Probably," Nathan admitted, his expression darkening. "But we can't let them dictate our lives. We need to take control of our own story."

I admired his determination, the fire that flickered in his eyes, a stark contrast to the chill wrapping itself around my heart. "And how do we do that?"

Nathan leaned in, his breath warm against my skin. "We fight. Together."

His words ignited something deep within me, a spark of hope that threatened to chase away the shadows. Together. The notion was intoxicating, a promise that whispered of unity and strength. But the deeper we fell into this connection, the more perilous the world around us became.

The door creaked, pulling us from our reverie. I jolted, a wave of panic crashing over me. Nathan tensed beside me, the warmth of our moment dissipating as reality encroached. I held my breath, straining to hear who might be intruding upon our sanctuary.

"Is someone in there?" The voice was unmistakable—Nathan's sister, Clara.

Nathan glanced at me, his expression a mix of concern and frustration. I nodded slightly, signaling him to answer. "Yeah, Clara, we're in here," he called, his voice steady despite the tension thickening the air.

The door swung open, and Clara stepped into the room, her eyes narrowing as she took in the scene. "What are you two doing?" she asked, crossing her arms over her chest.

"Just talking," Nathan replied, but I could hear the tension in his voice, the underlying note of defiance.

Clara's gaze darted between us, suspicion etched across her features. "You should be careful. There's talk... rumors swirling about you two. You know how our family is."

"Yeah, we're well aware," I said, irritation bubbling to the surface. "But we can't just hide away forever, can we?"

Nathan shot me a warning look, but the anger had already spilled from my lips, a hot rush of emotion that felt good and dangerous all at once. Clara hesitated, her expression softening slightly. "I get it. But you need to think about the consequences. If our parents find out..."

"Then they'll find out," Nathan interrupted, his voice rising. "I refuse to let them control my life."

"Your life? What about hers?" Clara retorted, pointing at me with a sharp finger. "You're dragging her into this mess, Nathan!"

"Enough!" I exclaimed, my voice cutting through the tension like a knife. "I'm not some damsel in distress. I can make my own choices."

The three of us stood in the charged silence, the air crackling with unspoken words and emotions. Nathan's hand found mine, squeezing it tight, grounding me amidst the chaos.

"Clara, we'll handle this," he said, his tone softer now, but firm. "But we need your support. I can't do this without you."

Clara's shoulders relaxed, the fight leaving her as she looked at us, vulnerability flickering in her gaze. "Okay. But you have to promise to be careful."

"We will," I assured her, knowing full well the risks that lay ahead.

As Clara left, the door closed with a quiet click, leaving Nathan and me alone once more. The room felt heavier now, the weight of our decisions settling on us like a mantle.

"Are we doing the right thing?" I asked, my voice trembling slightly.

Nathan turned to me, the fire in his eyes ignited anew. "We have to. For us. For everyone."

His words resonated deep within me, an echo of hope that spiraled into determination. Together, we would face the storm, battling against the tides of chaos that threatened to consume us. We would redefine our story, forging a path through the flames and ice that surrounded us, no matter the cost.

The evening sun dipped below the horizon, painting the sky with hues of orange and violet, as I stood on the balcony, lost in thought. The estate sprawled out beneath me, a testament to grandeur and excess, yet it felt like a gilded cage. The air was thick with the scent of lilacs, a reminder of fleeting beauty, as I clutched the railing, feeling the cool metal bite into my palms. Inside, the remnants of a lavish dinner party echoed, laughter and clinking glasses barely muffling the undercurrents of tension swirling within the walls.

Nathan joined me, his presence a comforting weight against my side. "You know," he said, leaning against the railing, "if I had known family gatherings came with such high stakes, I might have opted for a quiet life in a cabin somewhere."

I chuckled, the sound surprising even me. "And miss out on this delightful chaos? Never. Who else would I have to scheme with over fancy hors d'oeuvres?"

He grinned, a flash of mischief lighting up his eyes. "True, the crab cakes did leave a lot to be desired. If only we could have smuggled in a pizza."

"Now that's a party I'd gladly crash," I quipped, bumping my shoulder against his. It was moments like this—small, teasing exchanges—that reminded me why being with Nathan felt like breathing. He had a way of transforming the direst situations into something manageable, even humorous. But beneath that lighthearted banter was a heavy truth that settled like fog in my chest.

"I should have known better than to think we could have a normal family dinner," Nathan said, his voice lowering as his expression shifted to something more serious. "With the gala fallout, the tension is thicker than the sauce they served."

"Is it really that bad?" I asked, my stomach knotting at the thought.

"Let's just say I overheard my father and uncle arguing about 'keeping the peace' while my mother shot daggers across the table at everyone who dared to smile. You know, the usual family bonding experience."

"I'm surprised there were no actual daggers involved," I replied wryly. "Your family could teach a masterclass in passive aggression."

He chuckled, the sound lightening the mood, but I could sense the worry lurking beneath his laughter. The echoes of the gala still haunted us; whispers of betrayal had taken root, and the stakes felt dangerously high. We were walking a tightrope stretched between two families on the brink of war, our love a potential spark in a powder keg.

As if sensing my thoughts, Nathan reached for my hand, intertwining his fingers with mine. The warmth of his touch chased away the chill of uncertainty. "Whatever happens, I want you to know that I'm here. We'll figure this out together."

I nodded, trying to summon a confident smile. "Together," I echoed, but I couldn't shake the feeling that "together" was a promise fraught with peril.

The night wore on, and the party below swelled with energy, laughter piercing through the veneer of civility. We retreated into the shadows of the balcony, a hidden sanctuary where the chaos faded to a whisper. "I can't believe how much pressure there is," I said, leaning into him, allowing the warmth of his body to soothe my fraying nerves. "What if things don't settle down? What if they escalate?"

Nathan paused, his brow furrowed in thought. "If they escalate, we'll handle it. Together."

The assurance in his voice ignited a flicker of hope, but my mind raced with possibilities. "And if they drag us into their mess?"

"Then we'll fight our way out."

I turned to face him, the intensity of his gaze sending a thrill through me. "Fight? Is that your solution for everything?"

He smirked, his eyes sparkling with mischief. "Well, I'm good at it. You'd be surprised how effective a well-placed punch can be in a family feud."

"I'll keep that in mind if anyone brings out the dessert. I can see how chocolate cake might turn into a deadly weapon."

Nathan laughed, the sound rich and genuine. "See? We're already planning our defense strategy."

But as the laughter faded, a palpable tension returned, thickening the air around us. It was a reminder of the danger lurking beneath our playful banter. I knew that as long as Nathan and I were entangled in this web of familial loyalty and rivalry, we would have to tread carefully.

A sharp crack of glass shattering echoed from inside, followed by a flurry of raised voices. I exchanged a glance with Nathan, his eyes wide. "What was that?"

"Let's go check," he said, tugging me back inside.

The scene that greeted us was a whirlwind of chaos. Guests were clustered in small groups, their faces painted with concern, while my heart sank at the sight of Nathan's mother, her hands pressed to her temples, clearly overwhelmed. His father stood nearby, his face flushed with anger as he glared at Nathan's uncle, whose own expression was dark with contempt.

"Not a great family reunion," I muttered under my breath.

"Yeah, let's just say the ice is officially broken," Nathan replied, his tone dripping with sarcasm.

"Did someone lose their temper over the veal?" I joked, attempting to diffuse the tension, but my heart raced at the escalating situation.

As Nathan and I navigated through the crowd, I caught snippets of heated exchanges. Words like "betrayal" and "trust" ricocheted off the walls, heavy with accusation and regret. It felt as if the very air was charged, each breath I took thick with uncertainty.

"Do you think we should intervene?" I asked, glancing at Nathan.

"Not yet," he replied, keeping his voice low. "Let's just observe for a moment."

We edged closer to the center of the conflict, curiosity piquing with each passing moment. It was like watching a train wreck; I couldn't look away, even as my heart pounded in my chest.

Suddenly, Nathan's uncle raised his voice, "You think you can just control everything? This family isn't your puppet show, Nathan!"

I felt Nathan stiffen beside me, the tension rolling off him in waves. "This isn't about me!" he shouted back, his words cutting through the chaos. "You're all so focused on maintaining appearances that you're forgetting what matters!"

Gasps echoed through the room, and I felt my pulse quicken. This was the moment of reckoning, where the façade of family loyalty cracked under the weight of raw emotions.

"Enough!" Nathan's father boomed, stepping forward, his presence commanding silence. "This is not the time or place for this. We are family, and we must unite against our enemies."

"Enemies? Is that what you call them now?" Nathan shot back, his voice a mixture of anger and disbelief. "You don't understand what's happening here! You're too blinded by your own pride to see the truth!"

I squeezed Nathan's hand, willing him to step back, to retreat from the confrontation, but he stood his ground, his fierce loyalty igniting a fire in his eyes. The stakes had risen beyond our control, and I felt like a spectator in my own life as the drama unfolded before me, each moment building to an inevitable climax that neither of us could predict.

With every heated exchange, I knew we were teetering on the edge of something monumental, and no amount of bravado could shield us from the impending storm.

The tension in the room was palpable, thick enough to choke on, as Nathan and his father faced off like duelists at dawn, the air crackling with unspoken words and simmering resentment. I felt like a ghost caught in a storm, a witness to the unraveling fabric of a family that had long clung to the façade of perfection. Voices rose and fell like waves crashing against the shore, each syllable weighted with history and hurt, the air growing dense with the scent of unyielding pride and fear.

"You think unity will fix this?" Nathan shot back, his voice trembling with barely contained fury. "This isn't a game, Dad. Our lives are on the line, and you're still trying to pretend everything is fine!"

His father's jaw clenched, the muscle twitching ominously. "And what would you suggest, Nathan? We turn against our own? You're being reckless. You're putting everyone at risk."

"Everyone?" Nathan's voice turned icy, sharp enough to cut through the air. "What about us? What about me? You can't control my life forever!"

I held my breath, caught between the desire to intervene and the understanding that this confrontation was long overdue. In the depths of my mind, I acknowledged the truth: Nathan was right. The walls of this perfect family were crumbling under the pressure of secrets and lies.

"Enough!" His uncle's voice boomed across the room, drawing all eyes toward him. "This is not the time for petty squabbles. We need to address the threats lurking in the shadows, not tear each other apart."

A nervous murmur rippled through the crowd, and I felt Nathan's grip tighten around my hand, a lifeline in the tumult. The atmosphere shifted again, all eyes darting between Nathan and his family as if expecting a firework to explode at any moment.

"And how do you propose we do that?" Nathan's father asked, his tone a mixture of frustration and disbelief. "By ignoring our problems? By pretending that your choices don't have consequences?"

Nathan squared his shoulders, defiance radiating from him like a shield. "I refuse to live in fear of our own family. I will not hide who I am or what I feel. If you can't accept that, then maybe it's time we reevaluate what family truly means."

His words hung in the air like a challenge, and I felt my heart race in response. The bravery he displayed was nothing short of mesmerizing, a beacon amidst the chaos. But as the echoes of his declaration faded, a different kind of tension settled in—the kind that forewarns of imminent danger.

"Don't be naive," his uncle snapped, the venom in his voice unmistakable. "Your decisions could cost us everything. You think this is just about you and her? This is about our legacy!"

At the mention of "legacy," a shiver ran down my spine. My heart hammered against my ribs, the implications of his words sinking in. We weren't just pawns in a family drama; we were caught in a power struggle that could lead to catastrophic consequences.

"I'll do whatever it takes to protect what matters," Nathan declared, his eyes blazing with conviction.

The air turned electric as whispers and murmurs swirled around us, the room now a battlefield where allegiances were tested and loyalty was uncertain. I could feel the walls closing in, the weight of every gaze pressing down on me, forcing me to confront the reality that our love might not be enough to shield us from the fallout.

The shouting grew louder, the arguments escalating into a cacophony of accusations and half-formed threats. In the eye of the storm, I turned to Nathan, searching his face for reassurance, for a plan that would save us from the impending fallout. But before I could voice my fears, the door slammed open with a deafening crash, silencing the room.

All heads turned as Clara entered, her face pale and strained. "We have a problem," she said, breathless and frantic, her eyes darting around the room. "They've found us."

"What do you mean, they've found us?" Nathan demanded, his tone sharp as steel.

"The reports are true. Someone's been watching us. I saw them on the grounds just now." Her voice trembled, but the urgency in her tone was unmistakable. "They're not here for a family reunion."

I felt my stomach drop. The threat that had hovered just out of reach was suddenly real and pressing, a predator lying in wait, eager to pounce.

"Did you see who it was?" Nathan's father asked, suddenly alert, the anger in his features morphing into something more serious.

"No," Clara replied, shaking her head. "But I could feel it. I think... I think it might be them."

"Who are 'they'?" I interjected, my heart racing, the words slipping out before I could stop myself.

"The other families," Nathan explained, his voice low. "Those we've had conflicts with—rivals, enemies. They're not just rumors anymore. They're here, and they want to settle the score."

The gravity of his words crashed over me, a wave of cold dread sweeping through my veins. I had hoped our lives could return to normal, that love would be enough to shield us from external threats, but the reality was sinking in like an anchor, heavy and unyielding.

"Then we need to go," I urged, my voice rising slightly above the murmurs of uncertainty. "If they're here, we can't just stand around waiting for them to make a move. We have to prepare."

"Prepare for what?" Nathan's uncle scoffed, the arrogance spilling from him. "Running away won't change anything."

"Maybe not, but it gives us time," I countered, my resolve hardening. "We need to strategize and find a way to protect what matters most."

Nathan looked at me, a flicker of admiration in his eyes, and I knew we were united in our purpose. "She's right. We can't be caught off guard."

DANGEROUS ALLIANCES

In that moment, the decision was made. We would not succumb to the shadows lurking around us. We would fight, not just for our love but for our future.

Suddenly, a loud crash echoed from the back of the estate, sending a tremor of fear through the crowd. Panic erupted, and guests began to scatter, fear etched on their faces.

"Get to safety!" Nathan's father commanded, but the urgency in his tone felt too late. The danger was here, and it was no longer just a whisper in the dark.

In the chaos, I felt Nathan pull me close, his breath warm against my ear. "We need to move, now."

Before I could respond, the lights flickered ominously, plunging us into darkness, and a chilling silence swept over the room. The world around me dimmed, the chaos replaced by a suffocating stillness that screamed of impending doom.

And just as quickly, the power returned, illuminating a scene that sent ice through my veins: a figure stood in the doorway, silhouetted against the light, a smirk playing on their lips, eyes glinting with malice.

"Did you really think you could hide?" the figure called out, their voice dripping with disdain. "The game has just begun."

My heart raced as the realization hit me like a freight train. We were no longer just fighting against familial loyalty or rivalry; we were ensnared in a deadly game where the stakes were higher than we had ever imagined. The danger was real, and it was here to claim its prize.

Chapter 16: A Dangerous Game

The warehouse loomed ahead, a skeletal remnant of a bygone era, its corrugated metal walls shrouded in shadows. I could barely make out the jagged edges of broken windows, remnants of glass that glinted in the pale moonlight, resembling teeth in a decaying grin. This place, an echo of industry and ambition, had become a sanctuary for whispers of conspiracy, where secrets threaded through the air like smoke. My heart raced, caught in a delicate dance of fear and exhilaration. I was here, standing on the precipice of truth, and I had never felt more alive.

Nathan, always a steady presence beside me, scanned the perimeter, his brow furrowing as he peered into the darkness. "Are you sure about this?" His voice was low, reverberating with an edge of uncertainty that only heightened my resolve. "We could still back out. We don't need to take this risk."

I shook my head, my hair dancing around my shoulders in the cool night breeze. "No, we've come too far to turn back now." The adrenaline coursing through my veins fueled my defiance. We had pieced together fragments of a puzzle that loomed larger than either of us had anticipated. We were not just trying to expose a lie; we were preparing to dismantle an entire network built on deceit and manipulation. This was about reclaiming our lives and bringing justice to those who had suffered under the weight of the conspiracy.

Stepping into the warehouse was like entering another world, the air heavy with the scent of rust and damp wood, mingling with the ghostly remnants of oil and metal. Each step echoed in the cavernous space, a reminder of the danger that lurked in the shadows. Nathan's hand brushed against mine, a reassuring gesture that sent a jolt of warmth through me amidst the chilling atmosphere. We were in this together, bound by our shared determination.

As we navigated the maze of crates and machinery, a flicker of movement caught my eye. My breath hitched as I turned, adrenaline spiking once more. A figure emerged from the darkness, cloaked in a long trench coat, his face obscured by the brim of a hat. "You must be Nathan," he said, his voice smooth like silk, but with an underlying tension that hinted at danger. "And you must be the one who wants to play a dangerous game."

I couldn't help but shiver at his words, the implications hanging in the air like a storm cloud. Nathan stepped forward, his jaw clenched, ready to confront this stranger. "We're not here to play games. We need information. We know what you're involved in, and we want in."

The man chuckled softly, his amusement echoing in the cavernous space. "You're bold, I'll give you that. But boldness can lead to recklessness. You two are swimming in deep waters." He gestured toward the far end of the warehouse, where a flickering light illuminated a table laden with papers and documents. "Come. Let's see if you're truly ready to dive deeper."

We exchanged glances, the gravity of the moment sinking in. With a silent nod, we followed him, our hearts racing in unison. As we approached the table, I felt the weight of what lay before us—evidence, connections, names scrawled in hurried handwriting that hinted at a web of treachery sprawling beyond our comprehension. I could barely contain my excitement, the thrill of discovery propelling me forward.

"This is the crux of it all," the man said, his fingers gliding over the documents as if unveiling a treasure trove. "Everything you need to expose the network that has brought so much chaos to your lives." He leaned closer, his voice dropping to a conspiratorial whisper. "But understand this: you are now marked. Those who control this game will not let you walk away unscathed."

My heart raced, not just from the revelations but from the weight of his words. We had stepped into a world where danger was an inescapable companion, and I could feel its icy fingers creeping along my spine. "What do you mean?" I managed to ask, my voice barely above a whisper, laced with the thrill of fear.

He looked up, his gaze piercing through the shadows. "They are watching. Every move you make will be scrutinized, and any misstep could lead to dire consequences. You want to expose them, but the truth is a slippery fish. One wrong turn, and it could all come crashing down."

Nathan clenched his fists, determination etched into every line of his face. "We're not afraid. We have to do this. We won't let them control us any longer."

The man studied us for a moment, a flicker of respect crossing his features. "Then let's make sure you're equipped for the storm ahead." He handed us a dossier, thick with information, its pages crammed with names, dates, and connections that formed the backbone of the conspiracy. I felt the weight of the world resting in my hands, the power of knowledge intertwining with the looming threat of danger.

"Meet me here again tomorrow," he instructed, his tone shifting to one of urgency. "We'll strategize, but remember—trust is a rare commodity in this game. Choose your allies wisely."

With that, he slipped back into the shadows, leaving us alone amidst the chaos of the warehouse. Nathan and I exchanged a glance, the thrill of the unknown surging between us. I could feel the electricity in the air, the promise of what was to come swirling around us like a tempest. We were no longer just two kids caught in a game; we were players now, ready to unveil the truth.

"Are you ready?" Nathan asked, his voice steady yet tinged with excitement.

DANGEROUS ALLIANCES

I smiled, a fierce resolve igniting within me. "More than ever." We stepped back into the fray, armed with knowledge, ready to confront whatever darkness lay ahead.

A chill settled in my bones as Nathan and I stood in the warehouse, clutching the dossier that felt heavier than a stone. The flickering overhead light cast dancing shadows that seemed to mock our resolve, teasing us with the fragility of our plan. I glanced at Nathan, whose expression was a blend of fierce determination and barely concealed fear. "So, what's the plan?" I asked, trying to keep the tremor out of my voice. "We just throw these documents at the first person we see and hope for the best?"

He chuckled, the sound surprisingly light given the weight of the situation. "I mean, it might be more effective than we think. But I was thinking something a bit more strategic." The way his lips curled into that boyish grin gave me the courage I needed. We were in this together, and I had no intention of backing down.

With a quick glance around the dimly lit warehouse, I let out a slow breath. "Okay, so we gather our contacts. Who do we trust?" My mind raced through the names of the few people we had met in this murky world of subterfuge, each one tinged with uncertainty.

"Maxine, for starters," Nathan suggested, his voice steady. "She has the connections we need and the guts to pull it off."

"True," I admitted, remembering Maxine's sharp wit and fierce loyalty. She had a way of cutting through the noise, her instinct for danger almost palpable. "And if we can convince her this is serious, she might rally her contacts."

Just then, a loud clang reverberated through the space, slicing through the air like a knife. We both froze, hearts racing as the sound echoed ominously. "Did you hear that?" I whispered, gripping Nathan's arm.

"Yeah, and I'd prefer it if I didn't have to repeat myself," he muttered, eyes narrowing as he scanned the shadows.

"Should we check it out?" I felt a surge of reckless courage as I stepped toward the source of the sound, driven by an instinct that told me we couldn't ignore it.

"Maybe let's just stick to our plan and not add 'mysterious noise' to our list of problems," he countered, but I could see the flicker of curiosity in his eyes.

As I stepped cautiously forward, the sound of shuffling footsteps met my ears, drawing nearer with an unsettling quickness. My heart raced, but curiosity held me in its grip. Nathan followed close behind, his presence a steady anchor as we ventured deeper into the unknown.

Emerging from behind a stack of crates, we stumbled upon a scene that sent my heart plummeting. A group of men huddled together, their hushed voices laced with urgency. I recognized one of them—the wiry figure of Thomas, a low-level contact we had met through Maxine. "We need to move before they find out we're here," he said, his tone dripping with desperation.

"What the hell is going on?" Nathan blurted, stepping into the light. The men turned sharply, surprise flashing across their faces, quickly replaced by suspicion.

"Who are you?" Thomas demanded, his eyes narrowing as he took in our presence.

"Friends. Well, sort of." I raised my hands defensively, the tension thickening in the air. "We're looking for information about the conspiracy. We know something big is going down, and we want in."

"Big?" Thomas scoffed, but his expression shifted. "You two are in over your heads. You need to leave. Now."

I felt a pang of irritation. "Not happening. We came here to help, not to run away." The edge in my voice surprised me, but the reality of our situation pushed me forward.

Nathan stepped forward, matching Thomas's intensity. "We're not leaving without understanding what's happening. If you know something, you need to share it. We have evidence that can turn the tide."

The men exchanged wary glances, and I could see the gears turning in Thomas's head. After a moment of silence that felt like an eternity, he sighed, running a hand through his hair in frustration. "Fine. But you have to promise you'll stay out of it once you hear. It's more dangerous than you think."

"Danger is our middle name," I quipped, trying to lighten the atmosphere, though I knew how serious this was.

With a begrudging nod, Thomas beckoned us closer. "There's a shipment coming in tonight—something that could expose everything. But it's not just any shipment. It's the heart of the operation."

My stomach twisted. "What do you mean? What's in it?"

"Information," he replied, a hint of urgency in his tone. "Names, locations, everything. If we can get our hands on it before it reaches the other side, we can dismantle this network from the inside out."

"Then let's do it," Nathan said, determination igniting in his eyes. "We'll grab the shipment. No more playing around."

"Wait," I interjected, feeling a surge of panic. "What if it's a trap? We can't just waltz in without a plan."

Thomas's gaze turned steely. "We don't have time for hesitation. Either we act now, or we lose everything. And trust me, they won't hesitate to eliminate anyone in their way."

The gravity of his words settled heavily between us. The stakes had escalated once more, and I could feel the weight of my decision bearing down. "Alright," I said, my voice steadier than I felt. "But we need a plan. We can't rush in blindly."

Nathan nodded, his focus unwavering. "Let's gather more intel. If we're going to do this, we have to know the layout, the security, everything."

The tension was palpable as Thomas gestured for us to follow him deeper into the shadows. I could feel my heart pounding in my chest, anticipation mingling with trepidation. The night had transformed from a simple gathering into a dangerous game of cat and mouse, and I was ready to play. With every step deeper into the unknown, the thrill of rebellion surged through me, an intoxicating blend of fear and resolve, propelling us closer to the truth that lay just out of reach.

The shadows of the warehouse loomed larger as Thomas led us deeper into the maze of rusting machinery and crumbling concrete. Each step echoed like a heartbeat, a reminder of the urgency pulsing through our veins. I stole a glance at Nathan, who remained resolute, his jaw set with a determination that mirrored my own. We were no longer just kids trying to make sense of a world spiraling into chaos; we were on the brink of something monumental, ready to pull back the curtain on the truth that had haunted us for far too long.

"Okay, so what's the plan?" I asked, trying to keep my voice steady. The closer we got to the heart of this operation, the more my mind raced with possibilities—and dangers.

"We need to intercept the shipment before it reaches its destination," Thomas replied, his tone serious. "It's set to arrive in less than an hour at the old docks by the river. If we can get there first, we can secure the evidence and disappear before anyone notices."

"Sounds simple enough," I said, sarcasm lacing my words. "What could possibly go wrong?"

Nathan shot me a glance, half amused, half exasperated. "Let's keep the sarcasm to a minimum, shall we? We need to focus."

"Right, right," I said, waving my hands as if to banish my flippancy. "So how do we get there without getting caught?"

Thomas chuckled darkly. "That's the easy part. I have a car stashed out back."

"Of course you do," Nathan replied, a teasing glint in his eye. "You're practically a spy."

"I prefer the term 'informant,'" Thomas countered, leading us through a narrow passageway lined with old crates. "But let's save the banter for later. We have to move."

As we slipped out of the warehouse, the night air hit us like a splash of cold water, refreshing yet fraught with tension. The moon hung high, casting an ethereal glow over the empty streets. My pulse quickened as we approached the nondescript sedan, its dark paint absorbing the shadows. I slid into the backseat, the leather cool against my skin, while Nathan took the passenger side, his focus already shifting to our next steps.

"Where are we going exactly?" I asked, twisting around to face Thomas as he started the engine.

"To the docks," he replied, glancing at me in the rearview mirror. "You'll want to keep your heads down. If anyone recognizes you, it could be trouble."

"Great, trouble is my middle name," I muttered under my breath, though the reality of what we were doing sent a thrill coursing through me.

As we sped through the dimly lit streets, the city seemed to blur by, a ghost of what had once felt familiar. I watched the buildings zip past, each one a reminder of the life I had known—a life now intertwined with shadows and secrets. It felt surreal to be sitting in a car, planning to intercept a criminal operation, yet here I was, chasing a truth that had eluded me for too long.

"Do you think we're ready for this?" I asked, breaking the tense silence that hung in the air like fog. "What if we're not enough?"

Nathan turned slightly, his gaze steady and reassuring. "We've come this far, haven't we? We know what we're fighting for. That counts for something."

His confidence bolstered my resolve, but a flicker of doubt still lingered in the back of my mind. "Just remember, if we get caught—"

"Then we don't get caught," Nathan interrupted, a playful smirk dancing on his lips. "We're smarter than that."

I shook my head, a smile breaking through my anxiety. "Right. The smart part hasn't exactly been our strong suit lately."

"Just stick to the plan," Thomas chimed in, his voice laced with urgency. "We'll arrive in ten minutes. When we get there, you'll need to keep a low profile. No heroics."

As the car approached the docks, the atmosphere shifted dramatically. The sound of the water lapping against the old wooden pilings echoed ominously, and the air thickened with anticipation. Thomas slowed the car to a stop behind a cluster of shipping containers, their rusted exteriors hiding whatever darkness was to come.

"Here we go," he whispered, turning off the engine. The darkness outside was heavy and still, broken only by the distant glow of the streetlamps illuminating the docks like sentinels.

Nathan and I exchanged a glance, a silent agreement passing between us. We were in this together, for better or worse.

"Stay sharp," I murmured, heart pounding in my chest as we exited the car and crept toward the edge of the dock. The sounds of shuffling footsteps and low voices drifted through the air, drawing us closer to the source.

Peeking around a shipping container, I spotted a group of men unloading crates from a truck, their movements quick and precise. "That's them," I whispered, my pulse racing. "What now?"

"We wait for the right moment," Nathan replied, his breath hot against my ear, sending a thrill down my spine.

As we huddled behind the container, my mind raced with possibilities. We had to be careful, to find the right opportunity.

The stakes were impossibly high, and I could feel the weight of the moment pressing down on me.

Suddenly, a loud crash shattered the tension, reverberating through the air like a gunshot. My heart jumped, and I turned to see one of the men stumble, a crate spilling its contents onto the ground. Papers scattered like autumn leaves, fluttering in the breeze, and I caught a glimpse of familiar names and dates on the documents.

"That's it!" I gasped, my excitement bubbling over. "That's our evidence!"

But as I reached for Nathan, ready to make a dash for the documents, a shadow loomed behind us. "You really thought you could pull this off?"

The voice sent chills racing down my spine. I turned, my breath hitching in my throat, and there stood a figure cloaked in darkness, a smirk playing across their lips. My heart dropped as recognition washed over me, realization dawning with chilling clarity.

"Welcome to the game," the figure said, and just like that, the world around me tilted on its axis.

Chapter 17: The Confrontation

The air inside the diner felt thick, a blend of grease and unspoken fears clinging to every surface. The flickering neon sign outside cast an eerie glow through the cracked windows, illuminating the dust motes swirling in the stale air. I sat across from Nathan, his fingers drumming anxiously against the table. Each tap echoed in my mind, a reminder of the weight of our task. We had danced around the idea of rebellion for too long, but now, it was time to act. The underground network had become our only ally, a whisper of hope amidst the chaos of our lives.

I could sense the anticipation in Nathan, his eyes a mix of determination and trepidation. We had forged a bond over late-night discussions and shared glances that spoke volumes, but this was different. This was real. My heart thumped loudly in my chest, drowning out the clinking of dishes and the murmurs of the other patrons. We were on the precipice of something monumental, and the thought sent adrenaline coursing through my veins.

Just as I opened my mouth to speak, a shadow flickered at the edge of my vision. My gaze snapped to the corner booth where two figures huddled, their faces obscured by the dim light. I turned back to Nathan, his brow furrowed, and I knew he had noticed too. "Do you see them?" I asked, my voice barely above a whisper.

"Yeah, and they've been here for a while," he replied, his voice steady but tinged with concern. "Let's stay focused. We can't let them intimidate us now."

Right. Focus. I took a deep breath, steeling myself for the conversation ahead. This was our moment to outline the plan to expose the conspiracy that had wormed its way into our lives, the very foundation of our families' legacies. If we could just get this right, we could dismantle the tangled web of lies and deceit that had trapped us for so long.

DANGEROUS ALLIANCES

But before I could gather my thoughts, the diner door swung open with a jarring crash, sending the bell above it jangling like an alarm. The harsh light from outside spilled into the dim space, and in strode our families' security team, all sharp suits and even sharper glares. I felt the color drain from my face as their imposing presence filled the diner. Nathan's grip on the table tightened, the knuckles of his hands turning white.

"You two need to come with us," one of them barked, his voice as cold and unyielding as the steel of the door they had just slammed shut. The leader's eyes, as dark and unreadable as a winter storm, locked onto mine, and I could feel the dread creeping into my bones.

"No, we're fine here," I replied, forcing the defiance into my voice despite the tremor that lingered beneath the surface. "We're just discussing some business." It felt hollow, and I could see Nathan stiffen beside me.

"Business? Is that what you call it?" he snapped back, a hint of irritation breaking through his calm façade. "You know how serious this is. You're putting yourselves in danger."

"Danger?" I repeated, the word tasting bitter on my tongue. "I thought you were supposed to be the ones protecting us."

The leader stepped closer, his body a looming wall of authority. "And we intend to protect you—by taking you out of here. Now."

Nathan shot me a glance, and in that split second, I saw the resolve shift. It was the moment we both knew we had to choose: family loyalty or the freedom we craved. My heart raced, a pulse of panic sparking in my chest. I had never felt so trapped in my life, with our futures teetering on a knife's edge.

"We can't just walk away," Nathan said, his voice low but firm. "Not now, not when we're so close."

"Close to what?" the leader challenged, his patience wearing thin. "Close to getting hurt? You don't understand the gravity of this situation."

"No," I cut in, finding strength in the heat of the moment. "You don't understand. We're the ones who've been living in the dark. We're the ones who have to face this head-on." The words spilled out before I could catch them, a torrent of frustration and fear.

The leader's expression shifted, a flicker of something—maybe recognition—passing through his eyes. "You think you're the first ones to try this? You don't know what you're up against."

Nathan leaned forward, his voice intense. "Then let us find out. If we fail, we'll accept whatever consequences come our way. But you can't just take that choice away from us."

For a moment, silence enveloped the diner, thick and heavy. The other patrons had gone quiet, eyes darting between us and the security team. The tension hung like a taut string, ready to snap. I could feel the gravity of the moment, the world shrinking down to this standoff.

"Fine," the leader said at last, a reluctant resignation in his tone. "You have one hour. One hour to present your case, but know this—if anything goes wrong, if you're caught in the middle of this mess, it's on your heads."

Relief washed over me, a tide of adrenaline coursing through my veins. We had a chance. As the security team turned to leave, I felt the spark of determination ignite within me. Nathan met my gaze, a flicker of hope reflected in his eyes.

"We need to go now," he said, urgency lacing his tone. "Let's find the others and get this plan in motion. It's now or never."

With a nod, I stood, my heart racing with both fear and exhilaration. The diner, once claustrophobic, now felt like a launching pad into the unknown. The world outside awaited us, with all its chaos and uncertainty. We were stepping into the fray, ready to expose the truth and forge our own paths—together.

The moment hung in the air, thick with tension, as the words from the security team settled over us like a heavy shroud. The harsh fluorescent lights above flickered in protest, casting shadows that danced ominously along the cracked walls of the diner. I could feel the blood rushing in my ears, drowning out the murmurs from the other patrons, who were now watching us with a mixture of curiosity and concern. Nathan and I exchanged a glance, an unspoken agreement passing between us—a silent acknowledgment that we could not back down now.

"Really?" Nathan's voice dripped with sarcasm as he leaned back in his chair, arms crossed defiantly. "Is this how you greet two innocent patrons trying to enjoy their meal?" There was a flicker of mischief in his eyes that belied the gravity of the situation. I admired his ability to crack a joke in the face of danger; it was one of the many reasons I found him irresistibly charming.

The lead security officer, whose name I could never remember despite his frequent appearances, didn't flinch. "You think this is a joke? Your families are concerned for your safety. We're not here to play games."

"Then let us play our own," I interjected, feeling a surge of determination. "We're done hiding, done being coddled. We have our own plans now." The words felt powerful, almost liberating as I said them out loud. Nathan nodded in agreement, the glint of rebellion in his gaze.

"You two have no idea what you're dealing with," the officer retorted, a hint of frustration creeping into his voice. "This isn't just some petty conspiracy; it's a matter of life and death."

"Life and death?" Nathan echoed incredulously, leaning forward. "You mean like the death of our freedom? Or the life of a secret we're sick of carrying? Because that sounds pretty grim to me."

I felt a strange mixture of pride and anxiety swell within me as Nathan stood his ground. He was fearless, a quality I both envied and admired. But fear began to gnaw at my insides, reminding me of the very real consequences we faced. I leaned closer to him, whispering,

"We can't let them take us away. We've worked too hard to uncover the truth."

The officer's expression softened for a moment, a flicker of understanding crossing his face. "You think this is easy for us? We're trying to protect you. The last thing we want is to drag you back into the families' mess." His voice lowered, as if he feared being overheard, but his frustration was palpable.

"Then let us help," I pleaded, my heart racing. "We can't just sit back and let this happen any longer. If we're going to make a difference, we have to take the risk."

The atmosphere shifted slightly, the tension still taut but now laced with uncertainty. The officer exchanged a glance with his team, and I could see the cogs turning in his mind. "You really think you can take this on?" he asked, skepticism dripping from each word.

"Absolutely," Nathan shot back. "We're not asking for permission; we're telling you what we're going to do."

The standoff felt like a silent battle of wills, each side waiting for the other to blink. My mind raced, weighing the options like a delicate balance scale. I was aware of the stakes—our lives, our families, our futures hanging in the balance. But my resolve only hardened. We had no choice but to forge ahead.

Finally, the officer let out a long breath, his shoulders sagging slightly as if a weight had been lifted. "You have one hour. Just one. After that, we're coming for you. You need to understand that there's a real threat out there."

With that, the security team turned to leave, their exit as sudden as their arrival. The diner felt quieter now, the air heavy with unspoken fears and the remnants of the confrontation. I felt a rush of exhilaration mixed with trepidation as I turned back to Nathan.

"What now?" I asked, my voice barely above a whisper.

"We meet our contacts," he said, determination burning in his eyes. "We lay everything out, and we execute our plan. There's no turning back now."

The prospect of actually following through was thrilling and terrifying in equal measure. As we pushed ourselves up from the table, the weight of what we were about to undertake settled on my shoulders like a cloak. I glanced around the diner, taking in the faces of the other patrons. Some were engrossed in their meals, oblivious to the storm brewing just a few tables away. Others watched us with a mix of curiosity and concern.

"Let's go," I urged, my heart racing as we slipped out of the diner and into the night. The cold air hit us like a shockwave, invigorating and sharp, driving away the remnants of anxiety that clung to me.

The streets were eerily quiet, the shadows long and deep. Nathan walked beside me, a steady presence that calmed the tempest swirling in my mind. We moved quickly, adrenaline fueling our steps as we headed toward the rendezvous point.

As we approached the alley where we had agreed to meet the underground network, a familiar figure stepped out from the shadows—Rachel, one of our closest allies in the movement. Her face was pale, eyes wide with worry.

"I was starting to think you wouldn't show," she said, crossing her arms tightly against the chill.

"Trust me, we weren't hiding," I replied, forcing a smile despite the tension radiating from her. "We had a little encounter with our families' security team."

Rachel's eyes widened, and she looked between Nathan and me. "Are you serious? What did they want?"

"The usual," Nathan said with a wave of his hand, dismissing the gravity of the moment. "They're worried we'll expose the family secrets. But we're here to do exactly that."

Rachel nodded, determination flashing across her face. "Good. I've got intel that could change everything."

The three of us gathered in the flickering light of a streetlamp, our breaths visible in the cold air. Rachel pulled out a small notebook, her hands shaking slightly as she flipped through the pages filled with notes and sketches. "I've pieced together information about the conspiracy. It's bigger than we thought. There are connections to people outside our families—politicians, business leaders. It's all intertwined."

My stomach churned as the implications of her words sank in. This was more than just our families' hidden truths; it was a tangled web that reached far beyond our immediate lives. The thought of bringing this to light sent a thrill of fear and excitement coursing through me.

"Let's get started then," I said, feeling the urgency of the moment settle over us. "We have to act fast."

As Rachel began detailing her findings, I could sense the stakes rising. The shadows of the alley seemed to pulse around us, a tangible reminder of the danger we faced. But in that moment, I felt more alive than I had in years—charged with purpose, ready to confront the chaos head-on. The battle was just beginning, and we were determined to see it through.

As Rachel laid out the tangled threads of the conspiracy, the chill in the alley seemed to deepen, wrapping around us like a cloak of uncertainty. She pointed to her notes, her finger tracing the lines connecting various names and events, her eyes bright with fervor. "Look at this," she said, her voice barely containing her excitement. "This is more than just our families. It goes back years—corruption that's been festering in our town like a wound that won't heal. There are people here who would do anything to keep it hidden."

Nathan leaned in closer, his brow furrowed as he scanned the pages. "How deep does this go?" he asked, his tone serious. The gravity of Rachel's findings was palpable, and I felt the weight of it settle heavily on my shoulders.

"It connects to the mayor's office, shady dealings with developers, and even some state officials," she replied, her enthusiasm mingling with the gravity of the situation. "If we expose this, we might be able to bring everything crashing down."

"Crashing down," I echoed, the phrase sending a shiver down my spine. The thought was exhilarating and terrifying all at once. "But at what cost? We're not just going after our families' reputations; we could be taking on some powerful enemies."

"Enemies who are already after us," Nathan interjected, his voice firm. "We can't back down now. We have to strike first."

Rachel nodded, her determination shining through. "We need a plan. If we can gather enough evidence to present to the media, it'll create a storm that our families can't ignore. We need to make sure the truth comes out, no matter the fallout."

I felt my heart race again, not just from fear but from a budding excitement. This was our moment to take control, to transform the narrative that had always been written for us. "Okay, then let's figure out our next move," I said, the thrill of defiance sparking in my chest.

Just as we began plotting our approach, a distant sound echoed through the alley—a low, ominous hum that sent a jolt of panic through me. The hairs on the back of my neck stood on end, and I glanced at Nathan, whose expression mirrored my own unease.

"Did you hear that?" I asked, my voice barely a whisper.

Before Nathan could respond, the alleyway was suddenly flooded with light, blinding us momentarily. I shielded my eyes, squinting against the glare. When I could finally see again, a black SUV loomed at the mouth of the alley, its headlights slicing through the darkness like a knife.

"Get back!" Nathan shouted, instinctively pulling me behind him. Rachel's expression shifted from determination to fear as the vehicle came to a screeching halt, and the doors flung open.

From the vehicle emerged a trio of imposing figures, their silhouettes sharp against the light. The leader, a tall man with a cruel twist to his lips, stepped forward, his eyes glinting with malice. "Well, well, what do we have here?" he drawled, a predatory smile spreading across his face. "Looks like our little runaways have been busy."

"We're not going anywhere with you," Nathan spat, his voice steady despite the palpable fear radiating off him.

The man chuckled, a sound that sent chills down my spine. "Oh, I think you'll find that you don't have much choice in the matter." He gestured to the other two, who began to circle around us like wolves stalking their prey. "Your families are quite worried about you. We're just here to take you home."

"I don't want to go home," I said, my voice trembling slightly. "I want the truth to come out. You can't intimidate us into silence anymore."

The man's smile widened, revealing a hint of menace. "Ah, but you see, it's not about intimidation. It's about protection. There are forces at play here that are far beyond your understanding. You're better off staying quiet."

"Not a chance," Nathan replied, stepping forward defiantly. "We're going to expose everything, and there's nothing you can do to stop us."

A flicker of annoyance crossed the man's face, and in an instant, the atmosphere shifted from a standoff to something much more dangerous. "Then you leave me no choice," he said, his voice dropping to a low growl. "Take them."

Before I could react, the two men lunged for us. My instincts kicked in, and I shoved Rachel aside just as one of them reached for me. "Run!" I screamed, adrenaline surging through my veins. Nathan was already moving, his body a blur as he darted past the nearest figure.

We took off down the alley, my heart pounding in my chest as the sound of footsteps thundered behind us. The world around me blurred as I focused on the escape ahead. I could hear Nathan's breaths next to me, quick and steady, fueling my determination. We burst onto the street, the cool night air hitting my face like a splash of cold water.

"Where to?" I shouted, looking for any sign of safety in the chaos.

"The old factory!" Nathan called back, pointing toward the shadowy outline of the dilapidated building at the end of the street. "It's abandoned; we can lose them in there!"

Without hesitating, we sprinted toward the factory, the echoes of our pursuers growing louder behind us. I felt a surge of fear and exhilaration mingle together, driving me forward. The factory loomed closer, its broken windows and rusting metal promising a refuge from our relentless hunters.

As we reached the entrance, I glanced back and saw the men spilling onto the street, their expressions a mixture of anger and determination. Nathan pushed the door open, and we slipped inside just as the first man rounded the corner.

The inside of the factory was dark and musty, the air thick with dust and memories of a time long past. We stumbled forward, our footsteps echoing on the concrete floor as we navigated through the maze of old machinery and rusting equipment.

"Where do we go?" Rachel gasped, her voice a mix of panic and determination.

"Over here!" Nathan shouted, leading us toward a narrow staircase that spiraled upward. We ascended quickly, the creaking steps protesting under our weight.

At the top, we pushed through a door that led to a small office space, littered with the remnants of its former life—old files, shattered glass, and forgotten dreams. We ducked behind a desk, our breaths heavy and rapid as we tried to calm our racing hearts.

"They'll find us," Rachel whispered, her voice shaking. "What do we do?"

"We wait," Nathan said, his expression fierce. "We can't let them take us without a fight. We'll use this against them."

Just as he finished speaking, a sound echoed through the factory—a loud crash, followed by the sound of heavy boots stomping through the building. I felt a knot of dread tighten in my stomach as the voices of our pursuers grew closer.

"Where are they?" the man from earlier growled, his tone sharp and impatient. "They can't have gotten far."

As the voices neared, I glanced around the room, searching for anything we could use. My eyes fell on a metal pipe sticking out from the wall, an idea forming in my mind.

"Get ready," I whispered to Nathan and Rachel. "We need to create a distraction."

Nathan nodded, his jaw set in determination. As I grabbed the pipe, I could hear the voices of our pursuers growing louder, the tension in the air thickening like a storm about to break.

"On my count," I said, gripping the pipe tightly. My heart raced, and the world seemed to narrow down to the three of us and the impending confrontation. "One... two... three!"

I swung the pipe against the nearest window, shattering the glass in a shower of glittering shards. The sound echoed through the factory, drawing the attention of our pursuers.

"Over here!" I shouted, my voice ringing with adrenaline as I darted back into the shadows.

The footsteps changed direction, rushing toward the sound. The tension in the air was electric, and I could feel the fear and excitement coursing through me.

We had one chance, one moment to escape the trap closing around us. But as we crouched in the shadows, hearts pounding, I couldn't shake the feeling that this was only the beginning of something much larger than ourselves—a storm that was about to break, and we were right in its path.

Chapter 18: Chasing Shadows

The subway station loomed before us, its worn tiles and flickering fluorescent lights casting a ghostly glow on the graffiti-laden walls. I could hear the distant rumble of an approaching train, a comforting sound that reminded me of the life I had momentarily abandoned. It felt like a world away from the manicured lawns and pristine coffee shops of my Brooklyn Heights neighborhood, where my biggest worry was choosing the right shade of lipstick. Now, the stakes were infinitely higher.

Nathan's grip tightened around my hand as we slipped through the entrance, and I couldn't help but marvel at how familiar it felt—like fitting a missing puzzle piece into place. The chaos outside felt like a far-off dream, a distant echo of sirens and shouting. "We need to find a train that'll take us far from here," he whispered, his breath warm against my ear. I nodded, though my mind was racing, grappling with the swirling storm of emotions that threatened to overwhelm me.

As we descended the cracked stairs to the platform, I caught a glimpse of ourselves in the shattered mirror hanging by the turnstiles—two desperate souls, wild-eyed and breathing heavily. My heart hammered in my chest, each beat a reminder of what was at stake. I had never felt so alive, so aware of my surroundings; the musty scent of the subway mingled with the salty tang of sweat and fear.

The station was mostly empty, save for a few commuters who glanced at us with mild curiosity, their faces obscured by the shadows. I could sense Nathan's tension; he was a coiled spring ready to snap, and I couldn't shake the feeling that we were being watched. The darkness of the tunnel seemed to stretch endlessly before us, a gaping maw that promised safety—or doom.

"Where to?" I asked, forcing my voice to sound steady, though the tremor in my hands betrayed me.

He glanced down the platform, scanning the tracks. "We'll take the next train to Coney Island," he decided, his voice firm. "From there, we can figure out our next move." The idea of heading to a place synonymous with carefree summers and laughter felt surreal, a cruel juxtaposition to our reality.

"Are you sure that's the best option?" I couldn't help but question, though deep down I craved the thrill of running toward the unknown. "What if they catch up to us?"

Nathan turned to me, and for a fleeting moment, I could see the boy who was once so carefree, the one who made jokes about our high school drama and danced like nobody was watching. "We'll be fine. I promise," he said, though the uncertainty in his eyes made my stomach twist.

Moments felt like hours as we waited, the air thick with anticipation. I could almost hear the thundering of my heart matching the rhythm of the approaching train. It emerged from the darkness, a metallic serpent ready to whisk us away. As it screeched to a halt, I felt a pang of hope mix with the dread gnawing at my insides.

We boarded quickly, our bodies brushing against each other as we squeezed into the crowded car. The familiar jolt of the train was a welcome distraction, propelling us into the night. Nathan leaned close, his voice barely above a whisper, "Stay near me. We can't afford to lose each other now."

The train lurched forward, pulling us deeper into the underbelly of the city. My mind raced, replaying the events that had led us to this point—the secrets, the lies, and the revelations that had shattered my world. I was acutely aware of Nathan's warmth beside me, a beacon amidst the chaos. I turned to him, my heart swelling with an overwhelming sense of gratitude.

"Thank you for sticking by me," I said, sincerity lacing my words. "I don't know what I would do without you."

He smiled softly, though his eyes remained serious. "We're in this together. Always." The promise hung in the air, and I wanted to believe it more than anything.

But as the train barreled through the dark tunnel, I couldn't shake the feeling that we were hurtling toward something far more dangerous than we could anticipate. With each flicker of the overhead lights, I imagined shadowy figures lurking in the corners, waiting to pounce. The city above us felt like a distant memory, a façade hiding the monsters that prowled the streets.

Suddenly, the train screeched to a halt, jolting me from my thoughts. The lights flickered ominously, and an unsettling silence enveloped us. I exchanged worried glances with Nathan, whose expression mirrored my own dread. The doors remained closed, and the murmur of passengers transformed into whispers of confusion.

"Something's wrong," Nathan said, tension threading through his words. I felt it, too—the creeping sense of foreboding that wrapped around us like a suffocating blanket.

Then, without warning, the lights went out, plunging us into darkness. Gasps echoed through the car, and I could feel panic rising in my throat. I reached for Nathan, finding his hand and squeezing it tightly.

"Stay calm," he urged, though I could hear the underlying strain in his voice. "Just stay close."

The darkness seemed alive, a pulsating entity that threatened to swallow us whole. The faint sound of footsteps echoed in the distance, sending a shiver down my spine. Were they coming for us? I held my breath, listening intently, each second stretching into eternity.

And then, a flicker of light. A flashlight beam cut through the darkness, illuminating the faces of frightened passengers. Relief washed over me for a brief moment before I saw the figure standing at the end of the car. The familiar silhouette sent a jolt of fear through me.

It was him.

The one who had set this entire nightmare in motion.

"Get down!" Nathan shouted, pushing me to the floor just as the flashlight beam turned toward us.

I couldn't believe it—here we were, back where it all began, with our lives hanging by a thread.

The flashlight beam swept across the subway car, slicing through the darkness like a knife. My heart raced, pounding against my ribcage as I pressed myself against the cool, grimy floor. I could see Nathan's face contorted with a mix of fear and defiance, his jaw clenched as he tried to assess our options. "We need to get out of here," he whispered, urgency threading through his voice.

But the looming shadow at the end of the car—the figure that had haunted my dreams—was now a tangible threat. He was tall, clad in dark clothing that blended seamlessly with the shadows. I couldn't see his face clearly, but I could feel the weight of his presence, like a storm cloud ready to unleash its fury.

"What do we do?" I asked, my voice barely above a whisper, more a tremor of breath than a sound. The air felt thick with anticipation, each second pregnant with unspoken fears.

"We wait," Nathan replied, his eyes locked on the intruder. "We have to be smart."

As if sensing our stillness, the figure took a step closer, illuminating the space around him with a small handheld flashlight. The flickering beam caught the faces of the other passengers, their expressions a mix of confusion and growing panic. I held my breath, hoping the darkness would shield us from discovery.

Then, without warning, the lights flickered back on, harsh and unflattering, flooding the car with a glaring brightness that made me squint. For a brief moment, I thought I could breathe again. But then I saw his face, sharp and familiar, twisting into a sneer as he locked eyes with me.

"Fancy meeting you here, Emily," he drawled, his voice dripping with condescension. "Thought you could just run away and leave me behind?"

I felt Nathan's hand tense in mine, his body rigid beside me. I wanted to respond, to throw words back at him, but they caught in my throat. The world felt surreal, as if I were trapped in a nightmare where every twist was designed to keep me off balance.

"Get away from her," Nathan snapped, shifting slightly in front of me as if he could physically shield me from the danger emanating from the figure.

The intruder chuckled, a low, menacing sound that sent chills skittering down my spine. "You really think you can protect her?" he taunted, his eyes flickering with malice. "You're both in over your heads."

Panic clawed at my insides. I wanted to scream, to run, but I was frozen in place, caught in a web of fear and uncertainty. The other passengers were beginning to stir, their expressions shifting from confusion to alarm.

"Help!" I finally managed to shout, my voice breaking through the din of uncertainty. The cry echoed through the subway car, but I feared it would only add to the chaos, drawing more attention to our predicament.

The figure smirked, reveling in my distress. "Oh, don't worry, sweetheart. No one can help you down here."

With a sudden jolt, the train lurched into motion, the metallic screeching of the wheels on the tracks drowning out the mounting panic in my heart. As we sped away from the dark tunnel, I could see the glimmer of city lights outside the window, each flicker a reminder of the world I was desperately trying to escape.

But our pursuer wasn't finished yet. He stepped closer, his presence like a suffocating fog. "You have something that belongs to me, Emily. And I intend to collect."

I felt Nathan tense beside me, his body coiled like a spring ready to unleash. "What are you talking about?" he demanded, voice steady despite the tremor in his hands.

"The artifact," the figure hissed, his voice low and threatening. "You have no idea what you're messing with."

In that moment, clarity washed over me. I remembered the whispers of an ancient artifact, one that had been passed down through generations, a relic said to hold unimaginable power. My parents had kept its existence a secret, but the stories had lingered in the back of my mind like shadows waiting to be acknowledged.

"Why should we give you anything?" I challenged, forcing bravado into my tone. "You're the one who's threatening us."

He stepped closer, his breath cool against my cheek, and I could smell the faint trace of something sweet and metallic. "Because, dear Emily," he said, voice silky and sinister, "I have friends who would love to find you. And they don't play nice."

The train rattled on, jostling us as I exchanged glances with Nathan. His eyes were fierce, brimming with determination, but I could see the undercurrents of fear. The weight of the situation pressed heavily on us, a tangible force that threatened to crush our resolve.

I didn't have time to think about what to say next, but instinct kicked in. "We're not afraid of you," I said defiantly, even as a part of me trembled.

The figure laughed, a hollow sound that echoed around us. "You should be. You have no idea how deep this goes." He stepped back, allowing the light from his flashlight to dance around the car as he surveyed the other passengers. "And you," he pointed a finger, "better hope I don't have to come looking for you again."

Before I could process what was happening, the train lurched to a halt. The lights flickered once more, then went out, leaving us in darkness again. Panic erupted among the passengers, shouts and gasps filling the air. I felt Nathan pull me close, his body warm against mine, a grounding force in the tumult.

"We need to move," he whispered urgently. "Now."

Just as we began to inch toward the door, I caught a glimpse of the figure's silhouette against the faint glow of emergency lights. He was grinning, a predatory look that sent ice coursing through my veins. "Oh, you're not going anywhere. Not yet."

In that moment, as the weight of his words hung between us, I felt the world tilt on its axis. My heart pounded not just with fear, but with the reckless thrill of defiance. We were backed into a corner, but something inside me ignited—a spark that refused to be extinguished.

"Let's see if you can catch us," I challenged, adrenaline flooding my system.

Nathan looked at me, a mix of disbelief and admiration flickering in his eyes. Together, we surged toward the exit just as the emergency lights flickered back on, bathing the scene in a stark, clinical glow.

As we pushed our way through the throng of frightened commuters, I could feel the figure's gaze burning into my back, a searing reminder of the chase that had just begun. The world outside awaited us, a chaotic blur of sound and color, and we were determined to outrun the shadows that threatened to consume us.

The moment we burst out of the subway station, the cool night air wrapped around us like a refreshing embrace, and for a heartbeat, I felt as if we might actually escape. The cacophony of the city enveloped us—honking horns, snippets of laughter from late-night revelers, the faint strains of a street musician playing a soulful tune. It was a sharp contrast to the tension that had simmered within the subway walls, and yet, the fear still lingered in the back of my mind like a storm cloud refusing to dissipate.

"Which way?" Nathan asked, glancing around as if the streets might hold the answers. The uncertainty in his voice mirrored my own racing thoughts.

"Let's head toward the park," I suggested, pointing down the street. "There are more people there, and maybe we can lose them in the crowd."

Nathan nodded, and we set off, weaving through the throngs of pedestrians who milled about, blissfully unaware of the chaos shadowing our steps. I could feel Nathan's hand clutching mine tighter as we navigated the bustling streets, our hearts thundering in sync. The vibrant lights of the city blurred into a kaleidoscope of colors, each flicker a heartbeat in the city that never slept.

As we approached the edge of the park, the shadows deepened, and the laughter of the people faded into the background. "This way," Nathan urged, leading me toward a quieter path, lined with overgrown bushes and ancient trees that seemed to whisper secrets in the night. "We'll cut through here."

The deeper we ventured, the more isolated we became, and I could feel a sense of foreboding settling over me. "Do you think they'll follow us?" I asked, glancing back toward the street, half-expecting to see the ominous figure emerging from the darkness.

"I don't know," he admitted, his brow furrowing. "But we can't stay here for long."

We pressed on, our footsteps muffled by the carpet of leaves beneath us. The cool air began to feel heavier, charged with an energy that made the hair on my arms stand up. Just as I was about to voice my unease, we heard it—the unmistakable sound of footsteps crunching behind us, too deliberate to belong to casual park-goers.

"Run!" Nathan shouted, and we took off down the path, adrenaline propelling us forward. The trees blurred into a green haze as we darted through the foliage, weaving between the shadows. I could hear my breath coming in ragged gasps, the rush of fear driving us further into the unknown.

We burst into a clearing, and I skidded to a halt, taking in the vast expanse of the park under the moonlight. The grass shimmered like a sea of silver, but there was no time to appreciate the beauty. Nathan pulled me toward a cluster of benches, and we ducked behind one, hiding in the shadows.

"Do you see them?" I whispered, peering around the edge. My heart sank as I saw figures moving at the entrance to the park, their outlines menacing against the backdrop of streetlights.

"Just wait," Nathan urged, his voice low, his eyes fixed on the figures. "They'll have to search the paths; they won't expect us to go off the main route."

Minutes stretched like hours as we crouched in silence, listening to the thumping of our hearts and the rustling of leaves around us. The figures seemed to pause, their voices low and indistinct, and my stomach twisted in knots. I felt the familiar weight of fear pressing down on me, suffocating, as I clung to Nathan's hand.

"What if they find us?" I asked, my voice barely above a whisper.

"We won't let that happen," he replied firmly, squeezing my hand. "I won't let anything happen to you."

Just then, the sound of laughter echoed through the park, and the figures turned as a group of late-night joggers passed by, their voices bright and carefree. It was a moment of hope—until one of the figures stepped into the light, and I froze.

It was him—the man from the subway, the one who had followed us. He wasn't alone; two others flanked him, their eyes scanning the area with a predatory focus. "Split up," he ordered, his voice a dark growl. "We'll find them. They can't have gone far."

My heart dropped as I realized the danger was closing in. Nathan and I exchanged a panicked glance, and I knew we couldn't stay hidden for much longer. "We need to move," I urged, my voice trembling.

"Wait for the right moment," he replied, his eyes darting toward the jogging group as they disappeared into the trees. "We'll follow them out. It's our best chance."

Time felt suspended as we waited, hearts pounding in unison, every second stretched taut with tension. Finally, the man's voice cut through the night again. "They went this way! Keep looking!"

The urgency in his tone pushed us into action. "Now!" Nathan hissed, and we scrambled out from behind the bench, racing in the opposite direction of the search party. The park became a blur of shadows and moonlight as we sprinted toward the street, praying we could make it out before they caught on.

We dashed toward a row of trees lining the park's edge, the cool bark scraping against my palms as I pushed through. The city lights flickered ahead like a beacon of hope, but just as we neared the sidewalk, a sharp voice called out behind us. "There they are!"

Panic ignited within me, fueling my legs as I glanced over my shoulder. The figures were closing in, determination etched on their faces, and I felt the weight of dread wash over me.

"Run!" Nathan yelled, and we sprinted into the night, our feet pounding against the pavement. The sound of pursuit echoed behind us, a relentless reminder that we weren't free yet.

Just when I thought we might make it, a sudden jolt of pain shot through my ankle as I stumbled, crashing to the ground. "Emily!" Nathan shouted, his voice filled with terror as he turned back, rushing to my side.

"Go!" I cried, desperate to shield him from the danger. "Don't let them catch you!"

But his eyes burned with resolve, and he knelt beside me, determination radiating from him. "I'm not leaving you," he insisted, glancing back toward the darkness that was closing in.

I looked up, my heart racing as I struggled to rise, but a flicker of movement caught my eye—a shadow darting toward us from the alley. Time slowed as I realized we had mere seconds before they reached us. "Nathan, we need to—"

Before I could finish, the figure lunged.

Chapter 19: Into the Abyss

The air in the loft hung thick with a blend of paint fumes and lingering hopes, a potent mix that ignited my senses. Sunlight filtered through the tall windows, casting stripes of golden light across the worn wooden floor, illuminating dust motes that danced lazily in the afternoon glow. It felt as if the universe was conspiring to wrap us in a cocoon of comfort and solace, a stark contrast to the chaotic rhythm of Lower Manhattan outside, where sirens wailed and people surged like a restless tide. The hum of the city was a reminder of everything we were trying to escape, and yet here we were, trying to forge a new path amidst the rubble of our lives.

I could see the tension etched across Nathan's handsome features as he leaned against the counter, a half-empty cup of coffee forgotten in his hands. The creases in his brow deepened as he stared out the window, the view of the skyline both breathtaking and suffocating. The skyscrapers loomed like giants, their glass facades glinting under the sun, yet they felt more like prisons than pillars of strength to him. I wanted to reach out and soothe that furrowed brow, to banish the shadows that haunted his gaze.

"We can break free, Nathan," I whispered, the words almost a prayer. My fingers brushed against his cheek, igniting a spark that traveled from my fingertips to my heart. "Together." I believed in those words with every fiber of my being. It was a mantra that had kept me anchored through the turmoil of our lives, a reminder that we were not alone, even when the world outside felt overwhelming.

He turned to me then, his blue eyes filled with an unguarded vulnerability that took my breath away. In that moment, the weight of our shared burdens felt lighter, if only for a heartbeat. Nathan stepped closer, closing the distance between us, and I felt the familiar rush of warmth envelop me as he wrapped his arms around my waist. The world outside melted away, and all that remained was the two of us, suspended in our own bubble of defiance against the storm raging just beyond the walls of the loft.

The kiss that followed was tentative at first, a gentle exploration of unspoken promises and the lingering fear of what lay ahead. But as our lips moved together, the tenderness ignited into something more profound—a fire fueled by the urgency of our situation and the undeniable chemistry that crackled between us. I could feel the tension release, like a coiled spring finally letting go, and I melted against him, feeling safe and cherished in his embrace.

"I can't lose you, Nora," Nathan murmured against my lips, his voice thick with emotion. "Not now. Not ever." The sincerity in his words tugged at my heart, anchoring me in a way I hadn't anticipated. His fear was palpable, a heavy cloak that threatened to suffocate us both. It was a reminder of the stakes at hand, the realities we were trying to navigate, but it also served as fuel for the fire of determination burning within me.

"We won't lose each other," I promised, pulling back just enough to meet his gaze. "We'll fight. For us. For our future." My voice was steady, even as doubt flickered in the back of my mind. The world beyond our haven was full of danger, shadows that lurked just outside our line of sight, but in this moment, we were invincible.

Our shared dreams and fears intertwined, creating a tapestry of hope that enveloped us. Yet, as we stood in the loft, the enormity of the challenges ahead loomed like a storm cloud on the horizon. I could feel the weight of our decisions pressing down on us, the need to act before time slipped through our fingers like grains of sand.

"Okay, so what's next?" Nathan asked, breaking the spell that had enveloped us. His tone was light, yet the underlying seriousness was unmistakable. He was trying to pull himself together, to channel the energy we had just shared into something actionable.

I stepped back, collecting my thoughts, scanning the room for inspiration. The loft was a treasure trove of possibilities—sketches scattered across the table, remnants of Nathan's artistic flair clinging to the walls. The vibrant colors seemed to speak of dreams yet unrealized, echoes of a life that felt just out of reach. "We need a plan," I stated, my voice steady and resolute. "We can't let fear dictate our actions."

He nodded, determination settling on his shoulders as he pulled out a sketchpad and a pencil. "Let's map this out," he said, a flicker of his old self shining through the shadows that had clouded him. There was something invigorating about watching him take charge, his creative mind whirling into action, the artist's instinct coming alive in the midst of chaos.

As he sketched, I shared my thoughts, outlining a strategy that danced on the edge of audacity. We had to gather information, leverage our connections, and devise a way to confront the challenges we faced head-on. The more we spoke, the more the tension in the air shifted, transforming into a charged energy that pulsed with potential.

Moments turned into hours as we brainstormed, our laughter punctuating the seriousness of our task. Nathan's sharp wit sparked a series of playful banter, each exchange weaving a thread of camaraderie between us. The loft filled with a warmth that contrasted sharply with the chill of uncertainty outside, a sanctuary carved from our resolve and the bond we were forging.

But amidst the laughter and strategy, a gnawing doubt tugged at the back of my mind. What if our plans fell apart? What if the shadows outside were too powerful, too relentless? I pushed the thoughts aside, focusing instead on Nathan's smile and the glint of determination in his eyes. We had each other, and together, we would navigate whatever lay ahead.

The morning sun crept through the tall windows, painting the loft in shades of honey and amber, the light spilling across our hastily sketched plans scattered like fallen leaves on the wooden table. I watched as Nathan traced a line with his finger on the page, a map of sorts that captured our hopes and fears in one sweeping motion. It felt like we were architects of a new reality, crafting a blueprint for a future that sparkled with possibility.

"I think we should start with the gallery," I suggested, my voice breaking the comfortable silence that had settled between us. Nathan looked up, brow furrowed in thought, his blue eyes piercing through the morning haze.

"The gallery?" he echoed, his voice a mix of curiosity and skepticism. "You mean the one where my mother's art is displayed?"

"Exactly." I leaned in, the excitement bubbling up like a soda pop shaken too long. "We need to find out what she knows about the upcoming exhibit. Maybe there's something there we can use to our advantage."

Nathan sighed, running a hand through his tousled hair. "You know that's a double-edged sword. She's... complicated. The last thing I want is to drag you into her world."

"But I'm already in it, Nathan. We both are." My gaze locked onto his, a fierce determination fueling my words. "We can't shy away from our past if we want to shape our future. Besides, it might give us insight into the people we're dealing with."

He nodded slowly, conceding to the logic of my argument, but I could see the reluctance in his eyes. "Fine, but we go in under the radar. No big declarations, no emotional confrontations."

A laugh bubbled up, and I couldn't help but tease, "Since when did you become the master of subtlety?"

His expression softened, a playful glimmer sparking in his eyes. "Touché. Just trying to keep us out of the crosshairs."

With the plan in place, a new layer of energy filled the loft. It was a curious blend of anxiety and excitement, the kind that sends a thrill racing through your veins and makes your heart beat just a little faster. As we prepared to leave, I grabbed my jacket, feeling the fabric's weight as if it bore the weight of my hopes and fears.

Stepping out into the city, the cacophony engulfed us, a symphony of honking taxis and chatter that could drown out even the loudest of thoughts. The air was a patchwork of scents—street food mingled with the sharp aroma of coffee, the distant scent of rain hanging just beyond the horizon. New York thrummed with life, a vibrant reminder of everything we were fighting for.

"Let's make a pact," I said as we navigated the busy streets, my arm brushing against his. "No matter what happens at the gallery, we stick together. No secrets, no shadows."

Nathan's expression turned serious. "You think I'm going to let you face my mother alone? I wouldn't dream of it."

Our banter shifted into a comfortable silence as we walked, the city bustling around us while we shared our own quiet world. I could feel the tension between us, like the air before a storm—charged, electric. The gallery loomed ahead, its sleek exterior gleaming in the midday sun.

Inside, the atmosphere changed entirely. The clamor of the streets faded into hushed whispers and the soft rustle of art lovers discussing the pieces that adorned the walls. It was a world Nathan had grown up in, filled with beauty and creativity, yet shadowed by expectations and the ever-present weight of his family's legacy.

"Stick close," he murmured, scanning the room as if the walls might suddenly close in on us.

The artworks were captivating—each piece telling a story, each brushstroke a whisper of emotion. I marveled at the beauty around me, but my heart raced with anticipation. There was a sense of urgency in Nathan's demeanor, an urgency I mirrored as I followed him deeper into the gallery.

"Over there," he pointed discreetly to a cluster of patrons, his mother's unmistakable silhouette among them, her commanding presence hard to ignore. I felt my stomach twist—a mix of excitement and dread, like standing on the edge of a precipice.

"I'll approach her. Just stay behind me," he instructed, his voice low but steady.

"Got it. I'll be your secret weapon." I smirked, trying to lighten the mood, but Nathan's eyes were serious as he stepped away, ready to confront the very person who had shaped so much of his identity.

Watching him walk towards her, I felt a swell of admiration mixed with concern. He was brave, stepping into the line of fire, a soldier ready to wage war against the expectations that had once threatened to engulf him. As he engaged in conversation with his mother, I tried to eavesdrop, straining to catch fragments of their exchange.

Her voice was smooth and melodic, yet carried an underlying sharpness that sent a shiver down my spine. "Nathan, darling, you're looking well. I was starting to worry you'd become a hermit," she said, her eyes scanning the room, more interested in the art than her son.

"Just busy with my own projects, Mother," Nathan replied, his tone cool, but I sensed the tension beneath. "I wanted to talk about the exhibit."

The words hung in the air like an unspoken challenge, and I shifted closer, straining to hear. His mother's gaze finally settled on him, a flicker of interest crossing her features.

"Very well," she said, her tone dismissive yet intrigued. "What do you want to know?"

I could see Nathan take a breath, the calm before the storm. "What can you tell me about the pieces you'll be showcasing? Any particular artists we should be concerned about?"

"Concerned?" she echoed, a hint of amusement in her voice. "That's an odd word to choose, Nathan. I prefer to think of it as—opportunity."

As their conversation deepened, I felt the weight of their words like stones sinking in my chest. It was clear that the stakes were higher than I had anticipated. This wasn't just a simple family reunion; it was a game of chess, with every move calculated and fraught with potential repercussions.

I remained hidden, torn between wanting to intervene and respecting the delicate nature of their relationship. Yet, the atmosphere shifted abruptly when I heard her voice rise slightly. "You should remember, Nathan, that the world is not as forgiving as you might wish it to be. We have a legacy to uphold."

A rush of anger flared within me, igniting a fierce protectiveness over Nathan. I stepped forward, ready to confront her, but just then, Nathan's gaze caught mine—he shook his head, a silent plea for patience.

It was a pivotal moment, one that could either forge our path forward or fracture our resolve entirely. I held my breath, waiting for Nathan to navigate this treacherous terrain. In that charged space, surrounded by art and history, I understood that every brushstroke and every conversation was a step towards unearthing the truth.

The tension hung thick in the gallery, an almost tangible force that crackled in the air between Nathan and his mother. I could feel the weight of their unspoken history, layered and complex, like the brushstrokes on the canvases surrounding us. It was an odd juxtaposition: art that spoke of freedom and expression set against the backdrop of a conversation steeped in expectation and obligation.

Nathan's mother, with her elegantly coiffed hair and piercing gaze, radiated authority. Yet I sensed a crack in her polished facade, a flicker of uncertainty that made her more human, more relatable. As she spoke, her voice laced with practiced calm, I could see Nathan's resolve waver under the weight of her scrutiny.

"Opportunity?" he repeated, a slight edge creeping into his tone. "Is that what you call it? Because it sounds more like manipulation to me."

Her laugh was sharp, a sound that cut through the room, drawing the attention of nearby patrons. "Oh, Nathan, how dramatic you've become. You're still my son, whether you choose to embrace it or not. This world doesn't operate on idealism. It thrives on power and influence."

I took a step closer, heart racing, ready to jump in if this conversation took a turn for the worse. Nathan seemed to sense my presence, and his gaze flicked to mine, a silent plea for patience and understanding. I understood his need to navigate this minefield alone, even as my instincts screamed to defend him.

"Power and influence might be your currency, but I want no part of that world," he said, the strength in his voice surprising even me. "I'm done living in your shadow."

His mother's smile faltered, just for a moment, and I seized the opportunity to jump in, my own voice steady. "With all due respect, Mrs. Kline, your legacy shouldn't have to come at the expense of your son's happiness. Nathan deserves to forge his own path, free from the expectations that weigh him down."

The sharpness of my words hung in the air, and I felt the gaze of nearby patrons shift toward us. I could sense the collective intake of breath, a hush falling over the gallery as if we had crossed an unspoken line. Nathan's mother turned to me, surprise flitting across her features, and I braced myself for the inevitable backlash.

"Who are you to speak on family matters?" she shot back, her tone icy. "You're a distraction, a fleeting moment in my son's life."

My heart raced, but I held my ground. "Maybe I'm the reminder he needs. The world isn't black and white, Mrs. Kline. There's more to life than the family name."

Nathan's eyes widened slightly, a mixture of admiration and apprehension swirling in their depths. "Nora, it's okay," he murmured, but I could see the fire igniting within him, a reflection of my own determination.

"No, it's not okay," I pressed, daring to take a step forward. "We're not here to fight, but we need to acknowledge the truth. This isn't just about art or legacy—it's about people, feelings, and choices."

The gallery buzzed with murmurs around us, people casting glances like we were the main event at a bizarre circus. Nathan's mother seemed momentarily flustered, as if the winds of change had caught her off guard.

"I admire your passion, dear," she said, regaining her composure, "but you'd do well to remember that passion doesn't pay the bills. This isn't a fairy tale; it's life."

"Then let him write his own story," I shot back, emboldened. "Stop trying to script his every line."

Nathan shifted beside me, his expression a cocktail of pride and worry. "Nora's right, Mother. I want to paint my own future, not just color in the lines you've drawn."

The intensity in the room was palpable, a silent battle unfolding between mother and son, a war of wills that felt like it would erupt into flames at any moment. Then, as if the universe was conspiring against us, the gallery doors swung open with a dramatic flourish.

In walked a figure dressed in a tailored suit, exuding an air of confidence that silenced the room. My heart dropped as I recognized the sharp features and piercing gaze of Vincent Alaric, Nathan's father—a man whose reputation preceded him like a dark cloud.

"Is this a family reunion I wasn't invited to?" he drawled, his voice smooth as silk but laced with something more sinister.

Every eye turned towards him, the tension thickening like fog. Nathan visibly stiffened at the sight of his father, a mixture of dread and defiance flooding his expression.

"Vincent," his mother acknowledged, her tone shifting from defensive to wary, as if the stakes had just been raised.

I took a half-step back, my instincts screaming to retreat. The last thing I wanted was to be caught in the crossfire of this family feud, yet I couldn't ignore the sense of urgency that coursed through me. Nathan needed me. We had come too far to let the shadows of the past pull us under now.

"Why don't we take this to my office?" Vincent suggested, the glint in his eyes sharp enough to cut glass. "It seems we have much to discuss."

Before Nathan could respond, I felt a firm hand on my shoulder. "You should go, Nora," he said, his voice low, urgency threading through his words. "This isn't your fight."

"Like hell it isn't," I retorted, not wanting to back down now. But the look in his eyes was clear; he was concerned for my safety, a protective instinct that made my heart swell even as it twisted painfully.

Vincent stepped closer, casting an assessing glance at me. "And you must be the new muse. How charming." His voice dripped with condescension, and I felt a surge of anger.

"Not a muse, just a friend," I replied, crossing my arms defiantly.

Nathan turned to me, his gaze intense. "Stay here, please."

"No." The word slipped out before I could stop myself. "I won't leave you."

The tension hung thick in the air, a moment stretched to its breaking point. Vincent's lips curled into a smirk, as if relishing the drama unfolding before him. "Suit yourself. But remember, the art world can be a very unforgiving place."

With that, he turned and strode toward the office, Nathan torn between following his father and staying with me.

"Nora, I—" he began, but before he could finish, the gallery's fire alarm blared to life, shrieking through the tension-filled air.

People began to panic, moving toward the exits in a chaotic rush, and I turned to see Vincent's face transform from smug satisfaction to alarm.

"Stay close to me," Nathan commanded, his hand finding mine, and together we surged into the crowd, adrenaline pumping through our veins.

The blaring siren echoed in my ears, drowning out the panic and confusion swirling around us. I could see Nathan's jaw set with determination, the weight of our situation crashing down as we navigated through the throng of frantic bodies.

"Where do we go?" I shouted above the cacophony, gripping his hand tighter, feeling the pulse of the moment thrum through us both.

"Out! We need to get outside!" he replied, pulling me toward the nearest exit, urgency fueling our every step.

Just as we reached the door, a sharp crack echoed through the gallery, causing us both to freeze. I turned to see Vincent, his expression dark and menacing, gesturing toward us.

"Don't let them escape!" he shouted, and my heart dropped as figures moved to block our path.

With nowhere to go, my breath caught in my throat, and as Nathan's grip tightened around my hand, I realized we were on the brink of something far more dangerous than we had anticipated. In that instant, the gallery transformed from a sanctuary of art to a battleground for our freedom, and I knew we were diving headfirst into the abyss.

Chapter 20: The Revelations

The first light of dawn spilled through the tattered curtains, casting golden patches across the disheveled living room. I blinked against the brightness, the remnants of a restless night clinging to my eyelids. My heart was still racing, fueled by the whirlwind of emotions that had gripped me since we had fled the chaos of the previous night. I could still hear the echoes of the argument that had spiraled out of control, the shouts of desperation and betrayal hanging in the air like a thick fog.

Nathan was pacing back and forth, his brow furrowed in deep concentration, each step sending a ripple of anxiety through me. The soft creaking of the floorboards was a stark reminder of the home that once felt safe but had turned into a battleground for secrets and half-truths. His hands were shoved deep into the pockets of his worn jeans, a habitual gesture that betrayed his own turmoil. I could see the way the shadows danced across his face, accentuating the sharp lines of his jaw, a mix of determination and vulnerability that both comforted and unnerved me.

"Did you hear what I said?" Nathan's voice sliced through the thick silence, his tone heavy with urgency. "We need to go back. They took everything from us."

I swallowed hard, my throat suddenly dry. The thought of returning to the web of deceit we had barely escaped sent a shiver down my spine. Memories of the heated confrontation replayed in my mind—accusations flung like daggers, the betrayal stinging sharper than I could have imagined. I had felt like a pawn, maneuvered around the chessboard of our lives, every piece precariously placed by forces beyond our control.

"But what if they're waiting for us?" I countered, my voice barely above a whisper. "What if we walk into a trap?"

Nathan stopped pacing, turning to face me fully, those stormy blue eyes locked onto mine. There was an intensity in his gaze that made my heart flutter despite the fear curling in my stomach. "We can't let them dictate our lives. We can't let fear control us. If we don't confront this now, we might lose everything."

His words struck a chord deep within me. There was an undeniable truth in what he said. The stakes had never been higher, and I felt the weight of responsibility settle on my shoulders like a mantle. This was no longer just about us; it was about everyone who had been drawn into this tangled mess of secrets, lies, and betrayals. I thought of the families who had trusted us, of the friends who believed in our innocence. I had to believe that we could turn this around.

"What's the plan?" I asked, my voice steadier now, bolstered by the determination flooding my veins. "We can't just walk in there unprepared."

Nathan took a step closer, the air between us crackling with tension. "We gather what we can—information, resources—and we approach them directly. If we're going to salvage any chance of a future together, we have to face them. We need to get the evidence back before they use it against us."

I nodded, each heartbeat thrumming with a mix of dread and anticipation. This was our fight, our chance to reclaim our narrative, and I refused to back down. With a quick glance around the room, I grabbed my jacket, feeling the cool fabric against my skin as I slipped it on. Nathan watched me, a flicker of admiration in his eyes that fueled my resolve further.

Together, we stepped outside, the crisp morning air biting at my cheeks. The world felt different in the light of day, yet the lingering fear of what lay ahead twisted in my gut. I took a deep breath, inhaling the scent of dew-kissed grass and freshly turned earth. The sun was rising higher, illuminating the path ahead, but shadows still lingered in the corners of my mind.

As we made our way to Nathan's car, the gravity of our situation pressed down on me. Each step felt heavy, laden with the unspoken fears and unacknowledged truths that had built walls around my heart. The thought of confronting our families—of facing the people I had once trusted with my entire being—made me queasy. But I couldn't let my fears dictate my actions anymore.

"I know it's scary," Nathan said, his voice a soothing balm against the chaos inside me. "But remember why we're doing this. We're not just fighting for ourselves; we're fighting for everyone who's ever felt powerless in this game."

I looked at him, his unwavering gaze reassuring me. It was this belief, this fierce loyalty to one another, that had brought us to this moment. I couldn't help but smile despite the anxiety churning in my stomach. "When did you become such a philosopher?"

He chuckled, a warm sound that eased some of the tension. "Maybe I'm just trying to keep my sanity in check."

The banter felt light, a momentary reprieve from the weight of reality. It was a reminder that beneath the chaos and uncertainty, we still had each other—two rebels against a tide of expectation and control. As we drove away from the safety of our temporary refuge, the road stretched before us, and with it, the promise of confrontation, revelation, and ultimately, the chance to reclaim our future.

Each mile marker felt like a heartbeat, counting down to the inevitable clash with our past. I gripped the edge of my seat, the smooth leather cool against my palms, heart racing not just with fear but with a spark of defiance. We would emerge from this stronger, I told myself, more united. The thought of Nathan beside me, our shared determination shimmering in the air like electric static, filled me with a sense of purpose that no threat could extinguish.

As we approached the place that had once been a home, now turned into a battlefield of emotions and loyalties, I prepared myself for the storm ahead. Whatever lay waiting for us on the other side of that door, we would face it together, a united front against the tide of deceit that had threatened to drown us both.

The car's engine hummed softly as we navigated the winding roads that led us back to the heart of it all. Trees lined the route, their branches arching like sentinels guarding secrets that had yet to be uncovered. I glanced at Nathan, who gripped the wheel with a white-knuckled intensity, his jaw set in a line that spoke of determination. The air inside the vehicle crackled with tension, thick enough to cut with a knife, yet there was a quiet resolve between us—a silent agreement that whatever awaited us on the other side of that confrontation, we would face it together.

"What's the plan if they don't take kindly to our little homecoming?" I asked, trying to break the heavy silence that seemed to envelop us like a shroud. I attempted a smile, but it faltered under the weight of reality. "Should I start practicing my innocent face now?"

Nathan shot me a sidelong glance, a smirk tugging at the corners of his mouth. "Trust me, your innocent face needs no practice. It's the guilty one that could use a bit of work."

His attempt at humor was a much-needed balm, lightening the atmosphere just enough for me to breathe a little easier. I chuckled despite myself, feeling the tension in my chest ease, if only momentarily. The world outside the car window blurred by, a kaleidoscope of colors, a stark contrast to the storm brewing within me. I was grateful for Nathan's presence, for the way he could pull me back from the precipice of my worries, if only for a fleeting moment.

As we drew closer to the house, a sense of familiarity washed over me, intertwined with a wave of dread. The sprawling estate, with its ivy-covered walls and manicured lawns, had once been a sanctuary.

Now, it loomed before us like a fortress, an imposing reminder of the tangled relationships that resided within. I could almost hear the whispers of the past echoing through the hallways, secrets trapped within those walls, waiting to be unearthed.

"Ready or not, here we go," Nathan murmured, his voice low as he parked the car. I nodded, though my stomach churned with apprehension. I stepped out, the gravel crunching beneath my feet, each sound amplifying the sense of urgency.

The door creaked open, revealing a hallway that felt both welcoming and foreboding. The scent of polished wood mixed with the faint aroma of old books filled the air, an oddly comforting scent that was quickly overshadowed by the tension simmering just beneath the surface. I glanced at Nathan, who nodded, a silent reminder that we were in this together.

We moved through the house like shadows, our footsteps soft against the polished floors, careful not to disturb the fragile peace that hung in the air. I could hear muffled voices coming from the living room, their cadence laced with anxiety and uncertainty. As we approached, I could make out fragments of the conversation, the tone growing more heated with each passing second.

"—can't just sit here and do nothing!" The voice belonged to my mother, the fervor in her words unmistakable. "If they have the evidence, we're all at risk! We need to act now!"

"Act how, Maria? We can't just charge in without a plan!" came a deep voice I recognized as Nathan's father. "We're dealing with forces beyond our understanding."

My heart raced as I exchanged a glance with Nathan. The sense of foreboding grew heavier in the air, a palpable anxiety that enveloped us as we stood just outside the doorway, hidden from sight. I wanted to burst in and confront them, to demand answers, but a sense of caution held me back.

"Maybe that's exactly what we should do," Nathan murmured, his expression fierce and unwavering. "We can't wait for them to decide our fate. We have to take control."

Before I could respond, Nathan took a step forward and pushed the door open. The room fell silent, and I felt every pair of eyes turn toward us, a mix of shock and tension ricocheting off the walls. My mother stood frozen in place, her features a canvas of worry, while Nathan's father's brow furrowed, a frown deepening the lines on his forehead.

"Nathan! What are you doing here?" my mother exclaimed, her voice breaking the tense stillness. "You shouldn't have come back. It's too dangerous!"

"Dangerous?" Nathan shot back, his voice steady. "You mean more dangerous than sitting here and letting them take control of our lives? We're not just going to stand by and let that happen."

"Please, everyone, let's keep our voices down," Nathan's father interjected, his tone a mix of authority and concern. "We don't know who might be listening."

I stepped into the room, heart pounding, determined to assert my presence. "We need to talk about what happened. We can't ignore this any longer."

The tension in the room thickened as our families exchanged uncertain glances. My mother's eyes darted between Nathan and me, uncertainty etched across her face. "What do you mean, 'what happened'?" she asked, her voice softening. "We've been worried sick about you both. We thought you were..."

"Dead?" Nathan finished for her, a biting edge to his words. "You thought you could just sweep everything under the rug and it would all go away?"

"Enough!" my father's voice boomed, filling the space with authority. He stepped forward, his expression a mixture of anger and fear. "This is not the time for accusations. We need to focus on what's at stake here."

"Exactly," Nathan interjected, his intensity rising. "What's at stake is our future! If they have the evidence, they'll use it against us. We need to come up with a plan—together."

Silence descended upon the room, the weight of his words settling heavily. I could feel the gravity of the situation enveloping us, the realization of our vulnerability pressing down like a physical force. The tension was palpable, a living entity that crackled in the air.

"I'm not going to let them control my life," I said, my voice rising slightly as I took a step closer to my parents. "I deserve to know the truth, and so does Nathan. If we don't stand together, we'll lose everything."

At my words, a flicker of something passed between my mother and Nathan's father—a shared understanding that seemed to bridge the chasm of fear and distrust that had formed between us. "We need to find that evidence," my mother finally conceded, her voice steady. "We have to know what we're dealing with if we're going to protect our families."

A newfound determination surged within me. We were no longer pawns in a game played by forces beyond our control; we were warriors, ready to reclaim our narrative, ready to fight back against the unseen threats lurking in the shadows. As the discussions began to heat up again, strategies formulated, I couldn't help but feel that this was just the beginning—a spark igniting a fire that had been smoldering for far too long.

The room hummed with urgency as our families gathered, the atmosphere electric with a mix of fear and determination. Plans began to take shape, words cascading like the rushing water of a stream. "We can't just charge in without a strategy," Nathan's father insisted, the tension in his voice a clear reflection of the stakes involved. "We need to be tactical. We have to know what we're up against."

"I've had enough of playing defense," Nathan countered, his tone unwavering. "We need to take the fight to them. We know they have the evidence, and we know they're not going to stop until they destroy us."

I watched as the adults exchanged glances, their expressions a blend of concern and recognition. It was clear they understood the gravity of our predicament. In the past, I'd often felt like an outsider looking in—my parents navigating their world of alliances and conflicts while I remained on the periphery. But now, as I stood shoulder to shoulder with Nathan, I felt an unexpected swell of empowerment.

"If we're going to do this, we need to act fast," I chimed in, surprising even myself with the conviction in my voice. "Every second we waste gives them more time to fortify their defenses. We need to locate that informant and retrieve what they have."

Nathan's father nodded, his gaze sharpening. "There's a safe house nearby—one of our contacts might have seen something. We can start there."

My mother stepped forward, her expression resolute. "I'll contact our people and gather intel on the informant's last known location. We'll need all hands on deck to ensure our safety."

As the discussion unfolded, I felt a sense of unity forming—a bond that had been absent for far too long. Strategies were laid out, roles designated, and the lines of trust began to blur in a way I never thought possible. Each family member had their strengths, and I felt proud to be part of a team, no longer merely the sheltered daughter but a participant in the fight for our future.

"While we gather information, we need a distraction," Nathan said, a glimmer of mischief lighting up his eyes. "Something to draw their attention away from us."

My eyebrows shot up. "You're not suggesting we throw a party, are you? Because I don't think that's going to help our case."

He grinned, the tension easing slightly. "Not a party, but maybe something like a gathering—an event that looks perfectly innocent but allows us to move in the shadows. We can use it as a cover."

"Brilliant," I remarked, a wicked smile creeping onto my face. "What's more innocent than a family BBQ? Everyone loves a good burger and some backyard games. And I promise I'll even bring my famous potato salad, the one that always disappears faster than gossip in a small town."

"Noted," Nathan chuckled, but then his expression turned serious. "We'll need to be cautious. One wrong move, and everything could fall apart."

As the plan solidified, I felt my heart race, the pulse of excitement thrumming in my veins. Yet beneath the thrill was a current of anxiety—this could either be the turning point we needed or a catastrophic misstep.

As we divided tasks, Nathan and I found a moment to step away from the chaos. "Are you sure about this?" he asked, his voice low, concern etched into his features. "I don't want you to get hurt."

"I'm not going to sit on the sidelines while the world burns," I replied, my determination unwavering. "I need to be part of this. Besides, what's the worst that could happen? A little family drama? I think I can handle it." I added a wink for good measure, but the gravity of my words hung in the air like a dark cloud.

Nathan hesitated, his brow furrowing. "It's not just family drama. If things go south, it could get dangerous."

"Yeah, but if we don't do this, we risk losing everything. I won't let fear dictate my life anymore." The fire in my gut urged me forward, igniting my spirit.

With our roles established, the afternoon rolled in, bright and warm, as families began to prepare for the so-called gathering. The preparations were nothing short of elaborate. The scent of burgers sizzling on the grill mingled with the fragrant aroma of grilled vegetables. Laughter rang out, a deceptive veil over the tension simmering just beneath the surface.

Nathan and I worked alongside our families, playing the part of the blissfully ignorant hosts while our minds buzzed with strategy. It felt surreal, the juxtaposition of normalcy against the backdrop of our dire situation.

As the sun dipped lower in the sky, casting long shadows across the yard, I noticed a flicker of movement at the edge of the property. My heart skipped a beat. "Nathan," I whispered, urgency creeping into my tone. "Look over there."

He turned, his eyes narrowing as he followed my gaze. A figure lingered just beyond the tree line, hidden in the shadows. For a moment, my breath caught in my throat, my pulse quickening. The familiar chill of dread washed over me.

"Is that—?" Nathan began, but the figure took a cautious step forward, revealing themselves in the fading light. My heart raced, recognition hitting me like a punch to the gut.

"No way," I breathed, the world around me momentarily fading away. The figure stepped into view, and I could hardly believe my eyes. It was someone I thought I'd never see again, someone whose presence stirred memories both sweet and bitter.

Before I could call out, the air around us shifted, an unmistakable tension settling heavily. The backyard chatter faded, and the gathered families turned, sensing something was amiss. Whispers rippled through the crowd, a wave of confusion and curiosity as eyes darted toward the figure emerging from the darkness.

In that instant, my heart dropped. I could see the flash of fear and resolve in Nathan's eyes as we stood rooted in place, uncertainty hanging thick in the air. The gathering's cheerful facade was about to crack, the storm that had been brewing ready to unleash its fury, and I couldn't shake the feeling that everything was about to change in an instant.

Before I could even process what this figure meant for our plans or our families, the sound of a car engine revved in the distance. A sleek black vehicle rolled into the driveway, pulling up sharply. My stomach churned. I knew that car. A thrill of dread gripped me as I realized our carefully crafted evening was on the brink of unraveling.

The figure from the shadows stepped forward, revealing a determined expression, but before I could react, the car door swung open, and a second figure emerged, one I hadn't anticipated. This one held a promise of trouble, and as the sun dipped below the horizon, it was clear that the night was far from over.

Chapter 21: The Reckoning

The polished floors of Grayson Industries gleamed under the fluorescent lights, a stark contrast to the turmoil that churned within me. Each step I took felt heavier than the last, the weight of my family's legacy pressing down like a leaden shroud. The air smelled faintly of burnt coffee and desperation, a fitting scent for the battlefield I was about to enter. I glanced sideways at Nathan, who walked beside me with an intensity that mirrored my own. His jaw was set, determination etched into every line of his handsome face. We were a pair of misfits in a world defined by wealth and power, but today, we were prepared to challenge the very foundation of that world.

As we approached the boardroom, the imposing glass doors loomed ahead, a transparent barrier that felt more like a fortress. My heart raced, and I could hear the muted hum of voices on the other side. They were discussing us, I was sure of it—plotting, planning, and manipulating. The thought sent a shiver down my spine. I took a deep breath, allowing the cool air to fill my lungs, and with one last glance at Nathan, I pushed the door open.

The boardroom was a stark, corporate world—sharp edges and cold glass, filled with faces that reflected nothing but ambition. My parents sat at the long, mahogany table, their expressions unreadable masks. The flicker of anxiety mingled with determination in my chest. "We're here to talk," I announced, my voice slicing through the tense atmosphere like a knife.

"Talk?" my father replied, arching an eyebrow. "Is that what you call this little reunion? A chat over coffee?"

"It's more than that," Nathan interjected, his voice steady as he crossed his arms. "We know what's been going on behind the scenes. It's time to end the secrecy."

The silence that followed felt heavy, as if the air itself was holding its breath. My mother, always the picture of composed elegance, glanced at my father before leaning back in her chair. "You think you understand everything, don't you?" she said, a sardonic smile playing on her lips. "You have no idea what you're stepping into."

"Oh, I think I do," I shot back, anger sparking in my veins. "The lies, the manipulation, it all ends here. We deserve the truth, and so does everyone else affected by your choices."

"You're being naïve," my father countered, his voice low and controlled. "There are forces at play that are beyond your comprehension. This isn't just about family—it's about survival."

Nathan exchanged a glance with me, and I could see the gears turning in his mind. "No more games," he insisted. "We're done being pawns in your twisted game. If you won't come clean, then we will."

"You're threatening your own parents?" My mother's voice dripped with disbelief. "Have you lost your minds?"

The tension in the room crackled like electricity, and I could feel the walls closing in. I was caught between the desire to stand my ground and the instinct to retreat into safety. But I couldn't—couldn't turn back when the stakes were so high. "You don't get to decide our fate anymore," I said, my voice gaining strength. "We're taking control of our own lives."

"Control?" my father scoffed, his laugh harsh and bitter. "What do you know about control? You've lived in a bubble, sheltered from the consequences of our actions."

"And you think that gives you the right to manipulate everything around you?" Nathan's voice rose, cutting through the chaos. "You're wrong. We've seen the repercussions of your decisions, and we refuse to let it continue."

As Nathan spoke, I could feel the momentum shifting, the tides turning in our favor. The air grew thick with confrontation, each word igniting a fire in my belly. I leaned forward, emboldened by our shared resolve. "We want the truth about the company, about our family's legacy. And we want accountability."

My father's expression darkened, shadows pooling in the corners of his eyes. "Accountability? Do you think this is a game, a court where the guilty are punished? This is business, and in business, blood runs thick."

"It's not just business," Nathan shot back, his voice rising. "It's people's lives. You've hurt so many in the name of profit, and that ends now."

Suddenly, the atmosphere shifted; it felt as though a storm was brewing just beneath the surface. My father slammed his fist on the table, making the glasses rattle. "You think you can waltz in here and change everything? You have no idea what you're up against."

In that moment, the anger boiled over, and I realized we had stepped into a war zone. "We're not afraid of you," I said, my voice firm, a stark contrast to the chaos brewing within. "We're not backing down."

But as we stood our ground, the tension erupted. My mother stood abruptly, her chair scraping violently against the floor. "You foolish children!" she shouted, eyes ablaze. "You're playing with fire. Do you know what you're risking?"

"What I'm risking?" I replied, my heart racing. "What you're risking is our future, our lives! You've already lost so much—don't you see?"

The room erupted into chaos, voices overlapping in a cacophony of anger and betrayal. Accusations flew like daggers, and as the confrontation escalated, it became clear that we were on the brink of an all-out war. I stood, heart pounding, adrenaline coursing through me as Nathan's eyes met mine, a silent promise passing between us. This was our moment, our reckoning, and we wouldn't back down. The storm had arrived, and we were ready to face it head-on.

The chaos in the boardroom erupted like a volcano, spewing forth anger and resentment. My parents' polished masks slipped, revealing the raw emotions that lay beneath the surface—fear, frustration, and a stubborn refusal to relinquish control. My father's face turned a shade darker, his features sharpening into something almost predatory. "You think you can dictate terms to us?" he spat, leaning across the table, his voice a low growl that sent a chill through the air.

"You're the ones who have dictated everything!" I countered, refusing to back down despite the heat radiating from his fury. "You've made decisions that affect lives without even considering the consequences. We're not children anymore; we see through the smoke and mirrors."

Nathan's presence beside me felt like a lifeline. He was the anchor in this storm, his unwavering support bolstering my resolve. "This isn't just about you two," he added, his voice steady. "It's about the people you've hurt, the families you've torn apart in your pursuit of power."

"You're talking as if you're some kind of savior," my mother shot back, disbelief etched across her features. "You're both naive. The world isn't as black and white as you make it out to be. There are nuances—strategies—you wouldn't understand."

"Nuances?" Nathan scoffed, crossing his arms. "Is that what you call exploiting those who trust you? You've traded integrity for profits, and it's time someone held you accountable."

Just then, a sharp knock on the door interrupted our heated exchange. My father's expression shifted from fury to irritation, and I wondered who would dare interrupt this spectacle. When the door swung open, I was met with the sight of Derek, the company's legal advisor. He stepped in hesitantly, eyes darting between us and the board members.

"I'm sorry to interrupt," he said, adjusting his glasses, "but I believe we need to discuss the ongoing investigations into the company's practices." His presence added another layer of tension, like a tightrope stretched over a chasm. The atmosphere crackled, a mix of curiosity and dread hanging in the air.

"Now's not the time, Derek," my father snapped, waving a dismissive hand. "We're in the middle of something much more pressing."

"Actually," Derek said, his voice taking on a firmer tone, "I think this is precisely the time. We need to address the allegations that have surfaced. The board has been informed, and it's crucial we take a unified front."

"Unified front?" I echoed incredulously. "How can you speak of unity when you're the ones tearing this family apart?"

"Enough!" my mother's voice rose, laced with a thin veneer of control that barely masked her anxiety. "We will not discuss this here. This is a family matter."

"Is it?" Nathan challenged. "Is it truly a family matter when it's affecting so many lives outside these walls? This is about ethics, integrity, and a future that you seem hell-bent on destroying."

Derek looked between us, clearly caught in the crossfire. "What are you suggesting?" he asked, his brow furrowing as he tried to navigate the growing tension.

I took a deep breath, feeling the ground beneath me shift. "We're suggesting that it's time for transparency," I said, my voice steadying. "If you truly care about this company and its legacy, you'll allow the truth to come out."

The silence that followed was deafening. My father's jaw clenched, and I could see the cogs turning in his mind, weighing options, considering consequences. "You don't understand the implications of what you're proposing," he said, his voice dropping into a low, dangerous tone. "You could destroy everything we've built."

"Everything you've built on lies and manipulation?" I shot back. "Is that worth saving? What will your legacy be if it's built on the suffering of others?"

Just then, a flicker of uncertainty crossed my father's face, a crack in the facade that I had never seen before. "And what about you?" he countered, his voice sharp. "What legacy will you leave? Running from the truth won't make you any better than us."

The words struck a nerve, and I felt a flush of anger rise to my cheeks. "Running from the truth?" I repeated, incredulous. "I'm standing here fighting for it! I want to see change, not just for me, but for everyone impacted by your decisions."

The discussion hung in the air, thick with unresolved emotions, and I could feel the weight of generations bearing down on us. Nathan took a step closer to me, our shoulders almost brushing. "We're willing to take the risk," he said, his voice calm and resolute. "We'll expose the truth, and we'll fight for those who can't."

My father leaned back in his chair, visibly grappling with the situation. "And if you do this, what's to stop you from turning against us entirely?" he asked, eyes narrowing.

"Nothing," I admitted, my voice unwavering. "But if you truly cared, you'd find a way to turn this around, to make things right."

At that moment, the door swung open again, this time revealing a flurry of reporters, cameras flashing like a barrage of fireworks. "Mr. Grayson, what's your response to the allegations?" one shouted, shoving a microphone toward my father.

Panic flared in his eyes, and I could see the walls of composure he had built begin to crumble. The press had caught wind of our confrontation, and suddenly, we were no longer just a family squabbling behind closed doors. We were the center of a media storm.

"Get them out!" my father barked, voice rising in panic. But the reporters surged forward, eager to capture every moment of this unfolding drama.

"What will you do about the financial discrepancies?" another reporter shouted, pushing through the throng. "Is your family involved in unethical practices?"

"Enough!" my mother screamed, her voice cracking with desperation as she turned to us. "You've ruined everything! Do you have any idea what this means?"

"This means the truth is coming to light," Nathan said, his eyes sparkling with defiance. "And there's nothing you can do to stop it."

As the chaos enveloped us, I felt a surge of triumph amidst the uncertainty. We were on the precipice of something monumental—a reckoning that would shake the very foundations of Grayson Industries. The walls might be closing in, but with Nathan by my side, I felt ready to face whatever came next. The storm was brewing, and we were ready to weather it together.

The reporters surged forward like a tide, their voices rising in a cacophony of questions that filled the room with a chaotic energy. My father's expression twisted from defiance to panic, his carefully constructed veneer of control shattering as the cameras captured every moment. "You need to leave—now!" he barked, his voice barely rising above the din, but it was clear his authority was waning.

"Mr. Grayson, are you involved in the alleged cover-up?" a reporter shouted, the microphone thrust into my father's personal space like a spear. I felt an unexpected thrill run through me at the prospect of exposing our family's secrets, but it was quickly overshadowed by the realization of just how volatile this moment was.

"Stay out of this, Blake!" my father snapped, eyes darting toward me, a mix of anger and desperation flickering within. I felt the weight of his disapproval, yet it fueled my resolve. I would not let fear dictate our actions any longer. Nathan stepped forward, placing himself strategically between my parents and the encroaching press, his body tense but unyielding.

"Let's be clear," he announced, his voice cutting through the chaos. "We're here to discuss the truth behind these allegations. We've seen the destruction caused by your silence, and it's time for accountability." His words hung in the air, a bold declaration that sent a ripple of uncertainty through the assembled crowd.

"Are you saying the board has been complicit?" another reporter interjected, eagerness shining in their eyes. It was like a shark sensing blood in the water, and I could see how quickly this could spiral out of control.

"No, that's not what he's saying," my mother interjected, her voice rising in alarm. "This is a family matter, and it has no place in the media."

"Family?" I echoed, incredulous. "What family? The one that has been built on deceit and manipulation? We're done hiding from the truth. This is not just your company; it belongs to everyone you've affected."

The press seemed to sense the shifting dynamics and began to pounce. "What do you mean, affected? Can you clarify?" they asked, leaning in, eager to catch the next scandalous detail.

"Enough!" my father shouted, his frustration spilling over. "This is unprofessional. You're turning a family discussion into a circus!"

"It's already a circus, Dad," I said, a bitter edge creeping into my tone. "And you're the ringmaster."

Derek, the legal advisor, looked visibly uncomfortable, like a deer caught in headlights, unsure of which way to bolt. "Perhaps we should all take a step back and consider how to manage this..." he began, but the moment had spiraled too far for diplomacy.

"No more steps back," Nathan insisted. "This is a moment for truth, not more lies." He turned to the reporters. "There are people whose lives have been destroyed by the decisions made in this room. They deserve answers."

The room shifted, a palpable tension replacing the initial confusion. I could see the gears turning in my father's mind as he weighed the consequences of our defiance. "You're making a mistake," he warned, his voice low and dangerous. "This could backfire."

"Backfire? Or maybe it's time for a reckoning," I shot back, emboldened by the collective energy swirling around us. I could feel the reporters hanging on my every word, the balance of power shifting with each passing second.

But as I spoke, something flickered in my father's eyes—an emotion I couldn't quite identify, a flash of something dark and desperate. Before I could process it, he suddenly turned, storming out of the room with a fierce energy that stunned everyone into silence.

"What the hell?" Nathan muttered, exchanging a baffled glance with me.

"Is he really going to just walk away?" I asked incredulously, my heart racing.

As if in answer, my mother followed him, her heels clicking sharply against the floor, her face twisted in frustration. "We're not done here!" I called after her, but she didn't look back. The reporters, sensing a new twist, rushed to follow them, the sound of their footsteps echoing in the expansive boardroom.

"Let's get outside!" one shouted, and I knew this was spiraling out of our control.

But Nathan didn't move. He stayed rooted to the spot, watching the door through which our parents had just exited. "This isn't over," he said, determination settling over his features. "We need to follow them."

"Do you think they'll talk?" I asked, uncertainty creeping into my voice.

"I think they'll try to bury this," he replied, a fierce glint in his eye. "And we can't let that happen."

With a nod of agreement, we hurried after them, our hearts racing as we burst through the door and into the main reception area. The throng of reporters was already spilling outside, their eager voices a cacophony that echoed in the cool air.

As we reached the entrance, I caught sight of my parents at the edge of the parking lot, flanked by a few loyal board members who had joined the fray. They were surrounded by cameras, the flashbulbs popping like fireworks.

"What do you think you're doing?" my father shouted, his voice cracking as he tried to regain control of the narrative.

I felt the blood rush to my face as I realized I was about to step into the fray myself. "We're here for the truth!" I yelled, my voice piercing through the chaos.

My mother turned, her eyes wide with a mix of fear and rage. "You don't know what you're doing!" she shouted back, the desperation in her voice making my heart race.

Before I could respond, a chilling sound sliced through the air—a siren, loud and jarring. My stomach dropped as I turned to see flashing lights racing toward us. "What the—" I began, my mind racing as I processed the unfolding chaos.

The police arrived, a swarm of uniforms descending on the scene, their expressions stern and businesslike. "What's going on here?" one officer called out, assessing the crowd, the situation rapidly escalating beyond our control.

"Nothing! It's a misunderstanding!" my father shouted, his demeanor shifting to one of frantic defensiveness.

"Is it?" the officer countered, his gaze piercing. "We've received reports of possible misconduct. We need to ask some questions."

The tension that had been building erupted, and in that instant, I realized we were standing on the precipice of something far more dangerous than I had anticipated. My heart pounded as I exchanged a glance with Nathan, and we both knew this was just the beginning.

As the officer approached, the crowd surged forward, questions flying like arrows. The truth was finally within reach, but as the police closed in, I could feel the ground shift beneath me. Would we finally unravel the tangled web of deceit, or would the truth remain locked away forever, buried under layers of power and secrets? The sirens wailed louder, drowning out our voices, and I felt an icy grip of uncertainty settle deep in my gut.

Chapter 22: A Descent into Madness

The flickering fluorescent lights overhead cast an eerie glow on the stacks of dusty cardboard boxes that surrounded us. The basement of Grayson Industries, usually a quiet repository of old documents and forgotten machinery, had transformed into our makeshift war room. Each box we pried open spilled forth secrets—worn files yellowed with age, documents stamped with red warnings, and memos that hinted at the dubious dealings our families had engaged in. It was as if the very walls of the building were whispering tales of greed, betrayal, and corruption, inviting us deeper into their murky depths.

As I sifted through the papers, a sense of urgency hung heavy in the air. The conspiracies surrounding our families had evolved from mere gossip into a palpable threat. Every murmur of our names in the hallway felt like a dagger aimed straight at our hearts. It had begun as a search for answers—innocent curiosity driving us to uncover the truths lurking behind polished boardroom smiles. But now, it was a treacherous dance, each step fraught with peril, each discovery leading us closer to the edge.

"Can you believe this?" Jake exclaimed, his voice laced with disbelief as he held up a file emblazoned with our family crest. "They've been at this for decades!" His fingers trembled slightly, a mix of anger and disbelief reflected in his bright blue eyes. I couldn't help but admire how the shadows danced across his features, accentuating the strength in his jaw and the way his brow furrowed in frustration. At that moment, he seemed invincible, the embodiment of everything I admired.

"Yeah, and it gets worse," I replied, my heart racing as I flipped through pages revealing deals that had left lives shattered. "It's not just business. It's personal." Each page turned unveiled a web of manipulation, a tapestry of lies that entwined our families in ways we had yet to fully comprehend. I felt the weight of our discovery settle on my shoulders, a mantle I hadn't asked for, yet felt compelled to bear.

As we continued to dig, a low hum of anxiety surged through me, as if the very foundation of the building was resonating with foreboding. I glanced over at Aisha, who was pouring over a pile of contracts, her brow knit in concentration. The gentle flick of her pen against the paper seemed like a rhythmic countdown, each tap echoing the urgency of our task. "This doesn't make sense," she murmured, frustration seeping into her tone. "Why would they risk everything to hide these files?"

Before I could respond, a sudden chill swept through the room, snaking its way down my spine. It wasn't the cool air that lingered in the basement; it was something darker, something I couldn't quite name. I glanced around, feeling the hairs on the back of my neck prickle. "Did you guys feel that?" I asked, trying to mask the tremor in my voice.

Jake's expression shifted, a shadow crossing his face. "What do you mean?" he said, a hint of wariness creeping into his tone. Aisha looked up, her eyes wide, the laughter that had danced in them moments ago replaced by a steely resolve.

"It felt like—" I began, but my words were cut short by a sudden sound—a scraping, like metal against concrete. A shiver ran through me as I instinctively turned toward the source of the noise. In the far corner of the room, partially obscured by an old wooden crate, a figure stood motionless, their outline shrouded in darkness.

My heart raced as I took a hesitant step back, feeling the cool concrete wall press against my spine. "Who's there?" I called out, trying to project a confidence I didn't feel. Silence answered me, thick and suffocating, hanging in the air like an uninvited guest.

Then, without warning, the figure stepped into the dim light, revealing the unmistakable glint of a mask. My breath caught in my throat. It was one of the masked figures from the warehouse—a specter of our previous encounter now haunting the shadows of this room. Panic surged through me, my instincts screaming at me to run, but my feet felt glued to the ground.

"What do you want?" Jake demanded, stepping forward, his body a shield between me and the encroaching threat. I admired his bravery, but the fear that gripped my heart had no intention of loosening its hold.

The masked figure said nothing, but the air shifted, a palpable tension rising as they raised a gloved hand, gesturing for silence. I exchanged a glance with Aisha, and in that fleeting moment, I felt the world tilt beneath my feet. This was no longer just about our families; it was a life-or-death game that had spiraled far beyond our control.

"We need to leave," Aisha whispered, her voice urgent and fierce. But as we turned to make our escape, the figure lunged forward, moving with a predatory grace that sent chills racing down my spine. My heart pounded in my ears, drowning out reason, and I bolted for the door.

"Go! Go!" Jake shouted, pushing Aisha ahead of him as we made our frantic dash towards the exit. The sound of our footsteps echoed in the confined space, but the figure's pursuit echoed louder—a relentless predator on our heels. I could feel the darkness closing in, a weight pressing against my chest as we burst through the door and into the cool night air.

Outside, the stars glimmered like shards of broken glass against the velvet sky, a stark contrast to the chaos that had erupted within. But there was no time to pause, no time to reflect on the surreal nature of our escape. The mask-wearing figure was still out there, lurking, waiting for the right moment to strike again. We had stumbled into something far more dangerous than we ever imagined, and now we had to find a way to protect ourselves—and each other—from the impending storm that loomed over us.

The cool night air enveloped us like a heavy blanket as we stumbled into the dimly lit alley behind Grayson Industries. My heart raced, each beat echoing the chaos of the moment, a fierce reminder that danger lurked in the shadows, just beyond our sight. Jake and Aisha flanked me, their faces painted with a mixture of shock and determination, our breaths mingling with the faint scent of rain-soaked asphalt.

"Do you think they saw us?" I panted, glancing back toward the door we had just flung open. The weight of our discovery still pressed heavily on my chest, mingling with the adrenaline that coursed through my veins. The figure had loomed like a phantom, an omen of the uncertainty that now clouded our futures.

"Let's just get out of here," Jake urged, his voice tight with urgency. He took a step forward, but I could see the uncertainty flickering in his eyes. The confidence he usually exuded felt more like a mask now, just as real as the one we had just escaped.

"Where are we supposed to go?" Aisha interjected, her brows knitted in concern. "We can't go home. Not with... whatever that was following us."

Her words hung in the air, heavy with implications. It was one thing to confront the monsters lurking in the depths of our families' pasts, but another entirely to grapple with the reality that someone—something—was out to silence us.

"Let's head to my place," I suggested, the familiarity of home beckoning like a lighthouse in a storm. "We can regroup there, figure out our next move." The thought of returning to the sanctuary of my room filled me with a mix of comfort and dread. My sanctuary felt more like a cage now, the walls closing in with the knowledge that danger was just a heartbeat away.

The three of us dashed through the darkened streets, shadows chasing our heels. The city seemed alive around us, streetlights flickering ominously as if sharing in our fear. Each turn we took felt like a gamble, the specter of the masked figure looming large in my mind. I couldn't shake the feeling that we were being hunted, the thrill of adventure twisted into a terrifying game of cat and mouse.

As we rounded a corner, my heart sank at the sight of headlights sweeping toward us. I held my breath, half-expecting to see the figure emerging from the car like a dark angel of doom. But it was just an ordinary vehicle, the driver oblivious to our panic. Still, I felt a sense of urgency swell within me, the need to disappear from sight consuming my thoughts.

"Quick, behind that dumpster!" Jake hissed, pulling Aisha and me into the cramped space. The trash's rancid odor filled my nostrils, a sharp contrast to the crisp night air. I felt the cool metal of the dumpster against my back, the hard surface a stark reminder of our grim reality.

"What if they find us?" I whispered, peeking around the edge of the dumpster. My heart raced with each passing moment, the mundane rhythm of the city feeling like an unbearable backdrop to our peril.

"They won't. Not if we stay quiet," Jake replied, his voice low but firm, like the leader he had always aspired to be. I admired his bravery but knew that courage couldn't shield us from the impending storm.

As the car passed, its taillights fading into the distance, I let out a breath I hadn't realized I was holding. "Okay, we need a plan. We can't just sit here and wait for the darkness to consume us." I rubbed my arms, feeling the goosebumps rising as the cold seeped into my skin.

Aisha pulled her phone from her pocket, its screen glowing softly. "What if we record everything we found? Evidence that could protect us. If we go public, it might force our families to confront what they've done."

The thought sent a shiver down my spine. The idea of laying bare our families' secrets felt like opening Pandora's box. But what choice did we have? We were already in too deep. "That could work, but we need to be careful," I replied, feeling the weight of responsibility settle on my shoulders. "We can't let them know we're onto them."

"Let's go to your house," Jake urged again, and this time I nodded in agreement. The journey there felt like a maze, each twist and turn a small battle against the fear tightening around us. I could feel the pulse of anxiety throbbing in my temples, and with each step, I wondered if we were walking straight into a trap.

When we finally arrived at my house, I hesitated before opening the door. "You guys ready?" I asked, the familiar creak of the wood sounding like a warning.

"Ready as we'll ever be," Aisha replied, and we stepped inside, the warmth of the interior wrapping around us like a safety blanket. I locked the door behind us, feeling a momentary sense of relief wash over me.

The house was eerily quiet, the usual hum of life replaced by a suffocating stillness. My mom and dad were out, likely at some work function that felt more like a chore than an event. It was just us, the three of us huddled together in the living room, our breaths mingling with the scent of wood and old books.

"Let's set up in the basement," I suggested, gesturing toward the door that led to the realm of secrets and half-formed dreams. "We can spread out the files and start piecing together everything we know."

As we descended the narrow staircase, the darkness enveloped us, and I couldn't help but feel that we were venturing deeper into our own rabbit hole. The basement was cluttered but familiar, a collage of old furniture and forgotten memories that danced like specters in the shadows. I flicked on the light, illuminating the space, and the moment we settled into the dim glow, it felt like the world above us faded away.

We spread the files across the table, the papers resembling a chaotic map of our families' entwined histories. My fingers trembled as I picked up a document, the words blurring together as my mind raced to process the implications. "Look at this," I said, pointing to a name that sent a jolt of recognition through me. "This isn't just about us. It connects to... to them."

Aisha leaned closer, her brow furrowing as she scanned the text. "So they really are in this together. All those rumors... they weren't just whispers."

Jake's voice cut through the tension, laced with incredulity. "So, what do we do now? We can't just sit back and let them dictate our lives."

I felt a surge of determination welling up within me, pushing back against the fear that threatened to paralyze us. "We fight back. We expose them." The words hung in the air, heavy with their gravity, igniting a fire in the depths of my soul.

As we began to strategize, the weight of our discoveries sank in—this wasn't merely a battle for our families' reputations; it was a fight for our very lives, an urgent struggle against the darkness that sought to engulf us. The thought sent a shiver of both fear and exhilaration through me. We were not just pawns in this game anymore; we were players, and I was determined to rewrite the rules.

The tension in the basement thickened like a fog, wrapping around us as we tried to make sense of our surroundings. The dim light cast long shadows that twisted and curled along the walls, mirroring the chaos in my mind. I couldn't shake the feeling that we were being watched, our every move scrutinized by eyes hidden in the dark corners of our reality. The file I held trembled in my hands, a testament to the magnitude of what we were uncovering.

"Okay, let's stay calm," I urged, forcing the words out, even as my heart hammered against my ribcage. "We can't let fear paralyze us. Remember what we found—the records of the illegal trades, the cover-ups." My voice wavered, but I pushed through, desperate to rally us. "This is the evidence we need. If we can expose them—"

"Expose them?" Aisha cut in, her voice sharp, tinged with incredulity. "You mean if we survive this night! You saw what that guy was capable of. This isn't just a game anymore; it's a death sentence if we don't play our cards right."

Jake ran a hand through his hair, his usual bravado replaced by a hint of vulnerability. "So, what's our next move? We can't just sit here and wait for them to find us. We have to act, and we need a plan." The urgency in his tone urged me to think faster, but my mind felt like a scrambled puzzle, pieces slipping through my grasp.

"Let's use this basement to our advantage," I suggested, a flicker of an idea sparking in my mind. "It's hidden away, it's isolated. If we can rig it to trap any unwelcome visitors, we can buy ourselves some time."

"Like what? Build a moat?" Aisha quipped, though I could see the spark of interest in her eyes. "We could probably bribe them with old pizza boxes."

"Ha-ha," I shot back, rolling my eyes. "I was thinking more along the lines of the old crates. If we can create a barricade or even some kind of alarm system with noise, it might give us a few precious moments to escape."

Jake nodded slowly, the gears in his mind turning. "That could work. If we can block the entrance, we can take shifts watching the door while the other two get the files organized." His eyes flickered with a glimmer of hope, and I felt my heart lift slightly.

We set to work, our movements fueled by adrenaline as we moved the heavy crates and stacked them against the door, forming a makeshift barrier. The weight of the wood felt reassuring, a tangible symbol of our defiance against the chaos threatening to consume us. The sound of the crates scraping against the concrete resonated through the space, a rallying cry against the uncertainty that loomed outside.

With the barricade in place, we turned our attention to the files scattered across the table. "Okay, let's prioritize," I suggested, my fingers brushing over the documents like a pianist warming up. "We need to focus on anything that connects the Grayson family to the trades. It has to be in here somewhere."

"I'll take the top left," Aisha said, diving in with determination. "You take the right, and Jake can handle the center. Let's find the smoking gun before our friendly neighborhood psycho decides to drop by for a chat."

As we sifted through the papers, my mind raced, thoughts darting like fireflies in the night. The weight of our discovery pressed on me, each file a reminder of the lives our families had ruined in pursuit of power. I could hardly bear to think about the implications of what we were doing. We were digging up secrets meant to stay buried, and the price of our curiosity could be catastrophic.

Suddenly, the sound of footsteps echoed from the hallway above us, sharp and deliberate, sending a jolt of panic through my body. The three of us froze, hearts pounding in unison as the thud of boots grew louder. "Did you hear that?" Jake whispered, his voice a mere breath against the oppressive silence.

"Yeah," I replied, my heart racing. "It sounds like—"

The door rattled violently, and a menacing voice called out, "I know you're in there. You can't hide forever."

Aisha shot me a panicked glance, her eyes wide with fear. "What do we do?" she hissed, glancing at our barricade, then back at the door, as if willing it to magically absorb the threat outside.

"Stay quiet," I whispered, my voice barely more than a breath. "Maybe they'll think we're gone."

The doorknob rattled again, and my heart sank as I realized how futile that hope was. "You can't run from the truth!" the voice taunted, dripping with a sinister satisfaction. "You've unearthed things that were never meant to see the light of day. You don't know what you're dealing with."

"Yeah, and neither do you," I muttered under my breath, my grip tightening around the edge of the table. It was both a comforting and terrifying reminder of the stakes at play.

"Do you really think you can just waltz in here and scare us into submission?" Jake shot back, his voice steadier than I felt. "We're not afraid of you."

A laugh echoed back, chilling and hollow. "Oh, but you should be." The sound of footsteps grew louder, and my stomach twisted with fear.

In that moment, a crash erupted from above, sending a shiver down my spine. "They're coming," I said, urgency seeping into my voice. "We have to make a choice—now."

Aisha grabbed a file, her face resolute. "I'll hold the door. You two keep searching. If they come in, I'll delay them as long as I can."

"No!" Jake exclaimed, eyes wide with alarm. "That's too dangerous. We stick together, remember?"

"Sticking together means getting caught," Aisha replied, her voice firm. "If I can buy you a few minutes, you might find something we can use to turn the tide."

"Don't be ridiculous!" I protested, desperation clawing at my chest.

But Aisha was already moving, positioning herself against the door, ready to brace against whatever came next. "Just go!" she shouted, her determination shining through the fear.

The door shook violently, and I felt the floor beneath me vibrate with the force. "We can't lose anyone else!" I yelled, panic rising as the wood creaked ominously.

But the moment hung in the balance, the world outside closing in on us like a vice. With a final push, Aisha shouted, "I'll be fine! You have to trust me!"

Jake and I exchanged a look filled with fear and uncertainty, then made the split-second decision to follow her lead.

"Okay, but if you don't hear from us in five minutes—" Jake began, but I cut him off.

"I'll come back for you," I vowed, before we turned our attention back to the files.

With every second that passed, the pressure mounted. The door splintered as they began to force their way inside, and I could feel the weight of time slipping through our fingers. Just as we dug deeper into the stacks of papers, I spotted a folder tucked away in a dark corner, its spine worn and frayed. "Wait! This could be it!" I exclaimed, pulling it out.

The moment I opened it, the pages revealed a name that sent a chill coursing through my veins. The connections I had been searching for stared back at me, each line sparking a new realization, a new thread that could unravel everything. But before I could shout for Jake, the door gave way with a loud crash, and the shadows poured in, menacing and inevitable.

A figure stepped through, their presence swallowing the light in the room. "Found you," they said, and my heart dropped as I realized we were too late.

Chapter 24: Love in the Ashes

The city stretched out beneath us, a tapestry of glimmering lights and whispered dreams, a sprawling maze of streets filled with secrets yet to be unveiled. I lay nestled in Nathan's arms, the sharp tang of burnt rubber and charred wood still hanging in the air, mingling with the distant sounds of sirens and murmured conversations. My body throbbed with the remnants of the fight we'd just endured, but the sensation paled in comparison to the swell of relief I felt as the police rounded up the conspirators. The weight of uncertainty that had settled on our shoulders for so long began to lift, like the fog that had cloaked the city in a shroud of despair.

"Can you believe it? They're finally going to pay for what they did," Nathan said, his voice low, filled with a mixture of disbelief and triumph. His fingers brushed through my hair, a gentle reminder of the sanctuary we had found in each other amidst the chaos. The warmth radiating from his body was a balm to my battered spirit, and for a moment, the world outside faded into a distant hum, replaced by the intoxicating connection we shared.

"Not just them," I replied, trying to catch my breath, though my heart raced not just from the pain but from the enormity of what lay ahead. "We're free, Nathan. Free from all of this." I gestured vaguely to the night enveloping us, where the city glittered like a thousand tiny stars, each representing a possibility, a choice we could finally claim as our own. Our families had woven a complex web of deceit, manipulation, and power, and we had been ensnared in it longer than we cared to admit. But now, as the sirens blared in the distance, I felt the fragile threads of that web unraveling, leaving us standing at the edge of a new beginning.

Nathan's eyes glinted with an intensity that took my breath away. "We have each other," he said, his voice steady and resolute. "No matter what happens next, we'll face it together." The sincerity in his words wrapped around me like a comforting blanket, soothing the remnants of fear that threatened to resurface. I nodded, unable to find the words to express the depths of my gratitude, the love that had blossomed between us like wildflowers in the cracks of a concrete jungle.

Just then, the commotion around us grew louder, as police officers began cordoning off the area and directing bystanders away from the scene. A sense of finality hung in the air, mingling with the lingering smoke that curled like spectral fingers into the night. I could hear snippets of conversations—people speculating about the details of the conspiracy that had nearly consumed us, the betrayal that had festered within our families, the darkness we had fought so hard to illuminate.

"Nathan," I murmured, looking up at him. "What do we do now?" My question hung between us, a fragile thread woven into the fabric of our newfound reality. It was exhilarating and terrifying, the vast unknown stretching before us like an open road at dusk, ripe with promise yet shadowed by uncertainty.

He hesitated, his brow furrowing as he considered the weight of our choices. "I think we need to leave this behind. We can't stay here, not after everything. We need a fresh start, a place where we can build a life without the shadows of our families looming over us." His words ignited a flicker of hope within me, illuminating the darkness that had clung to my heart for so long.

"What about school? What about our friends?" The questions tumbled out, as I felt the pull of responsibility, the fear of abandoning everything I had known. But even as I spoke, I realized that those ties had been strained by the revelations of the past weeks, frayed by the deceit that had wrapped around us like a chokehold.

"We'll figure it out," Nathan said, determination lacing his tone. "What matters is that we're together. We can create our own narrative, write our own story. And I want you by my side." His sincerity washed over me like a tide, pulling me closer to him, filling the chasms of doubt that had threatened to engulf my heart.

The city beneath us seemed to pulse with life, each twinkling light a beacon guiding us forward. "Okay," I said, my voice trembling slightly with the weight of my decision. "Let's do it. Let's find our own place." A rush of exhilaration surged through me, the thrill of stepping into the unknown, hand in hand with the boy who had become my anchor amidst the storm.

As we descended the steps leading away from the remnants of our old lives, I glanced back one last time. The scene was chaotic, yet the sight of the police, the lights flashing, the sirens fading into the distance, marked the end of a chapter that had held us captive for far too long. We were free, unbound by the legacies that had once defined us.

Nathan's grip tightened around my waist as we moved through the crowd, weaving past curious onlookers and officers busy documenting the scene. I felt a sense of liberation wash over me with each step, and I knew that together we could navigate whatever lay ahead. With each heartbeat, the certainty grew; we were ready to carve out our own destiny, away from the ashes of the past.

In that moment, I understood the profound truth of our journey. It was never about escaping our families or running from the chaos that had defined our existence. It was about embracing the unknown, the exhilarating rush of possibility that awaited us as we took our first steps into a world where our choices belonged solely to us.

As we slipped into the lively streets of the city, the cool night air kissed my cheeks, mingling with the warmth radiating from Nathan's side. The world was alive with the sounds of laughter, the sizzle of street food vendors, and the distant hum of music spilling from nearby bars. Each step felt like an act of rebellion against the shadows of our past, a defiance I hadn't known I craved until now. We were like explorers setting sail for uncharted waters, eager to discover what lay beyond the horizon.

Nathan glanced down at me, a mischievous glint in his eyes that suggested he was hatching a plan. "How about we grab something to eat? You look like you could use a slice of pizza, or is it too soon for carbs?" His smile was infectious, a beacon of light cutting through the remnants of our earlier turmoil. The tension of the evening evaporated, leaving behind a giddy excitement that danced in my chest.

"Carbs are always a good idea, especially after facing down a conspiracy," I replied, my voice teasing as I nudged him playfully. "Besides, pizza is basically a food group in this city." My heart fluttered at the way he laughed, the sound warm and inviting, reminding me that joy could exist even after chaos.

We ventured into a small pizzeria that smelled of bubbling cheese and fresh basil. The interior was cozy, with low-hanging lights that cast a warm glow over the mismatched tables. A few scattered patrons were lost in their own worlds, punctuating the atmosphere with laughter and the clatter of forks against plates. Nathan ordered a large pepperoni pizza and two sodas, his demeanor relaxed as he leaned against the counter, casually flipping a quarter in the air.

"Is that your new party trick?" I quipped, arching an eyebrow at him. "Because if so, I'm not sure it'll win you any friends, but it might distract the waitstaff."

"Oh, come on. A little flair never hurt anyone!" He grinned, the youthful mischief returning to his features. "Besides, this is just the warm-up. Wait until I show you my impressive skills with a napkin."

I couldn't help but laugh as he attempted to juggle the flimsy napkins, his focus so intense that it bordered on comical. For a moment, we were just two kids in a pizzeria, leaving behind the weight of our families and their mistakes. When the pizza arrived, steaming and generously topped, we settled into a corner booth, the aroma wrapping around us like a comforting embrace.

"Okay, so what's the plan?" I asked, taking a bite of the perfectly crispy crust. "Do we run away to start a new life on a tropical island, or are we just getting ahead of ourselves?"

Nathan leaned back, eyes sparkling with mischief. "I mean, a tropical island sounds tempting, but I think I'd miss the pizza too much. Maybe we should stick to more realistic goals, like figuring out how to pay rent."

"Fair point," I replied, chuckling. "What if we just focus on finding jobs first? I can't imagine our parents will be thrilled if we don't at least pretend to adult for a while."

He raised an eyebrow, pretending to be deep in thought. "Pretend to adult? Sounds like my entire high school experience."

Our laughter filled the air, a sweet reminder that even amidst uncertainty, we could still find joy. But as the pizza vanished and our banter flowed, a quiet shadow loomed over my thoughts. The truth about our families' misdeeds had been unearthed, but what did that mean for us? The idea of a fresh start was exhilarating, yet the weight of our past still lingered, an uninvited guest at our table.

As if sensing my shift in mood, Nathan leaned closer, his expression turning serious. "Hey, I know it's a lot to take in. But we're in this together. Whatever happens next, we'll face it side by side."

I looked into his eyes, where I found the steady resolve that had become my anchor. "You're right. I just—sometimes it feels overwhelming, you know? Like we've traded one mess for another."

Nathan reached across the table, taking my hand in his, the warmth of his skin grounding me. "We can only control what happens from here. No more family drama, no more secrets. Just us."

I squeezed his hand, drawing strength from his unwavering belief in our shared future. "Just us. I like the sound of that."

The rest of the evening melted away, filled with small talk and shared glances, each moment weaving a tighter bond between us. We wandered through the city afterward, allowing the sights and sounds to envelop us as we explored the vibrancy of life after darkness.

As we passed a bustling park, I spotted a small group of people gathered around a makeshift stage. Curious, we edged closer, discovering a local musician performing a soulful ballad. The melodic notes floated through the air, capturing the essence of the moment, the beauty of new beginnings wrapped in the warmth of community.

"Let's stay," Nathan suggested, his excitement palpable as he pulled me toward the crowd. "I want to dance with you under the stars."

I hesitated, glancing around at the other couples swaying gently, lost in their own worlds. "Dance? I don't know if I'm ready for that."

"Trust me," he said, his voice low and reassuring. "I'll lead. Just follow my rhythm."

Before I could protest, he took my hand and guided me into the thrumming heart of the crowd. With each sway of the music, I felt the tension in my chest release, melting away into the air around us. He spun me into the embrace of the moment, his laughter ringing out as we moved, lost in our own little bubble.

The world faded, leaving just Nathan and me, the city illuminated by the glow of the moon and the distant laughter of strangers. I found myself surrendering to the rhythm of the music, my heart dancing in tune with his as we twirled beneath the starry sky. It was in that simple act of surrender that I realized the true weight of our choices.

With every spin, we carved out a space that belonged solely to us, free from the burdens of our past. Each note of the song echoed the promise of a fresh start, of a love that could bloom in the ashes of our former lives. And in that moment, I knew we were on the cusp of something beautiful—a shared future that had the potential to redefine who we were, one step at a time.

The music swelled around us, enveloping us in a cocoon of warmth and intimacy as Nathan pulled me closer, our bodies swaying together beneath the scattered stars. Each note danced through the night air, weaving a tapestry of sound that blended seamlessly with the soft rustling of leaves. My heart raced, not just from the exhilaration of the moment but from the realization that I was standing here, with him, free to be whoever we wanted to be.

"You know, for someone who claims they can't dance, you're pretty good at it," Nathan teased, his breath warm against my ear, sending a delightful shiver down my spine.

"Flattery will get you everywhere," I shot back, a playful grin spreading across my face as I twirled away from him, my laughter ringing out as I spun back into his arms. "Just don't get too cocky, or I'll start demanding pizza-flavored compliments."

He chuckled, his eyes sparkling with mischief. "Pizza-flavored compliments? Now that's a niche market. I'm sure we could make a fortune."

The world around us blurred into the background, and for those fleeting moments, it was as if nothing else mattered—just the rhythm of our bodies, the laughter, and the warm glow of connection. As the song ebbed and flowed, I found myself lost in the moment, letting the joy of the evening wash over me. It was a precious respite, but the weight of our reality loomed like a specter at the edge of my mind, reminding me that this newfound freedom came with its own set of challenges.

As the music faded into a final, lingering note, Nathan pulled back slightly, his expression shifting to something more serious. "I've been thinking," he said, his voice steady. "About what happens next. We've escaped one mess, but there's still so much to figure out."

I felt a twinge of anxiety at his words, the magic of the evening fading ever so slightly. "Yeah, like how to get jobs and maybe even find a place to live without our parents' support," I replied, trying to keep the mood light despite the heaviness creeping in. "Not to mention, I have no idea what the job market looks like in this city right now."

He nodded, his brow furrowed in thought. "And we have to deal with our families too. They might have been arrested, but they won't just disappear. This isn't over."

My stomach twisted at the mention of our families, the turmoil they had caused, the webs of deceit they had spun. "What if they try to pull us back in? What if they won't let us go?"

Nathan squeezed my hand, his grip firm and reassuring. "They can't control us anymore. We have each other, and that's what matters. But we need a plan."

A wave of determination surged through me. "Okay, then let's make one. We could look for jobs together, maybe even find an apartment. We could live like normal people!" The idea sent a thrill through me, igniting a spark of hope that I hadn't fully allowed myself to feel until now.

"Normal people, huh?" Nathan mused, a teasing smile returning to his lips. "I'll believe it when I see it. But I'm game. Let's give it a shot."

We stepped away from the makeshift stage, the remnants of the concert fading into the background as we made our way back through the bustling streets, our hearts lighter with each passing moment. But as we rounded a corner, my heart sank.

There, standing beneath the flickering streetlamp, was a figure I recognized all too well. My breath hitched in my throat as I came face to face with someone I thought I'd left behind.

"Jessica?" I breathed, a wave of disbelief crashing over me. She looked different, her hair tousled and her expression filled with a mix of relief and something darker. "What are you doing here?"

Nathan tensed beside me, his eyes narrowing as he shifted protectively closer. "Do you know her?" he asked, his voice low, an undercurrent of warning woven into his tone.

"Of course I know her," I replied, trying to keep my composure. Jessica was not just a familiar face; she was part of the chaos that had ensnared us all, the girl whose family had been a central player in our shared history of deception. "But why are you here?"

She stepped closer, a desperate look on her face. "I came to find you! You don't understand. It's not over, not yet. You have to listen to me."

The urgency in her voice sent a chill through me, but I couldn't shake the feeling of betrayal that tightened around my heart. "Why should I trust you? Your family—"

"I know what my family did! I know about the conspiracy. They're not just going to let you walk away!" Her eyes were wide, frantic, and for a moment, I hesitated, caught in the web of confusion that had plagued me since this all began.

"What do you mean?" Nathan's voice was tense, his protective instincts flaring as he stepped in front of me, creating a barrier between Jessica and me.

"I can't explain everything now, but there's something you need to know," she said, glancing around as if she were afraid someone might overhear us. "They're planning something—something big. And you two are at the center of it."

My heart raced, a mix of fear and uncertainty swelling within me. "What do you mean? What kind of 'something'?"

Jessica took a deep breath, her gaze flicking to Nathan and then back to me, a look of genuine concern replacing the desperation.

"They're coming for you. They won't stop until they get what they want."

Before I could process her words, a sudden commotion erupted further down the street, sirens blaring back to life, echoing ominously in the night. My pulse quickened as I turned my head toward the noise, the fear in the pit of my stomach growing heavier.

"Look, we need to go," Nathan said, urgency lacing his voice as he took my hand again, his grip tight. "Now."

But as I turned back to Jessica, ready to demand more answers, she had vanished into the shadows, as if she had never been there at all. My heart pounded, confusion swirling in my mind.

"What just happened?" I asked, panic creeping in as I scanned the street for any sign of her. "Did she just... disappear?"

Nathan shook his head, eyes narrowed with determination. "We need to get out of here, now. Whatever she knows, it's not safe. They're closing in."

My heart sank as I looked into his eyes, realizing that the freedom we had fought for might already be slipping through our fingers, like sand in the wind. The promise of a fresh start felt like a distant dream, one that was being threatened by the very shadows we had sought to escape.

As we turned to leave, I couldn't shake the feeling that we were not just running from our past but toward an uncertain future—one that loomed before us, dark and unyielding, ready to reveal its secrets at the most inopportune moment.